My Best French Wedding

Also by Amanda Sellet

Hate to Fake It to You

The Odds of Getting Even

YOUNG ADULT NOVELS

By the Book

Belittled Women

Flirting with Murder

My Best French Wedding

A Novel

Amanda Sellet

ST. MARTIN'S GRIFFIN
NEW YORK

This is a work of fiction. All of the names, characters, organizations, places, and events portrayed in this work are either products of the author's imagination or used fictitiously.

First published in the United States by St. Martin's Griffin, an imprint of St. Martin's Publishing Group

EU Representative: Macmillan Publishers Ireland Ltd, 1st Floor, The Liffey Trust Centre, 117–126 Sheriff Street Upper, Dublin 1, D01 YC43

www.stmartins.com

Designed by Meryl Sussman Levavi

The Library of Congress Cataloging-in-Publication Data is available upon request.

ISBN 978-1-250-90630-4 (trade paperback)
ISBN 978-1-250-90631-1 (ebook)

First Edition: 2026

10 9 8 7 6 5 4 3 2 1

For Frédéric, my very own French archaeologist

My Best French Wedding

87th Annual New Voices in Media Awards: Celebrating Journalism's Next Generation

Finalists for the Game Changer Prize

Life, Styled. Hildy Johnson, editor in chief. In an era when even the most venerable magazines are shuttering their print editions, Johnson boldly staked her claim to a renaissance of the glossy. The compact monthly combines glamorous art direction and a cheeky editorial sensibility with serious long-form reporting, as Johnson and her team introduce readers born long after the glory days of the "slicks" to the pleasures of tangible media.

"Meet Me in Montauk: A Wedding Three Decades in the Making," by Walter Burns. Bursting onto the scene with this gritty yet empathetic deep dive into the human story behind a glitzy party, Burns injected relevance and urgency into the sleepy realm of wedding coverage. His Bells and Whistles column is a must-read for society mavens and those who breathlessly follow their every move, making it the ultimate "get" for wedding planners and publicists.

Death and Taxes: The Murder of an Accountant. Multimedia reporting and podcast by *New Jersey* magazine. Cam Lin, editor. Wake up, Gray Lady. A team of novice reporters—including two J-school interns—produced one of the most downloaded true-crime podcasts of the year, exploring the suspicious circumstances surrounding the final days of a number cruncher from Trenton.

Balls in the Air, an e-sports gazette. Gia Hamline and Greg Brown, founders. It's in the game for Hamline and Brown, who managed to make the world of virtual competitions as riveting as anything on the gridiron. Bonus points for not being afraid to bite the hands that feed them, with their coverage of ongoing legal challenges to collegiate e-sports "teams" under Title IX.

NOW

1

Walter

FIVE WEEKS BEFORE THE PRESCOTT-SCHAFER WEDDING

NEW YORK—If anyone had asked five minutes ago, Walter Burns would have described himself as a rational person, by nature and training. A journalist's job was to observe and report, not embroider the truth with fanciful notions—and Walter was nothing if not a consummate professional.

Most of the time.

So how to explain his immediate awareness that Hildy had entered the ballroom of this nondescript Midtown hotel, even before he looked up and saw her standing near the entrance? Maybe it was the force of her personality, sending out vibrations strong enough to register on the Richter scale. Either that or he'd turned psychic, and this was a forewarning of imminent doom.

He tried not to stare as she moved across the room, nevertheless noticing that her hair was a little longer than she usually wore it, pinned back on one side with a sparkly clip. That was the "now" version of Hildy, a sleek and sophisticated woman of business. She turned her head to greet someone, and he saw that the rest of her riotous curls had been set free, reminding him of the lightly electrocuted look she'd sported in her youth. It was like this every time their paths crossed.

The weight of their history made for a double whammy, the

impact of adult Hildy layered over the damage she'd done to him back then.

Hildy smiled at someone Walter didn't recognize, her dark eyes bright with interest. The shimmery stuff on her lids matched the silver of her dress—if you could call that a dress. It looked more like liquid mercury, dancing over her skin. His arm lifted on autopilot, raising his glass to his lips.

Wine dribbled down his chin. Walter swiped at it with the back of his hand. Leave it to Hildy to reduce him to a drooling imbecile.

At least that snapped him out of his haze, as if a giant thumb had unmuted the background noise. Of course Hildy was here—and fully expected to win, if that outfit was any indication. He practiced his poker face. The one that said, *I am a neutral bystander*. As opposed to someone who had been concussed by the sight of his competition.

The effort was wasted, because she didn't turn in his direction. It seemed his prickling physical awareness of Hildy was a one-way street. Walter chose a table at random, only realizing after pulling out a chair that he'd met two of the occupants before.

"Basketball, right?" He leaned across the table, arm extended.

"Hoop D's. Derek and Dean," the larger of the pair confirmed, shaking Walter's hand. His thick neck and coat-straining shoulders suggested football, while the lankier Dean looked like he might actually have played basketball. Not that you needed real-life experience to report on a topic. It wasn't as if Walter had been married before.

"That's Oliver," Derek added, indicating a weedy blond with round tortoiseshell glasses and a sweater vest who looked like he'd be more at home in a rare-books room. "He's Mr. Wine."

"My YouTube channel," Oliver supplied.

Walter nodded as if he'd heard of it.

"We're doing viognier next week. You should tune in. It's the next albariño."

"Good to know," Walter replied, as though he had a burning personal interest in wine fads. He'd gotten better at pretending to care about hoity-toity lifestyle trappings, though it was still an uphill battle trying to catch up with all the class signifiers he'd missed during his normie childhood. Obscure shellfish rules. To eat the cheese rind or not? Socks vs. no socks. How to disassemble an artichoke with the finesse of an open-heart surgeon.

Sometimes Walter worried that if he lingered too long in that world, he'd lose sight of reality. He was a tourist, not a transplant. It was important to remember that.

"Who is *that*?" Mr. Wine asked, sounding way too interested.

Walter guessed who he meant, but feigned ignorance so he'd have an excuse to look. Hildy was laughing with a woman he recognized as a political reporter from the *Times*. He wondered what they were talking about. It had been a long time since he'd heard Hildy laugh, unless you counted the occasional *ha* of scorn.

"He knows her," Derek informed the half-filled table, jerking a thumb at Walter.

"Knew." Walter ignored the expectant pause as they waited for him to elaborate. If he started that story, they'd be here all night. "She's the editor of *Life, Styled*," he said, keeping it dry and factual. "Hildy Johnson."

"Youngest editor in chief I ever heard of," Dean chimed in.

"They keep stats on that?" Walter's snappish response garnered a disapproving frown from Derek. That was fair; he sounded like a jealous ass.

Oliver stroked his wispy goatee. "She's like a glass of champagne," he began, breaking off at Walter's glare of warning. "The color of her dress, I mean. And those heels," he added, as if he couldn't help himself.

Walter's scowl intensified. This Oliver person had no right to talk about Hildy's appearance. Would he have waxed poetic about a male colleague's looks? Also, she was none of his business.

"A lot of history there, huh?" Derek managed to sound both sympathetic and eager for details, while Oliver blinked hard, as if he couldn't quite picture Hildy Johnson rubbing elbows with someone like Walter Burns.

Joke's on you, Walter thought, tugging at the cuffs of his shirt. Once upon a time, he and Hildy had been . . . after an internal debate, he settled on the term "friends." It was both ironic and insufficient.

"It was a long time ago," he said out loud.

"She broke your heart?" Dean guessed.

"Not like that," Walter replied, a shade too quickly.

He could tell from their *mmkay* expressions that his denial had been less than convincing, even though it was mostly true. Hildy had shredded Walter's trust and his professional prospects, but he'd built back since then—entirely on his own, without handouts or shortcuts.

"Who told you that?" he asked Derek. "About Hildy. And me." If Hildy ever mentioned Walter, he assumed it was to curse his name. He'd be lying if he said it wasn't perversely satisfying to get under her skin—metaphorically speaking.

As opposed to the real thing, so abundantly displayed in that dress.

Derek shrugged. "I heard what happened at that wedding in the Catskills, with the mud wrestling. Seemed like a safe assumption the two of you had some baggage."

Not Walter's proudest moment, though there had been extenuating circumstances. What did people expect when they held a wedding at a summer camp, complete with crafts, campfires, and guided nature walks? Messiness went with the territory—especially after a certain magazine editor showed up in her white jean shorts and immaculate hiking boots.

If you were going to point fingers, how about the wedding planner who'd had the brilliant idea of sticking Walter and Hildy on opposite sides of the grown-up tug-of-war?

"We tend to compete for the same stories," Walter explained. Surely fellow journalists would understand how chasing a story could become all-consuming, until it was hard to think about anything else. "It's a professional rivalry."

"Sounds very professional," Dean murmured.

"You must see that all the time in sports. Like Duke and . . . that other team." Walter's usual facility with metaphors seemed to have deserted him.

"UNC," Derek supplied.

"You're saying the two of you are like the Packers and the Bears?" Dean glanced at Hildy, so naturally Walter had to follow the direction of his gaze. What was holding that dress up anyway? The straps looked as structurally sound as cobwebs.

"It's not like the Super Bowl or anything." Walter tried to sound casual, and also like he knew about sports, despite the fact that the only one he'd watched with his mom growing up was figure skating. "There are plenty of weddings to go around."

Although they didn't all cast the same spell as the over-the-top celebrations he and Hildy vied for. The general public seemed to have an insatiable appetite for reading about the nuptials of the ultrawealthy, the glitzier the better. It wasn't necessarily the kind of journalism he'd dreamed of doing as an idealistic teen, but those stories got so much traffic, businesses fell over themselves to buy ad space. His beat might lack world-changing impact, but it was hard to top for job security.

"Hey, Wally."

He'd been too caught up in not staring at Hildy to notice Corinne's approach.

He stood to give her a hug. "You look nice."

"Thanks." She slid her belt to one side, centering the buckle. "Do you like my dress as much as Hildy's?"

Walter opened his mouth to deny any knowledge of Hildy's whereabouts, much less what she was wearing, but Corinne held up a hand. "It looked like you were trying to read the care instructions on the label. From across the room." She pretended to nudge Walter's jaw back into place with the tip of her index finger. "She smells incredible too. And I can tell you her moisturizing game is on point."

"Good for her." Good for both of them, letting bygones be bygones. He wondered what that would be like. Not that he was envious of Corinne's relationship with Hildy. "Did you bring a date?" he asked, casually counting the number of remaining seats at their table.

"Besides Hildy?" Corinne gave him her most patronizing smile, which was saying something. "No. Although I am seeing someone. She's not in the biz, thank God. Some of us know better than to lust after our colleagues."

Walter forced a smile. "You were always the smart one."

"Someone has to be." She studied his face. "Glad to see you're keeping it classy tonight."

He resisted the urge to check his hair. "Is that more sarcasm?"

"No, Mr. Sensitive. You look fine. I mean vis-à-vis you-know-who." She tipped her head in Hildy's direction.

"It's ancient history." Walter rearranged his silverware so he wouldn't have to look Corinne in the eye.

"You're both super over it," she said with a faux-wistful sigh. "It's inspiring."

Derek cleared his throat. "Incoming."

Hildy's dress was closer to gray than silver at this distance, like dolphin skin—or the sky before a storm. What a useful observation, when Walter should have been bracing for impact. Somebody needed to slap some sense into him.

Hildy would probably volunteer.

His thoughts skidded backward, to the first industry event he'd ever attended. It was Hildy who'd coached him on how to dress, make small talk, and style his hair. Walter felt the phantom memory of her hands tugging lightly as they tamed the mushroom cloud on his head.

"We're over here, Corinne." Hildy's voice snapped Walter back to the present in time to feel her glance slide over him like a raindrop against glass. "Gentlemen," she said to the table at large before treating them to a view of her departing figure.

The dress dipped almost to her tailbone in back.

She sat down at the next table over, directly in Walter's line of sight. It was no big deal. He'd seen shoulder blades before—including hers.

"Great posture," Dean whispered.

"Like a dancer," Oliver chimed in.

One thing they didn't teach you in J-school was that reporters were a bunch of pot-stirring gossips.

"I hate all of you," Walter said.

* * *

As the plates were being cleared from dinner, Walter excused himself to stretch his legs. He took his time, doing a full circuit of the lobby. A former boss had encouraged him to take up smoking so he could corner sources when their guard was down, but Walter figured he already had enough self-destructive habits—chief among them the woman who was sitting in his chair when he returned to the banquet hall.

His traitorous tablemates appeared delighted by this development.

"Walter!" Derek beamed at him. "We're playing a drinking game."

That explained the flushed cheeks and goofy grins.

"I'm not sure—" Walter broke off when Hildy's dark eyes dared him to say no.

He was sitting down before he realized he'd made up his mind. As fate would have it, the only empty spot was right next to Hildy.

Good thing he was wearing several layers of clothing, or their bare arms might have accidentally brushed. "What are the rules?"

"Choose a buzzword." Oliver held up a bottle of tequila of unknown origin. Did he travel with his own bar cart? "If they say yours, the rest of the table drinks."

"What if one of us has to go up there?" Walter angled a thumb at the stage, thinking of Hildy's deathtrap stilettos, which he had only noticed because of their vivid scarlet hue. As opposed to a prurient interest in her wardrobe.

"Sounds like somebody's already planning his speech," Hildy said, not quite under her breath. She touched her collarbone, and Walter's gaze snagged there before trailing up the column of her neck. No jewelry that he could see, but maybe you didn't need accessories when your dress was made of starlight.

It occurred to him that he was staring, and the rest of the table was watching him do it. "Things going well at the magazine?" he asked.

"Extremely," Hildy replied. "As I'm sure you've noticed."

"The subscription someone mailed to my home address? It was hard to miss. Once I realized it wasn't a Restoration Hardware catalogue."

Hildy's nostrils flared, though she had to know he was lying through his teeth. Her magazine was as sharp and stylish as its editor in chief.

"Don't be jealous, Burns. We know we look good. It's that tactile quality newsprint can't match." She skimmed a finger along her silk-clad thigh.

Derek notched an invisible mark in the air, like he was keeping score.

"Forget it," Corinne stage-whispered. "It's a permanent stalemate. Minus the mating."

Walter made a desperate attempt to redirect the conversation. "Working on anything interesting?"

"As opposed to our usual drivel?" She fanned her lashes at him, an expression of innocence that would fool no one who had known her longer than ten minutes, never mind ten years.

"Yes, I was insulting you. Because what I do is so different."

"Some would say it's practically identical." Hildy took a casual sip of wine. "Almost derivative."

"And yet you're the one who always seems to be following me."

"I suppose you'd rather I just roll over and let you have your way?" Hildy let that idea dangle between them, twisting a curl around her index finger.

Walter did his best to match her tone. "It's no fun if you don't participate."

"Are they talking about what I think they're talking about?" Derek whispered to Corinne.

"Always," she sighed.

"The wedding beat," Hildy said, before returning her gaze to Walter. "That's the only thing the two of us have in common."

Walter broke eye contact first, draining the contents of the nearest water glass before slamming it on the table. "My word is 'disruptive.'"

"Mine is 'ignite,'" Hildy said half a second later, like even this was a competition.

Dean flicked a not-subtle glance between the two of them. "I'll take 'agitate.'"

"I'm going with 'elevate,'" Corinne said. "As in, the thing we should all strive to do with our behavior."

"Fine," Oliver whined, as if this happened to him every time. "I'll take 'core values.'"

At the podium, the emcee announced the keynote speaker, a rumpled city editor with a few wisps of hair draped over his bare cranium like tinsel.

"If it ever gets to that point, I need you to do an intervention," Dean said to Derek, patting the top of his head.

"Deal," Derek promised.

"Welcome, game changers. We are here tonight to honor the vanguard of our profession. Voices who have elevated the field—"

Corinne pounded the table with her fist. "Line 'em up, losers."

By the time the second speaker stepped to the microphone, Walter was shit-faced. It was a miracle Hildy was still upright, though her posture had gotten a lot less perfect. He imagined running a knuckle down her back to iron out the curve of her spine.

That would be a good way to get his hand bitten off. He poured himself another shot and tossed it back.

"What?" he asked, when the rest of the table stared at him.

"Nobody said any of the words," Derek whispered.

Hildy shook her head, like his lack of gamesmanship came as no surprise. "Walter likes to play fast and loose with the rules."

That was rich, coming from her. "What rules?"

"Like you don't know." She stood abruptly, shimmying her dress back into place. Walter squeezed his eyelids shut, too late to prevent that image from searing itself into his retinas.

When he opened them, Hildy was on the move.

"Have you ever tried walking in heels?" Derek asked, conversationally. "It's a lot harder than it looks." He paused to watch Hildy sashay across the carpet. "She's got skills. The red is a nice touch too. Gives the look that little pop."

"He has a great sense of color," Dean informed the table, slurring slightly.

Walter ignored the unsolicited commentary, looking around for Corinne before pushing his chair back. He didn't like the idea of Hildy wandering hotel corridors alone with that much tequila in her system.

* * *

The hallway was empty. Walter peered around the corner. "Hildy?"

The hangers on a wheeled coatrack slid apart to reveal her face.

"Who wants to know?" When she saw it was Walter, she groaned like a toddler. "Figures."

He strolled around the line of hanging jackets to join her. "What are you doing?"

"Decompressing. What are *you* doing?"

"Looking for you."

"Ta-da." She waved a hand at herself, and Walter noticed she'd kicked off her pointy red shoes. It was like seeing a gladiator post-combat, without their armor.

"Those can't be comfortable."

"You get used to it. Once the circulation cuts off." She rubbed her instep against the opposite calf, and Walter had the insane urge to offer to massage her foot.

"Are you enjoying looming over me?" Hildy tipped her head back to look up at him with an exaggerated squint. Walter found that he missed having her right there in his face. It hadn't occurred to him until then that she almost always wore some kind of heels.

"Yes, looming is one of my top hobbies."

"Lucky for you there are plenty of other shadowy corners in this hotel."

That was probably his cue to leave, but his feet seemed to be stuck to the carpet. He wondered if it was only the urge to free her toes that had brought Hildy out here. "Are you worried about the awards?"

"Maybe," she replied, after a microscopic pause.

"Too much tequila?" he guessed.

"Are you implying I can't hold my liquor?"

Walter shook his head, not rising to the bait.

"Can I be honest?" Hildy asked, before the silence got too heavy.

"Honest or transparent?" he countered, after biting back a knee-jerk *I don't know, can you?*

"What are you, the copy desk?"

"I just meant it's not like you to hold back. Or ask permission to speak freely."

"You'd be surprised how much I keep inside."

She might as well have poured lighter fluid on his curiosity. Walter tried to play it cool. "Such as?"

"Wouldn't you like to know." She mimed turning a key in front of her lips—and then dropping it down the front of her dress. He tried not to look, but it was a losing battle.

"Don't you ever get tired?" She gestured between them. "Of this. It's exhausting."

"Is that all it is?"

Her lips puckered with suspicion, or possibly annoyance. "What do you mean?"

"Isn't it just a teensy bit exciting?" he teased, pinching his thumb and forefinger together. "Gets your blood pumping?"

"Speak for yourself." She leaned back until her shoulder blades touched the wallpaper, springing forward again so fast Walter instinctively reached out to steady her. "It's scratchy," she said, ignoring his outstretched hands. "The wall."

And that dress would offer as much protection as a soap bubble. "Did you hurt yourself?"

She took another step toward him, chin raised in defiance. "Like you care."

Walter forgot to reply, distracted by her closeness. A beat of silence passed. He'd lost the conversational thread. *Don't ask about her perfume*, he silently ordered his mouth. It smelled like jasmine.

Hildy shivered under the weight of his gaze.

"Do you want my jacket?" he asked, sliding it off.

"Why, am I nipping out? I put those little things on." She circled a finger in front of the peak of each breast. "You know what I'm talking about."

He shook his head, not trusting himself to speak.

"I figured one of your brides would have told you. Tricks of the trade. Especially with a backless dress." When he said nothing, Hildy leaned closer, watching him with one brow raised. It felt like playing chicken, to see which of them flinched first.

"What are you doing, Hildy?"

"Waiting for you to run away."

"That's funny." It wasn't. "I could have sworn you were the one who runs."

"Ha! I'm not scared of you."

"Then why are you trembling?" He looked down at the smooth skin of her shoulders, with those whisper-thin straps.

"Rage, most likely."

Walter draped his jacket around her shoulders, careful not to make contact with her skin. "There. In case it's cold *and* rage."

"I am known for my ability to multitask."

He pressed his lips together to keep from smiling, offering a wordless, "Mmm."

"That's all you have to say?"

"What do you want me to say?"

"Nothing."

He shrugged, keeping his mouth shut. Hildy watched him through narrowed eyes, as if she didn't trust such easy obedience.

She edged closer. "Too bad you're not wearing a tie."

"Why?" Walter pressed a hand to the front of his shirt, suddenly insecure about the dress code.

Hildy wet her lips, maybe on purpose—or maybe she was nervous too. "Because I'd grab it." She made a fist and held it under his chin. There was a reckless gleam in her eyes, as if she'd just changed the rules of engagement and was daring him to back down. But Walter was many years (and several shots of tequila) past that kind of caution. If she wanted to escalate their game of brinkmanship, he could kick down a few guardrails too.

"And choke me to death?"

She shook her head. "And pull—like a leash. Then you'd always be right where I want you. No running away."

He lowered his chin, until he was close enough to whisper. "Who's running?"

Her throat moved as she swallowed. "I promised Corinne I wouldn't fight with you."

"We're not fighting."

"Yet."

"It's your call." He indicated the imaginary leash. If Walter were honest, he'd admit it had been there since the day they met: an invisible tether pulling him back into her orbit time and again. "Where do you want me, Hildy?"

When she lifted her hands, he figured the odds were fifty-fifty that she was about to shove him away. He held his breath as her fingers came to rest on his shoulders. Hildy's palms skimmed his collar before traveling up his neck and over his ears until she'd worked her fingernails down to his scalp.

"Who taught you to do this?" she asked, kneading lightly.

"Do what?" How was he supposed to focus when she was touching him? It was like forcing yourself to climb out of a warm bed on a winter morning. He'd keep hitting that snooze button forever.

"This." She smoothed his hair back from his forehead.

His jacket started to slip off her shoulders, so naturally Walter had to put his arms around her to hold it in place. "You did."

"Really." Her hands stilled, like her whole body was skeptical of that answer. "Not a girlfriend?"

He shook his head, taking the opportunity to bring his face closer to hers. She pressed a finger to his mouth. Walter waited for her to tell him to stop, get over himself, read the room. He was dreaming if he thought she was going to . . .

Slowly rub that finger along his lower lip, staring at him with heavy-lidded eyes. When he inhaled sharply, her finger slipped inside his mouth. Walter tasted her on his tongue as his lips closed.

It lasted only an instant before she pulled away, sliding that same finger into her own mouth and sucking it like a candy cane. It was almost a kiss—but not close enough.

Yanking her against him, Walter spun so his back was to the wall. And then his tongue was in her mouth, or vice versa, and his hand was sliding up the thigh she'd wrapped around his hip. She made an impatient noise, and he hoisted her higher, until they both gasped.

"You're touching my ass," Hildy observed.

He squeezed the smooth flesh, wondering hazily if she was planning a complete play-by-play. It wouldn't be the strangest thing about this moment. "You're not wearing underwear."

She bit his earlobe. "Try again."

Walter's hand traveled slowly over her hipbone until he encountered a delicate scrap of lace. It felt like the slightest pressure would snap it in two.

"Ah," he said, giving the fabric an experimental tug.

Hildy choked out an "ah" of her own that he swallowed with another kiss.

They'd kissed before, but not like this. Walter wasn't worried about accidentally banging teeth or what to do with his tongue. He only wished he'd had less tequila so he could taste more Hildy as his mouth slid down to the base of her throat. Pushing the strap of her dress aside, he pressed his lips against the delicate skin of her shoulder.

"I swear to God if you give me a hickey I will end you, Walter Burns."

Hearing her growl his name was almost too much, a phantom wish from his subconscious escaping into the light. And now all he wanted was to leave a mark on her perfect skin to say *I was here. She liked me enough to let me do this*. Every time Hildy looked in the mirror, she'd remember this—remember *him*.

He pulled back, wondering if this was a fever dream. Since

when did Hildy let him hold her like this, all loose and flushed in his arms with her hair mussed and her dress askew?

She flicked him in the shoulder. "Did I tell you to stop? You used to be better at taking direction."

There she is, he thought as Hildy tilted her head to give him access to her neck. It was a pleasure to do her bidding.

"Walter," she asked, breathless.

"Mmm?"

"Are we really doing this?"

"Probably not a good idea." But he didn't stop.

"Because we hate each other?"

"Hate" was a strong word. Maybe their decade of sparring had been more like a scrimmage than a war.

"I was thinking about the public setting," he said. "And we could be drunk."

"But if we don't do it now, we might never get another chance."

"Why?" They were both young and healthy. Walter felt like he could run a marathon, though that wouldn't have been his top choice of aerobic activity.

"We can't go on like this forever."

He tried to frown, but it was hard to focus with his mouth against her throat. A future without Hildy was not something he'd ever contemplated.

"Eventually one of us is going to come out on top. Not like that," she chided, when he hummed his approval. "For real."

This isn't real? Walter didn't give voice to the question, for fear she'd say no.

"I'm talking about settling this for good." Her palms traveled slowly down his chest, leaving a trail of heat in their wake. "Winner take all."

Finally something clicked. "You mean tonight. The award?"

"Maybe." Her eyes slid sideways, and a distant corner of his brain catalogued her brief hesitation as suspicious. "Watch this space, as they say."

"I'm always watching." Apparently it was his night to blurt out things he should have kept to himself.

"Not for long, creeper. You'll be off licking your wounds after I wipe the floor with you."

He captured her mouth again. "I'd rather lick yours."

"Except I won't have any," she said, breathless.

"Somebody's feeling confident."

"I have every reason to be."

Walter fully intended to ask why, until Hildy started undoing the middle buttons of his shirt.

"Guess we better strike while the iron's hot." She suited action to words, slipping her hand inside.

His eyes flickered shut as her fingers skimmed his pecs. "You always did like a good hard deadline."

"Oh yeah. It really gets me going." She gave his nipple a pinch. "This wouldn't even count. It's like a do-over."

"Is that how it works?" He liked this rule—a hall pass for unfinished business—especially when Hildy pulled her hand out of his shirt and reached for the buckle of his belt.

Fuck me, Walter thought. *Please*.

The hangers on the garment rack rattled. The reality of the situation came crashing down on him a second before Corinne shoved a pair of raincoats aside.

"Do I need to get a hose?" She gave them her most withering stare. "I was gone for five minutes."

"At least we weren't arguing." Hildy had already stepped away from him to yank her dress back into place.

"You know what you also weren't doing?" Corinne crossed her arms like a disappointed teacher. "Showing up for the awards announcement. As in, the entire reason we're here."

"It's happening now?" Hildy frantically removed her barrette, sweeping stray tendrils behind her ear before fastening it again. "Can I borrow your lipstick?" she asked Corinne, barely glancing at Walter, who was probably wearing most of Hildy's.

"Too late," Corinne informed her. "They already called it."

Hildy sucked in a breath, like she'd had the wind knocked out of her. She flashed Walter a look heavy with accusation, as if he'd done this on purpose.

Did she really think he'd hatched an evil plot to waylay her with a scorching make-out session? She seemed to have forgotten that Walter had also blown off a career-making milestone to be with her.

And I'd do it again, he realized. If Hildy showed the slightest interest in picking up where they'd left off, Walter would follow her right off that ledge. If he was pissed at anything, it was his own idiocy.

"Who won?" Hildy asked.

Corinne's grimace said it all.

Walter braced for Hildy's reaction. He was ready for her to breathe fire, but she had gone perfectly still—a statue of herself. A second later, she stooped to pick up her shoes.

"Hildy!" he yelled when she slipped past him without so much as a parting glance.

"Whatever," she snapped. "It doesn't matter."

His mouth opened, ready to throw questions after her like grappling hooks. Surely she wasn't going to just *leave*. That would be . . .

Exactly her MO, Walter reminded himself, watching Hildy's curls sway. Was she shaking her head or shuddering?

Even after she turned the corner, her parting salvo rang in his ears. She had to be bluffing. What the hell was all that talk about victory and defeat if the award didn't matter to her?

Unless she meant *Walter* didn't matter. In which case everything that had just happened between them was a nonevent, of negligible importance.

Amazing how she could make him feel like a massive loser even when he "won."

He really should have been used to it by now.

Wedding Bells for Prescott Heiress?

A *Gratz on That* Special Report

Ever since news of Fiona Prescott's engagement to Robin Schafer leaked (pro tip: don't sport a five-carat pink diamond on *that* finger if you don't want people to know your business), the world has been waiting to hear where (and how) they would tie the knot. Lake Como? A private island? One of the family estates? Mount Kilimanjaro?

Well, guess what, C-listers and wannabes: Privacy is the new celebrity. News about the Prescott/Schafer nuptials is locked down tighter than a freshly Botoxed forehead. Rumor has it invites went out this month. If you, like us, were left off the list (boo-hoo!), we'll have to wait for someone to spill all the behind-the-scenes details, because you know this is going to be one for the books.

NOW

2

Hildy

TWO WEEKS BEFORE THE PRESCOTT-SCHAFER WEDDING

NEW YORK—Sometimes Hildy liked to pause in the middle of a staff meeting to pat herself on the back. Not literally, because she didn't want to pull focus from junior members of the editorial team. This was more of a quiet inhale of satisfaction. *I fucking did it. Built my own magazine from the ground up*.

Maybe their offices weren't on the top floor of a skyscraper with million-dollar views, and their bottom line could be more robust, but you had to savor your victories. This sage advice came directly from a guest columnist in one of the first issues of *Life, Styled*. What was the point of winning if you didn't enjoy it? Or pretend to be happy just to be nominated, if the occasion demanded.

Hildy shook off that unpleasant memory. Nothing but blue skies from now on. Total domination of the lifestyle journalism market was almost within reach.

Good luck stealing this *prize, Walter.* Hildy was about to checkmate him so hard he'd be seeing stars.

The thought of scoring the ultimate victory after all this time was like turning her face up to the sun following a decade of winter. Was there a greater feeling in the universe than being in possession of a hot scoop? Especially when the intel was this juicy—and you knew beyond a shadow of a doubt your nemesis didn't have a clue. This time, Walter Burns was going down for the count.

She fought to contain a smile as she made a note for a future listicle (Better than Sex: Feelings We Wish We Could Bottle), earning a sharp glance from her managing editor. Corinne would find out soon enough. The only thing more delicious than holding on to a secret this big was blowing someone else's mind with the reveal. Plus they needed to pack, so time was of the essence.

"Thank you," Hildy said when the last report had been delivered. Ordinarily she would have had follow-up questions about the concept of vegan ceviche, but today there were bigger fish to marinate. "Corinne, could you hang back for a minute? I need to pick your brain."

Judging by the speed with which her features, fashion, and food editors fled the room, they must have assumed the discussion was about to turn to data and metrics, aka Corinne's domain.

"Spill before your head explodes," Corinne said as soon as they were alone. Her refusal to pander to Hildy's moods was both her best and worst quality as a co-worker.

Hildy propped her elbows on the table, leaning forward to make intense eye contact. "Guess who's going to France?"

"You know I hate guessing games. And rhetorical questions, if that's what you were going for."

It occurred to Hildy that she could have found a more receptive audience for her headline news, but she couldn't risk the information leaking beyond this room.

"You and me," Hildy informed the curmudgeon in the charcoal wool dress.

Corinne's frown deepened. "We don't have time for a vacation."

"Good thing this is work." Which would strongly resemble a vacation, but that was a fringe benefit.

"What kind of work?" Corinne asked, still wary.

"We're changing up the August issue." Hildy made a show of

looking over both shoulders. "I have a hot lead for Turning the Page."

"Who's getting married?"

"How do you know it's a wedding?" The entire point of their most popular monthly column was to commemorate all kinds of major life events, from weddings to graduations, house buying to divorce, childbirth to empty nests, with a lavish full-color photo spread and accompanying feature. Part of the *Life, Styled* mission was to show there were many chapters in a person's story, including ones that didn't come with presents and cake.

"Wild guess," Corinne deadpanned. "Unrelated to your general obsession with wedding coverage, which I'm pretending not to notice."

"Fine. It's a wedding. But not just *any* wedding." She let the pause expand until Corinne looked up, then treated her to a double-barreled brow lift.

"Fiona Freaking Prescott's wedding."

Corinne stared at her for several beats. "Are you fucking kidding me. You got it?"

"One hundred percent in the bag."

"Hell yes." Corinne savagely ripped off a bite of bagel with her teeth, chewing like it was the flesh of her enemies. "What kind of clambake are we talking?"

"The social event of the century." As she spoke, Hildy imagined the words in bold type, splashed across a two-page spread. Maybe they'd do a bleached-out effect, give it a retro feel. Or saturate the whole thing with a golden glow. "An American take on the royal wedding. The most hush-hush, closely guarded, A-list-only gathering of one-percenters and corporate titans since the Rockefeller era. The *Vanity Fair* Oscar Party of the business world, only a hundred times more exclusive."

"Are you going to wrap this up today or should I get more coffee?"

"Do you know how hard it's been to keep this inside? I've been bursting to tell someone." Hildy spun her chair in a quick circle, releasing some of the pent-up energy. "This is the culmination of *months* of scheming. The lunches, the brunches, drinks and DMs, hitting up friends of friends, the aunt of a cousin's roommate's yoga instructor, working my way closer and closer to the center of the web." She held up a clenched fist. "Sometimes I amaze myself."

Corinne sighed with what Hildy chose to read as affection. "So what's the deal?"

"The party starts in two weeks, at an undisclosed location in France. Mysterious, no? A full slate of prewedding events, and then the big day itself. Secrets within secrets." Hildy made woo-woo fingers. "Which we will exclusively share with *Life, Styled* subscribers one month postwedding. They get privacy on their big day, we get a massive circulation boost." And permanent bragging rights over their main competitor for wedding coverage. She wasn't going to let *anyone* forget that part.

"I'm going to need maps, flight schedules, weather data." As the tiny calculator that lived inside Corinne's brain whirred to life, Hildy zoned out. She was picturing Walter's face when he realized she'd beaten him to the punch. The tight jaw, flushed cheeks, hands digging through that thick dark hair in frustration . . . if only she could see it for herself. But that would be hard to swing without surveillance, and she'd promised Corinne not to do anything legally compromising. It was the high road all the way: making him cry for mercy from a safe distance.

"Earth to Hildy." Corinne snapped her fingers. "Are we talking vineyard? Riviera? Cathedral? Shit, is it Notre-Dame?"

"Country, not city," Hildy corrected. "I'm thinking remote and private. Secluded yet lavish. Apparently it's going to be very *Sleeping Beauty*–core."

"I have no idea what that means."

Neither did Hildy, but she was willing to roll with a vague aura of fairy-tale magic, presuming tiaras would be involved. She gave Corinne the few establishing details she'd managed to wheedle out of the bride. "We fly into Bordeaux, and then they transport us to the destination. That's all they're telling us so far."

"Are we going to be blindfolded?"

"The vibe I'm getting is less 'sex cult' and more 'European refinement.' The word 'terroir' was used."

"Wines of the Bordeaux region," Corinne voice memoed herself. "Should we start researching tonight?" She mimed tipping back a glass.

"I booked a hot oil treatment." Hildy fluffed her curls. "Might do a little shopping on the way home. I'm thinking linen everything, definitely a new straw hat." She shivered with anticipation. "This is a major turning point for us. It's going to put *Life, Styled* on the map. You want to know the best part?"

"Securing the financial future of our magazine?"

Hildy shook her head. "Fiona said I'm the only one she trusts to do the story justice. Which means no Walter Burns lurking around like a fox, or—a wolf. No, a weasel." Because foxes and wolves suggested a certain level of charisma, and the only thing Hildy wanted to imply was that Walter was underhanded. "The point is, he may have won a stupid award, but that doesn't mean anything except the judges are probably misogynists."

"In your unbiased opinion."

"As a journalist," Hildy agreed, hand to heart.

"Let's hope you're right." Corinne rapped her knuckles against the surface of the table. "Knock on fake wood. We can't afford another episode of the Walter and Hildy show."

"That was not my fault. You know I never back down from a challenge."

Corinne blinked in mock confusion. "What exactly was the

challenge? 'Hildy, I bet you can't lick my tonsils.' Or no, 'Hildy, I dare you to show up at the awards ceremony in an itty-bitty silk dress that leaves nothing to the imagination.'"

"It's called cross-promotion. We feature the designer in *Life, Styled*, I wear their work at a high-profile public event. Representing our brand is part of my job description."

"What's our brand again—eat your heart out, Walter Burns?"

"Presenting a glossy package so alluring and fresh no one can look away." That was the genius of a bias-cut slip dress with a daringly low scoop in back, if you knew how to move. *Feast your eyes on this, journalists of the tristate area!* And yes, that list happened to include Walter, but as far as Hildy was concerned, her only mistake had been letting him get close enough to touch.

Corinne shook her head. "I guess it was naïve of me to think we'd finally hit the statute of limitations on this situation."

"De-escalation takes two."

"Does it, though? Seems to me that as an adult woman you are fully capable of letting go of a grudge from high school." Corinne lowered her voice on the last two words, like they were too embarrassing to say at full volume.

"It doesn't matter how old we were. That was the starting line of my professional career."

"What some might call your villain origin story."

"Thanks to Walter!" Hildy closed her eyes. He wasn't going to dim her shine today of all days. "Fine, yes, I'm partly responsible for what happened at the banquet. Like twenty-five percent."

"And Walter is the other seventy-five?"

"No, at least forty percent of the blame belongs to the tequila. The rest is Walter. You know how ruthless he is. There's no limit to how low he'll stoop to sabotage me."

"He certainly looked like he was ready to get down and dirty. Right there behind the coatrack."

Hildy pretended to inspect her cuticles, even though she'd had her nails done three days ago. If she didn't replay the memory, maybe she wouldn't betray herself with a blush. "Like I said, that won't be an issue. Walter Burns can read about the wedding of the century at the same time everyone else does—on the pages of *Life, Styled*."

"I expected an evil laugh at the end of that monologue. But I appreciate the restraint."

Hildy flicked her hair over her shoulder. "I am a classy bitch."

Wedding Week Itinerary

On behalf of the bridal couple and their families, bienvenue en France! Thank you for being part of this celebration of the union of Fiona Prescott and Robbie Schafer. We hope you will take the opportunity to immerse yourselves in the rich history of the region, as well as its vibrant contemporary culture, by joining the daily excursions.

The Welcome Soiree: An Evening of Roses and Rosé

Day 1: Jardins in the Sky: Feast your eyes on cutting-edge horticultural design surrounded by stunning views of the Vézère Valley at this clifftop art garden, followed by lunch at the château.

Day 2: Gastronomical Exploration: Luxury meets terroir on a private tasting tour of artisanal local delicacies, including magret de canard fumé, vin de noix, and, of course, foie gras.

Day 3: Architectural Majesty: Even in the Land of 1001 Castles, the Romanesque keep of the Château de Beynac stands out as one of the most stunning examples of the form, towering above the eponymous village.

Day 4: Un Jour à la Campagne: Try your hand at the sports of kings and queens, including archery, falconry, games of strategy, the catapult, and, of course, the joust. All equipment provided.

Day 5: Journey to the Center of the Earth: Among the most extensive of the legendary decorated caves of the region, Rouffignac boasts more than two hundred images of prehistoric animals.

Day 6: On the Rivière: Whether you choose a kayak, a canoe, or a more leisurely tour on one of the traditional gabarres that have ferried passengers along local waterways since the Middle Ages, spending time on the river is a must.

Day 7: The Moment: Be ready to board your shuttle by 3 PM for the trip to a wedding venue beyond your wildest dreams. A cocktail hour precedes the ceremony, which will be followed by a seated dinner, after which Fiona and Robbie invite you to join them in dancing the night away.

> *We hope this week will be a time of relaxation and enrichment for our guests. For questions or assistance of any kind, wedding staff will be available at the main and satellite hotels as well as during the day trips. The families respectfully request that you refrain from sharing information or photos until after the wedding, to protect everyone's privacy.*
>
> *The media presence will be discreet.*

NOW

3

Hildy

ONE WEEK BEFORE THE PRESCOTT-SCHAFER WEDDING

BORDEAUX, France—"You know they have wine everywhere," Hildy pointed out. "We didn't have to go to a museum to find it."

Her preference for their first day in France would have been shopping, followed by people watching at an outdoor café, after which they could have strolled along the river thinking deep thoughts about love, death, and fashion. You had to embrace the local culture or what was the point of travel?

"I'm sorry, is my desire to learn things killing your buzz?" Corinne checked her phone. "Is it weird we haven't heard anything from the office?"

"What are you picturing, a hostage situation?" Hildy grabbed the phone out of her hand and shoved it under a napkin. "It's still super early in New York, and if there was a crisis, they'd let us know. We'll video chat with them later, okay?"

"Maybe not while we're drinking."

"We're in Bordeaux. We're not going to *not* drink the wine. It would be rude. Besides, they should see us living our best lives. It's aspirational."

Corinne narrowed her eyes. "You're surprisingly calm about being away from the magazine."

"We're away from the *office*," Hildy corrected. "The magazine is with us always."

"If you say the words 'in our hearts,' I'm not responsible for my actions."

"Fine." Hildy made a heart sign with both hands anyway, just to see Corinne's eyelid twitch. There was nothing like day drinking in a fancy ultramodern museum after minimal sleep to give you a sense of reckless abandon.

Corinne frowned at Hildy's wineglass. "Are you almost finished?"

Hildy obediently chugged the rest, hoping a French gendarme wasn't going to march up and arrest her for failing to savor every sip.

"Because we have limited time here, so we need to keep it moving."

"I got the judgy subtext the first time," Hildy assured her. "But thanks."

Despite their intense predeparture strategizing, they'd managed to arrive in France with starkly different visions for the first stage of the trip. Hildy assumed their primary agenda during these two days would be making sure French women hadn't made a massive evolutionary leap on the fashion front that had yet to reach American shores and then updating their own wardrobes accordingly.

Ha! Corinne was far too busy dragging her from reflecting pool to fountain and then on to another ancient stone gate. Even their meal breaks had parameters.

"We should taste as many walnut products as possible," Corinne had informed Hildy on the way out of the hotel that morning. "Candied walnuts, walnut liqueur, walnut ice cream. Also duck. We need to hit that hard."

And so they had, for the last twenty-seven or so hours, by Hildy's estimation. It wasn't that she didn't enjoy these cultural highlights. She simply preferred to have herself in order first, and sweaty and footsore had not been on her list of goals for the day. When she told Corinne they needed to hit the ground running, Hildy had been imagining the two of them sinking into the pampered-wedding-guest mindset so that by the time the actual festivities began, they'd be in peak form.

At least the wine museum was a reasonable compromise: atmosphere and refreshments plus educational value! After an aperitif and snacks, Hildy felt fortified enough to ask, "What's next on your list, Rick Steves?"

"We need to eat some of those canelés. They look like tiny Bundt cakes, but the consistency is closer to a baked custard. It's the signature pastry of Bordeaux."

"Noted," Hildy said.

"And then we have a lot more old buildings to look at." She glanced at Hildy's shoes, which had admittedly been chosen for style rather than comfort. "We can take the tram."

"Hallelujah." Beyond giving her feet a break, Hildy appreciated the aesthetics of the experience, the sleek modern vehicle gliding past the narrow streets and weathered stone of the ancient city center. It was like seeing a martini shaker in a thatched cottage, or those glass pyramids at the Louvre.

She was thinking about the visual impact of combining elements from different worlds, and whether that was something to discuss with the magazine's graphic designers, as the tram slowed ahead of the next stop. Some primal instinct made her turn, her body recognizing danger before her conscious mind received the news.

Hildy's fingers clamped onto Corinne's arm, interrupting a description of one of the bridges that spanned the Garonne River. "We need to get off *now*," she hissed.

"Not yet." Corinne pointed at the map on the wall showing their route. "I told you, our stop is Hôtel de Ville."

"Change of plans." Hildy tugged at Corinne's arm, ready to drag her through the doors if necessary. "Excusez-moi," she said to the people in front of them as she angled her body toward the exit.

"What the hell was that?" Corinne asked when they were on the platform.

Hildy held a finger to her lips, beckoning Corinne to follow as she hurried around a group of schoolkids in matching uniforms. Reaching into her tote, Hildy grabbed the first thing that came to hand. Last month's *Life, Styled* wasn't the ideal camouflage for the situation, but she held it in front of her face anyway.

"Are you doing some kind of mime?" Corinne didn't bother lowering her voice. "Is it because we're in France? I think I'd prefer a beret, if you're going to pick up an affectation. Or a jaunty little scarf."

The tram running in the opposite direction finally pulled away from the station. When the last car had disappeared from view, Hildy lowered the magazine. "You didn't see?"

"See what?" Corinne jerked from side to side, no doubt panicked at the thought of missing a historical marker or famous statue.

Hildy took a deep breath. It was important not to panic. "We have a situation on our hands. Code red."

"You got your period?"

"No! He's here."

"The groom?"

"The Walter!"

Corinne shot her a skeptical look. "That second glass of wine was a bad idea."

"I'm not drunk!" Hildy hadn't meant to yell but her nerves were shot. "I saw him," she insisted. "On the tram."

"Pretty sure I would have noticed if *Walter Burns* was on our train. Especially after your head started spinning around."

"Not ours. The one going the other direction." She needed to fast-forward this part of the discussion, because they didn't have time to argue over whether Hildy was or was not delusional. "Do you seriously think I wouldn't recognize him?"

Corinne opened her mouth and then closed it again. "No," she finally conceded. "You could probably dig his femur out of a shallow grave and be like, 'Aha! Definitely Walter's thigh bone.'"

"Okay," Hildy said, ignoring the macabre undertones. "So we accept the basic premise that Walter is here, in Bordeaux."

"Coincidence?" Corinne ventured.

Hildy shook her head. "He's here for the *wedding*. This is one billion percent an attempt to steal my story."

"Did he cackle and twirl his mustache when he spotted you?"

"He didn't see me." The acid taste at the back of her throat didn't fade when Hildy swallowed. "Too busy chatting up Fiona Prescott's sister."

It had taken a minute to place the woman's face, but Hildy's recall for names was excellent, especially when the person in question had flirted shamelessly with Walter in her presence. Maude Prescott, the older sister of the bride, was some kind of fancy plant expert with multiple degrees and an austere personal style that made Hildy feel ever so slightly unsophisticated.

"Fuuuuuuck," Corinne groaned, to the delight of the nearby French children, who immediately began imitating her pronunciation, like a miniature Greek chorus.

Hildy smiled an apology at the teacher while backing away. It was cold comfort knowing she and Corinne were finally on the same page, existential dread-wise.

"I thought we had an exclusive." Corinne rubbed her temples.

"We do."

"Then she can't turn around and let Walter write about the wedding too."

It wouldn't be the first time a bride had wriggled out of an agreement. The soon-to-be-married were prone to eleventh-hour freak-outs. Fortunately, most of them could be talked around if you knew which buttons to push.

"We need to get there ASAP." The plan was already coalescing in Hildy's mind. "He can scheme all he wants. Anyone who gets between me and this story will live to regret it."

"This feels like the moment to remind you it would be hard to edit a magazine from prison."

"Don't worry. Plan A is to cut the head off the snake."

"I feel so reassured," Corinne muttered, as Hildy pressed a contact on her phone.

"Fiona? It's Hildy. Bonjour to you too. Listen, I have some fun news!" She squeezed every last drop of false cheer she could muster into the words, hoping it would hide the undercurrent of panic. "We are so excited to get started, we're coming today!"

NOW

4

Walter

ONE WEEK BEFORE THE PRESCOTT-SCHAFER WEDDING

ON THE A89 AUTOROUTE, France—No one told Walter that jet lag would feel like coming out of general anesthesia.

The strangeness of his current circumstances—in the back of a luxury town car, next to a woman he barely knew, in a foreign country—kept fading in and out like a radio signal. All the snap decisions that had led to this moment felt remote and unreal, as if he'd been sleepwalking at the time.

It started at a wedding, and Hildy was involved: Those were the essential facts. Then again, that described most of the mistakes Walter had made in the last decade.

Maybe it would have been different if he'd met Maude under other circumstances. Or if Hildy hadn't been there. Or let's be real: if Walter had never gotten tangled up with Hildy in the first place. But you couldn't rewind time, so he needed to focus on the present—starting with the woman who was actually here beside him.

Maude wasn't the first wedding guest who had propositioned Walter. He might be new to transatlantic travel, but there was very little about the marriage industrial complex that surprised him, and behind-the-scenes assignations were as central to the experience as white satin. The steps were as familiar as the electric slide: a glance at his ring finger, a question about whether he was staying on-site, a casual mention of a room number. In his case, the tacit invitations had an undertone of *you're here to do a job; why not provide this additional service?*

But Maude's approach was different. She was much more subtle, for one thing. When he accepted her invitation to meet for coffee, Walter's only thought had been maintaining friendly relations with a source. He certainly wasn't banking on a trip to France.

Some offers were too good to refuse.

"Mineral water?"

It wasn't until Maude spoke that Walter realized how long they'd been sitting in silence, apart from the muffled sounds of traffic.

"I'm fine, thanks."

He considered the woman sitting beside him. Maude was intelligent, ambitious, dark haired—on paper, totally his type. So what if the conversation wasn't flowing? Walter was fried, and she was distracted. There were worse things than an uninterrupted stretch of quiet. At least he and Maude weren't at each other's throats.

A phantom memory of the silken warmth of Hildy's skin taunted him. Walter could almost feel the throb of her pulse against his lips.

If he was sharing this back seat with Hildy, the air would be buzzing with tension.

That was probably what happened when your first infatuation was an epic clusterfuck: a warped sense of what a relationship should be. Once you confused danger with attraction, you were doomed to keep wanting things that were bad for you, instead of seeing the potential in someone calm and mature like Maude.

"What?" Maude asked.

"I didn't say anything."

"You were staring."

Walter shook his head. "Sorry. Zoning out."

"We're still about an hour away, if you want to take a nap. I'll wake you up when we get there." Maude had been here for weeks, supervising preparations. She was fully adjusted to the local time zone. Or maybe she was just more accustomed to the jetsetter lifestyle than Walter, who'd gotten his first passport two years ago.

"Thanks." He was grateful for an excuse to close his eyes, though he had no plans to sleep. Walter had passed through exhaustion and come out the other side. Thoughts darted in and out of his consciousness, slippery as fishes, until he managed to latch onto one.

Where was Hildy right now?

NOW

5

Hildy

ONE WEEK BEFORE THE PRESCOTT-SCHAFER WEDDING

ON THE A89 AUTOROUTE, France—"What if it's a cave?" Corinne asked, after they survived a hair-raising series of roundabouts to merge onto the expressway.

"What if what's a cave?"

"The wedding venue."

"I don't see Fiona Prescott as the spelunking type." It was a wish as much as a prediction, since helmets would wreak havoc on Hildy's curls. Not to mention her general dislike of dark and creepy spaces.

"Speaking of going deep," Corinne continued, "we need to talk about the history before we get there. It's definitely going to come up."

"You know it's not my fault that Walter's here." Hildy flinched as another French driver whizzed past like he was auditioning for Formula One. What was the speed limit? She didn't have the brain power to translate kilometers into miles.

"Narcissism, party of one. I'm not talking about *your* history. This is cave art country. Prehistory central. I've been doing a lot of reading about Lascaux."

That explained her wedding theory. "We can do a sidebar," Hildy promised. "Once we lock down the main story."

"Right." Corinne exhaled heavily. "It all depends on that." She turned to face the window a beat too late to hide her worried expression.

"We just have to remind Fiona that working with us was *her* decision and people need to respect her autonomy because it's her damn wedding. There's a history of tension in that area, which should play to our advantage."

"Okay, Machiavelli."

Hildy's conscience gave a guilty twinge. She generally preferred to use her powers for good. "Blame Walter! He's forcing me to take the gloves off."

Corinne fell into a ruminative silence. Hildy wasn't sure whether she was silently judging or looking for landmarks as they zoomed past green hillsides dotted with occasional signs proudly advertising the local gastronomy. Ducks! Wine! Walnuts! The French made no secret of their priorities in life.

Unlike some people Hildy could name, who specialized in being as opaque as possible, even when they were chasing you across two continents.

"What's the deal with the sister?" Corinne asked.

"They're close, but there's a pretty big age gap. And then when their mom died, the dynamic totally shifted. Maude has a tendency to treat Fiona like a child."

It was one of the first things Hildy and Fiona had bonded over, this strange combination of being motherless and yet surrounded by controlling relatives. Although the circumstances were not identical, since Fiona's father was still alive and her mother had died of natural causes, as opposed to signing away parental rights to continue her career as an ethnographer in a remote South American rainforest while Hildy was raised by an overbearing uncle and succession of step-aunts, plus two boneheaded cousins who treated her like a combination little sister and household pet.

Everybody had their own story—as Hildy had pointed out

more than once during an editorial meeting. In her case, there was even a peer-reviewed journal article about her disappearing parent's decision to "repudiate the first-world Western trap of the patriarchal nuclear family" to pursue the "higher goal" of research. Maybe if her mom (aka the egg donor) had known Hildy's father was a few short years from a fatal car accident, she might have stuck around. Or not! It wasn't like Hildy had a window into her mother's thoughts, beyond what she'd shared with the rest of the world.

Hildy assumed her coloring and her curls were her mother's legacy, since she didn't resemble the rest of the Johnson clan. Sometimes she worried she'd also inherited her missing parent's relentless ambition, though hopefully Hildy was less cold-blooded about it. If she had to manipulate Fiona, it would be gently—and with her best interests at heart. As well as Hildy's. And her magazine's.

"I mean in terms of Walter," Corinne clarified. "What's his connection with the sister?"

"They met at a wedding." Hildy made a conscious effort to loosen her grip on the steering wheel. "Remember the nouveau agrarian paradise bride last fall? That was Maude's cousin."

"Met as in they were introduced or . . . ?" Corinne let the question trail off, though they both knew what she was really asking: Did they hook up or what?

"Allegedly he was interviewing her," Hildy said, before Corinne could go there. "About *plants*."

Corinne snorted as if she'd heard that line before. It was gratifying to know Hildy wasn't the only one who found that excuse a little thin.

THEN

6

Hildy

TEN MONTHS AGO

NEW HOPE, Pa.—There were farms and then there were *farms*, Hildy reflected, taking in the scene. A perfect blue sky, a puff or two of white clouds, blowsy flowers and rippling grass, rustic indoor furniture arranged on the lawn in conversational vignettes: The effect was very urban-sophisticate-moves-to-the-country-to-grow-a-perfect-pint-of-berries. Which she would then sell at the farmer's market and somehow earn enough to support her chenin blanc habit.

Hildy would watch the shit out of that movie, but this was supposed to be real life. Or at least the aesthetic version of "real." They had animals and everything, including a trio of sheep so immaculately groomed they could have competed at the Westminster Kennel Club. Were there stylists who specialized in livestock, or did they pay a human beautician to give the animals a blowout? She made a mental note to investigate further for a possible feature. Today, she had a different agenda.

"Earthy but sophisticated," she murmured. "Natural without the tang of dirt. The mason jar aesthetic on steroids, refreshed and rejuvenated. A kale smoothie for the eyes."

Naturally, Walter chose that moment to stroll around an artistic arrangement of hay bales. He acted surprised at seeing her there.

"Friend of the bride?" he asked.

"I have a lot of friends," Hildy replied, with what she hoped was an air of mystery. If he thought she was there to party, like the spoiled socialite he presumed her to be, it would blindside him when *Life, Styled* published their superior coverage.

Walter stared into the distance, as though captivated by the miniature donkey being led on a harness like this year's golden-doodle. Guests could "borrow" one for the day, if they wanted to add a little animal husbandry to their sojourn in the country. Hildy had been tempted, but she needed both hands free for taking notes.

"Don't let me keep you," Hildy said, with a transparently false smile.

"Why? Are you here with someone?"

"Is that so hard to believe?"

"Just making conversation."

As if either of them ever said anything to the other without packing in at least two layers of hidden meaning. Every sentence was a baklava of sneak attacks and coded insults. "I'm surprised you made it out of the last one alive."

"Sorry to disappoint you."

She shrugged, watching his eyes catch on the sweetheart neckline of her gingham sundress. "Hopefully you won't catch anything from the livestock."

"And leave you to report on this wedding all by yourself? That would be tragic."

"I think you mean 'awesome.'"

"You don't get to edit me, remember? I don't work for you."

"Thank God for that." She steepled her hands, casting a grateful look skyward. "I have more important things to worry about than keeping you in line."

"My sentiments exactly."

A server approached, offering them hors d'oeuvres. Walter

shook his head like the buzzkill he was, so naturally Hildy had to take one to be contrary.

"How is it?" he asked, when her mouth was full of puff pastry and chili oil and some kind of leaf.

She took her time swallowing before slowly running a finger over the corner of her lips. Stepping closer, she tapped the old-school notebook tucked into the lapel pocket of his suit. "Do your own research."

His hand closed around her fingers, holding them for a beat before gently removing them from his person. Even after releasing her hand, he maintained eye contact, voice lowered to a confidential rumble. "I've done *plenty*."

"Something in your throat?" Hildy held up a finger, and another server glided over with a tray of cocktails.

"I don't drink when I'm on the clock," Walter said.

She shrugged, taking a long sip of a beverage that tasted like a more acidic V8. "Yum," she lied. "Maybe I'll run the recipe as a sidebar."

"Really?" His little *hmm* of surprise was like a mosquito bite on the back of Hildy's knee.

"What?"

"It seems to me the real story is the setting." Walter spoke as if it pained him to have to point out something so obvious. "This property has been in the bride's family for generations. Her grandparents were married here—"

"And she had her grandmother's dress remade for today," Hildy cut in. "Speaking of historical tidbits."

"They also added a saltwater swimming pond to the grounds, converted the main house to solar energy—"

"Installed a dance floor in the barn."

"With wooden beams from an old dairy," Walter hastened to add, before Hildy could say it. "But of course the real cherry on top—"

"Is the plantscaping." She choked a little on the word, for its intrinsic silliness and because the botanical consultant had ignored Hildy's request for an interview. So they'd grown their own flowers. It wasn't *that* revolutionary.

Walter's eyes lit up, like he knew exactly what she was thinking. "You heard about the sunflowers?"

The temptation to bluff was powerful, but Hildy kept her mouth shut.

"No?" he correctly surmised. "Must be because she promised the story to me."

"Congratulations." She gave him a dead-eyed smile. "Stop the presses, we have breaking news: Flowers spotted at wedding!"

"It's not a *bouquet*, Hildy. We're talking about a room made entirely of sunflowers. Four green, growing walls, a carpet of grass, nothing but sky overhead. Can you imagine the happy couple saying their vows at sunset?"

"It sounds like a glorified arbor," Hildy lied.

"I guess you'll find out when you read my story, since that part of the ceremony is private." He sighed as if he sympathized with her plight. "It really is a piece of living art."

"I'm glad you think so," said the tall, spare brunette who had approached from Walter's other side. She was all angles and monochromatic clothes, with a sleek bob and oversized jewelry. Hildy would have guessed art dealer or spy before gardener.

"Hello, Maude." Walter turned on the charm, beaming as if he hadn't already bamboozled a story out of her. Hildy might have thrown up, if her drink hadn't already burned through her stomach lining.

Maude offered Hildy her hand. "Cousin of the bride."

"You're a lot more than that." Walter sounded like he was auditioning for a role as her personal hype man. That was an awful lot of pride to take in a source—unless he and Maude were exchanging more than horticultural trivia.

"She has a degree in plant sciences from Cornell," Walter informed Hildy. "Maude grew half of what we're eating tonight. I'd tell you about it, but that would spoil the surprise."

Hildy kept her smile locked in place even when Maude put a hand on Walter's arm. It seemed like a superfluous gesture when their hips were already touching, but it did confirm the vibe she'd been sensing.

"I'm sorry I had to cut our conversation short." Maude pitched her voice low, for Walter's ears only. "I have a few minutes now, if you're free. I could give you a tour."

He gazed at Maude as if the two of them were alone at a candlelit restaurant. "I would love that. If you're sure you don't mind?"

"Knock yourselves out," Hildy replied. Not that she wasn't having a super fun time being the third wheel.

Walter frowned at her. "I was talking to Maude. She must be incredibly busy today."

Unlike Hildy, who was standing there with a froufrou drink, twiddling her thumbs. It was so typical of Walter to make her feel like a vapid afterthought.

"My part is mostly done," Maude assured him.

"Lucky me." He smiled down at Maude-the-talented in that ingratiating way Hildy vaguely remembered from their youth. He probably used it all over the wedding circuit: *Tell me more about your table settings! I find your choice of napkins deeply compelling!*

What would the fawning bridesmaids and plantscapers say if they met high school Walter, before his frame filled out and his skin cleared and someone analyzed his colors? (Though Hildy could have told him back then that this shade of green would make his eyes pop.) When they first met, it had been a toss-up whether Hildy wanted to kiss him or give him the other half of her BFF charm. *Maybe*, she remembered thinking, *this is what it's like when you meet someone really special*. They could be your friend *and* your crush.

Now that she was older and wiser, Hildy's feelings about Walter were a lot less ambiguous. She wanted to take him apart, slowly and methodically, with her bare hands. *Psychologically*, she course-corrected, when the wrong kind of image popped into her head. It had nothing to do with removing his clothes.

"Excuse us," Walter said, his arm not quite touching Maude's lower back.

He could play the respectful gentleman all day. Hildy wasn't fooled. This was Walter waving a red flag in her face. Look at me, stealing the scoop right out from under you!

Let Walter think he'd won. What was one minor skirmish in the grand scheme of their war? Hildy was already working another angle, with the potential to deliver a truly epic victory. And then they'd see who really excelled at nurturing a tiny seedling of an idea into a brilliant blossom of a story.

Hildy pictured a faceless woman poring over the pages of *Life, Styled*. She might be at a nail salon, or a sticky kitchen table, or the doctor's office, or on a crowded train, but for those stolen moments she'd be in this pastoral idyll, on a summer afternoon, walking on plush grass while a light breeze ruffled her hair. Maybe it seemed superficial to *some* people, but Hildy believed she was providing a public service. Who needed a sunflower room when you could take your mind on vacation for the price of a magazine? Hildy held her hand out to the side, dropping an invisible mic.

"Was that Walter's wallet?" Corinne asked, strolling up beside her. She pretended to check the grass for evidence.

"No." Though that would have been a neat trick, had Hildy trained as a pickpocket. "I have a much bigger score in mind."

"Looks like you have competition," Corinne shot a pointed look at Maude, who was holding up a sprig of something green for Walter's inspection.

"I'm not talking about scoring with Walter. The goal is to score *on* him. Or against him. Over him." Damn it. "You know what I mean."

"That makes one of us," Corinne murmured into her drink.

Hildy didn't dignify that with a response. "Rumor has it the Prescott clan may be gathering for another wedding in the not-too-distant future."

"Shit!" Corinne's face drained of color. "You mean Walter—"

"No!" Hildy was superstitiously glad to have cut her off before she could finish the thought. "Don't be ridiculous. Not that it matters to me. Except for pitying whoever ends up with him. Why do you look so relieved?" she asked, before Corinne could argue.

"I was afraid I was going to have to hog-tie you, what with the open flames and pointy skewers."

How would it feel to have a second-in-command who respected your executive functioning? Hildy would probably never know. "For your information, I'm totally in control—and in possession of a very important piece of knowledge."

"Feel free to tell me once this dramatic pause is over."

"There's another Prescott daughter." And Hildy was going to make sure she got to this one first.

NOW

7

Walter

ONE WEEK BEFORE THE PRESCOTT-SCHAFER WEDDING

TAMNIÈS, France—The roads grew increasingly narrow after they exited the highway, carrying them deeper into the countryside until they turned onto a paved track that wound around a steep hill. Perched at the top was a picturesque village with a commanding view of the surrounding fields and forests.

"The main hotel is over there." Maude pointed at an entryway draped in wisteria, beyond which Walter glimpsed a sparkling infinity pool. "That's the restaurant," she added, indicating a building on the other side of the clay tennis courts that must have predated the hotel by several centuries. "A lot of the houses on the main square are actually guest cottages. Basically this whole town is part of the hotel complex, except for the church. And the cemetery."

Walter assumed it would set the wrong tone for a resort to have its own graveyard. Definitely not in keeping with the overall vibe of French country charm.

He climbed from the car, arching his back in a long-overdue stretch. The air was warm and fragrant. Overflowing flower boxes adorned the windowsills, attracting bees that buzzed lazily in the honeyed light. It was hard to remember a world of airports and toll roads and deadlines.

"It's beautiful," he said, too exhausted to come up with a better word.

Maude gave a distracted *hmm*, sliding her sunglasses to the top of her head. "Obviously it's not the *main* attraction." She glanced at his hands, as if he might be taking notes. "Shall we go in and get you settled?"

Walter started in the direction of the trunk, but Maude waved him off. "They'll bring your luggage."

Ah. His middle-class roots were showing. He followed Maude down a covered walkway lined with potted trees. The door to the hotel swung open before they reached it. Walter expected a uniformed doorman, but it was the bride herself who stormed outside.

"Maude!" She held both hands out in front of her, like a flight attendant having a tantrum mid-safety demo. "What is going on?"

Walter shifted slightly, feigning a sudden interest in the canopy of tree branches overhead. There came a point in every wedding when family tensions spilled over. No one wanted a reporter to witness those scenes, so he'd gotten good at being invisible when the occasion demanded.

"Calm down, Fee. What's the problem?" Maude reached for her sister as if to squeeze her shoulder, but Fiona jerked away.

"You can't just show up here with *him*." A manicured hand flicked in Walter's direction. He blinked in surprise. Apparently he wasn't an innocent bystander on this one.

"Why not?" Maude sounded faintly amused by her sister's outburst, in what Walter suspected to be a habitual older sibling attitude.

"Because he wrote about our cousin's wedding," Fiona replied, as if it should have been obvious. "What's next, you're going to tell me to wear her dress? Hire the same band? Maybe we should copy her menu too?"

A cool breeze danced across the back of Walter's neck, leaving a trail of gooseflesh in its wake. And yet the leaves on the trees didn't so much as rustle.

"I already hired someone to do the wedding coverage," Fiona was saying, all but stomping her foot. "By myself. Because it's *my* wedding."

Slowly, Walter turned around.

"Walter," Hildy said, in a voice so cool it would have frosted glass. Which was ironic, considering her sleeveless yellow dress looked like liquid sunshine. Her bare shoulders were already bronzed.

"Hildy," he replied. Adrenaline burned off the jet lag in an instant.

She turned her back on him with the regal disdain of a cat, watching the Prescott sisters.

"I'm not stepping on your toes," Maude chided, grabbing Fiona's hands. "He's here for *me*, Fee."

Had he imagined the sharp intake of breath from Hildy's direction?

"You're dating?" Fiona's gaze swung from Maude to Walter. "Why didn't you tell me?"

"Well," Maude started to say, but whatever explanation or excuse she planned to offer was cut short by the arrival of an older man with white-streaked hair.

"A date? Let's hope this one speaks English." He laughed at his own joke, chucking Maude under the chin.

"Daddy," Fiona protested, leaping to her sister's defense as if they hadn't been butting heads thirty seconds ago.

Mr. Prescott sighed. "So sensitive." He extended a hand to Walter. "I didn't catch your last name?"

"Burns."

"Don't know it."

"He's going to write about the castle," Maude said, before her father could ask to see Walter's family tree.

"What's this about a castle?" Hildy looked from Fiona to Maude, skipping over Walter as if he didn't exist.

"It was hidden in the forest," Maude began, with the practiced air of someone who had told this story a hundred times. "The trees grew up around it until everyone forgot it was there. I've been overseeing the restoration of the grounds. It's something of a passion project."

Hildy nodded as if Maude was speaking her language. Walter guessed she must be thinking of *Life, Styled* as her castle.

"Maude named it Château Fiona, because I'm going to be the first one ever to get married there!" Fiona's expression fell. "Only Maude made me promise not to tell anyone so it wouldn't spoil the big reveal, even though *she* gets to spill to whoever she wants."

"I only told Walter," Maude protested.

If he hadn't been watching so closely, Walter might have missed Hildy's eye twitch.

"If there's one thing he loves, it's a castle." Someone who didn't know her might have believed Hildy was making polite conversation, but Walter recognized the sound of an incoming grenade. "I bet he's just *bouncing* with excitement."

"I have no idea what you're talking about," he lied.

THEN

8

Walter

ONE YEAR AGO

MILFORD, Del.—In his idealistic youth, Walter had envisioned a journalistic career that made a difference: exposing corruption, holding polluters accountable, bringing medical advancements to light. Nowhere in that list of Pulitzer-worthy investigative series had he predicted covering the Dark Carnival–themed wedding of two crypto bros.

The setting—on the grounds of an abandoned fertilizer plant in Delaware—would have been creepy enough without the truckloads of dead leaves that had been brought in for the occasion. Walter had not previously been aware that autumn foliage was available out of season, especially in this quantity, but according to the wedding designer, the leaves were a crucial element of the Macabre Attraction aesthetic.

"It's that crunch underfoot, like desiccated insect bodies," she'd explained, with the air of someone who expected to be quoted in print. "Enhancing the awareness of decay and mortality."

Certainly, the people in graffiti-covered hazmat suits wielding electric leaf blowers added to the apocalyptic mood. To each their own, Walter reminded himself, fighting to keep his balance as the world shifted beneath him. The bouncy castle had seemed like a less disturbing option than any of the rides, much less the fun house, plus it would be hard for any of the cyberpunk stilt-walkers to follow him inside.

Technically it was more of a bouncy maze, with one inflatable leading to another. To the fleet of strobe-equipped drones zooming overhead, it probably looked like a quivering subdivision. He glanced at his watch, making a silent bargain with himself. If no one came through in the next five minutes, Walter would venture back outside. Until then, he would sit . . . if not quite still, then almost stationary.

There was a telltale jerk beneath him the instant before a black-clad figure stumbled into view. Walter was about to announce his presence when the person removed their beanie, and a halo of curls spilled free.

"Hildy?"

She bounced to face him, landing in a half crouch with her arms extended.

"Are you here to rob someone?" Walter asked, taking in her head-to-toe black Lycra.

"I left my tutu in the car. With the glowsticks." Hildy wobbled closer. "Nice vest, by the way. Wouldn't have pegged you as a purple person."

"There's a lot you don't know about me." Like the fact that wearing a purple-and-lime striped "waistcoat" had been a condition of his attendance because the grooms didn't want anyone to "adulterate the vibes."

"Yes, I'm sure you're very complex." It would have sounded more cutting if she hadn't delivered the line while swaying like a drunken sailor.

"Is that why you're stalking me?"

She swayed toward him, and then back again. "You wish."

"Don't tell me *you're* covering this wedding."

"Why wouldn't I be?"

"Because it doesn't seem like your kind of scene."

"Delaware?"

"All of it. Not exactly a Tiffany's-and-champagne crowd. Besides, don't you have minions you can send to do your bidding?"

Hildy gave a hop of outrage. "I don't have *minions.* Our staff is a *team*. The kind that doesn't bail on me at the last minute."

Walter chose to ignore the silent accusation. Like she was one to talk about trust and loyalty.

"And what, you were the only member of the team who didn't have plans tonight?" He tipped toward her like a bowling pin. Hildy took a wobbling step back before Walter managed to right himself.

"No, I had to cancel my *extremely* exciting social engagement to deal with *you*." She moved to poke him in the chest. Thanks to Walter's evasive stagger and Hildy's overcorrection, her finger landed closer to his belly button. He choked down a laugh, but only because it was a ticklish spot.

"So you did follow me here," he taunted. "Obsessed much?"

"In your dreams," she hissed, with a bounce of frustration. "I'm here to deliver a message."

"You could have texted."

She scoffed at that. "As if I have your number."

That shouldn't have stung. Then again, his reactions to Hildy had never been entirely logical. "You found me," he said, as if he were eager to move along and see what the contortionists and fire-eaters were up to, or swing by the Nightmare Parlor for one of the wedding favors, a complimentary mystery tattoo. "What's the message? Or is that code for 'someone's about to give me a beatdown'?"

"Stop messing with my people." Hildy loaded each word with menace, hands fisted at her hips.

"*Your* people?" Walter shook his head in mock confusion. "I thought you were a team."

"Don't play innocent with me. I'm wise to your tricks."

"Who's playing? I have no idea what you're talking about."

"Let me refresh your memory. Two months ago, at that Edwardian LARPer wedding in Queens. A freelancer named June? Strawberry blond hair, with the little barrettes in front?"

She waited for Walter to fill in the gaps, but he could only shrug. He knew which wedding she meant—the fashions were hard to forget—but couldn't see how his actions that day had been problematic, unless it was the fact of his existence Hildy objected to.

"I loaned her a pen. Did it leak in her bag or something?"

"I'm not here about a *pen*. How petty do you think I am?"

"I feel like I probably shouldn't answer that."

Hildy stomped in frustration, then had to dance her feet around to regain her balance. "You told her to quit her job!"

Walter was shaking his head before she finished. "I definitely did not do that." They'd chatted a bit before the ceremony, sure. And now that Hildy mentioned it, Walter vaguely recalled a young and nervous June bringing up her interest in macroeconomics. Since most of his career was built on random confessions from strangers, it hadn't struck Walter as a particularly significant detail.

"That's funny, because she left before the freaking vows and came racing back to the office to tell us about meeting this super 'wise' older man who helped her see that her real passion was going back to school to finish her PhD. I asked myself who she could possibly be talking about," Hildy continued, walking in a slow yet lurching circle around him. "It was the 'wise' part that threw me."

"Of course," Walter murmured, when she glanced at him to make sure the insult had landed.

"But then it hit me—"

"Sounds painful."

She held a finger to her lips for silence. "The only person who would do anything possible to undermine my magazine is *you*."

"Believe it or not, I don't spend my days thinking about how to thwart you, Hildy." Walter waited for a bolt of lightning to strike him down for lying.

"Then why did you use your Jedi mind tricks on her?"

"All I did was listen. It's called empathy."

"Maybe you should invest in a thesaurus because I'm pretty sure the word you're looking for is 'sabotage.'"

It was possibly the dweebiest argument they'd ever had, and that was not a low bar. "Listen, Hildy—"

"Ooh, are you going to mansplain something to me?" She lowered her voice to a rumble, in apparent imitation of him. "'Listen, Hildy, sometimes people don't want a job at your silly little magazine. Get over it.'"

"That's not what I was going to say." Nor was it something he believed. Once upon a time, before he realized their worldviews were fundamentally incompatible, Walter had imagined sharing an office with Hildy. Even now, he maintained a grudging respect for her editorial skills, however much she annoyed him personally.

"Good, because *Life, Styled* is a fantastic place to work. We have an awesome time. In a serious professional way. And it's *not* a vanity project."

Walter raised both hands in a show of innocence. "I never said it was."

"My sources beg to differ."

"What sources?"

"It doesn't matter. I'm not here to talk about that because I don't need your approval."

"What do you need?"

"From you? Nothing. Except to stay out of my way." She squinted at him. "Do we understand each other?"

"Um," he hedged. Had they ever really, even at the beginning? "Signs point to 'No.'"

Hildy squared off with him, posture pure belligerence even

as her lower body shifted like she was on a StairMaster. Walter's pulse kicked up a notch.

Before she could unleash her tirade, a procession of clowns bounced through the entrance, laughing and shoving each other. It was a terrifying parade of white makeup and lurid red mouths. Walter could feel a brand-new phobia developing in real time.

The clowns jounced and collided, setting the floor beneath them into violent motion. It felt like trying to surf on a damp sponge. Hildy toppled to her knees, one hand grabbing Walter's thigh on the way down.

A few inches to the left would have put them in a far more compromising position, though Walter was trying not to think about that possibility. Crouching, he reached for an elbow or a shoulder to help her up.

"Stop it," she hissed, when he accidentally brushed one of her curls.

Something dry and leathery crunched between his fingers. It was too solid to be styling-product residue, which left one possibility.

"There was a leaf," he informed her, in case she thought he was copping a feel.

Hildy's fingers tightened warningly against his quad. "That's because I had to crawl through a freaking *hedge*."

Her voice rose in anger, which had the unfortunate effect of alerting the nearby clowns to their presence. The beam of a flashlight washed over them.

"Shit, sorry!" a clown sporting a candy-red pompadour called out, swinging the light up and away. "We're totally leaving."

"And don't worry, we didn't see anything," another member of the party assured them, attempting to tiptoe across the heaving surface in a pair of giant yellow shoes.

As the first clown ducked to enter the tunnel leading farther into the castle, the smallest member of the party paused, plucking at her neck ruff. "Be careful. Somebody could get hurt."

"What was that about?" Hildy asked, frowning as the tremors from the clown parade faded.

Walter hesitated, hoping she would catch on before he had to say it. He raised his eyebrows at her, but she shook her head.

"A misunderstanding." He cleared his throat, fully intending to leave it at that.

Hildy frowned at her hand—still clutching his thigh—and then Walter's crotch, conveniently located in front of her face. After an agonizing silence, she tipped her head back to look at him. "Did they seriously think I was going down on you in a bouncy castle?"

As if the location was the improbable part. Walter made an unsuccessful attempt to laugh.

"Your fly isn't even open. Not even speaking of the logistics."

"I think your hair was blocking that area," he pointed out. "They couldn't see—you know."

"Whether Little Walter had come out to play?" She was enjoying herself now, in inverse proportion to his discomfort. "You could have been permanently incapacitated. One bad bounce and that's all she wrote."

"Can we stop talking about this?" It would have been a painful subject even if Hildy wasn't speaking to his zipper.

"Oh please. We're both grown-ups. It's not like I'm corrupting you."

Walter reached for her, thinking to put an end to the argument by helping her up.

She scrambled away on all fours, so of course he had to give chase.

"Dream on," she taunted when he ricocheted off the nearest wall.

He lunged for her, almost getting an arm around her waist. At the last second, Hildy reversed course, knocking into him like a wrecking ball.

"Take that." She rolled sideways, but didn't make it far enough. Walter collapsed on top of her at a diagonal, as if they were a human *X*.

"Stop breathing so hard," Hildy panted. Their stomachs were pressed together, pushing back and forth with every inhale.

"I'm sorry my need for oxygen offends you." Walter tried to shift his weight without kneeing her, but every movement resulted in more of his body rubbing against hers.

The strangest thing about being this close to Hildy was that it didn't feel strange enough, despite how long it had been since they last touched. Then again, strangeness was a relative term in the current setting. It occurred to him that they might have been better off all these years communicating through light wrestling, instead of using words. It was a relief to set down their weapons for a few minutes.

He wondered if Hildy had noticed it too.

"Is this how a waterbed feels?" she mused. "Must have been like trying to have sex on a trampoline. I wonder if that's why the birthrate fell off in the 1970s."

It was hard not to admire the workings of her brain, sniffing out possible stories in the most random places. "I think it was the economy. And birth control."

"I like my version better," she said, wriggling out from under him. Walter rolled onto his back, lifting his hips to make it easier for her. When she was free, he sagged back onto the floor, watching her crawl closer.

"Yes, Hildy?" he said, when she was kneeling at his side, staring down at him.

"See? That is how you should always address me. 'Yes, Hildy. Whatever you say, Hildy. Your wish is my command, Hildy.'"

"Whatever you say, Hildy."

"Never mind. Your delivery is all wrong."

"So much for my career as a ventriloquist's dummy."

"Pretty sure they already have one at this wedding, and it is one hundred percent possessed." She brushed her curls out of her face. "Here's what I came to tell you. Are you listening?"

"You have my attention." Walter saw no need to admit that this was a permanent state.

"The party's over."

"Which party would that be?"

"The one where you run amok all over my beat. Reporting and pillaging. From now on, you'll be dealing with me."

"*You're* going to do the reporting?"

"Yes, Walter. I appreciate your lack of faith."

That wasn't what he'd meant, though he doubted Hildy would believe him. "I didn't think the mighty editor had time for that kind of thing."

"I do whatever needs to be done. I'm a Jill of all trades. The Swiss army knife of journalists." She leaned closer. "Not some dewy-eyed intern who thinks you're fabulous because you used to chase celebrities."

"Funny, that's exactly what it says on my CV."

She did not look amused. "Consider yourself warned, okay?"

"Is that a threat?" Because he could think of worse things than the prospect of running into Hildy all the time.

"Yes. So don't fuck with me." Hildy pressed a finger to the slight divot at the base of his chin. "Are we clear?"

He gave a slow nod, careful not to dislodge her hand.

Her gaze locked on his mouth. "Is that a smile? Are you laughing at me right now? You should be taking this a lot more seriously, Walter."

"I'm not laughing at you."

"Don't lie to me either."

He wasn't. But he also couldn't admit that he was glad not to be alone in the freaky darkness, even if she was here to deliver an ultimatum. "I'm afraid you're not as frightening as the clowns."

Hildy grunted, unable to argue. "Next time I'll do the makeup."

"Don't forget the wig."

"I never forget anything, Walter." She paused to let the barb strike home before lurching to a stand. He watched her sway drunkenly toward one of the exits.

"Where are you going?"

"Home."

"You're not staying for the paintball rave?"

"Hell no. I'm just here to mess with you."

"Seriously?"

"Like you said, not my scene."

"Too scared? Don't want to sully your shiny brand with something edgy and dark?"

"So what if I like pretty things? You can pretend that makes me a lightweight, but the truth is that I choose where to put my focus. Which means nightmare on emo street is all yours."

After she bounced out of sight, Walter let his head flop back against the floor. He always needed recovery time after a run-in with Hildy, and tonight was no different.

His thoughts swarmed like bees. Jealousy that she'd left while he had to stay. Annoyance that Hildy got the last word. Confusion as his body replayed every scrap of physical contact, like a miser counting the contents of a piggy bank.

If what she'd told him was true, he was looking at a lot more encounters like this one—minus the bouncy castle and (God willing) the clowns.

And here he'd been worried the wedding beat might be getting a little stale.

NOW

9

Hildy

ONE WEEK BEFORE THE PRESCOTT-SCHAFER WEDDING

TAMNIÈS, France—"What do you mean, he loves castles?" Fiona rounded on Hildy with eyes so wide she looked like a horse catching the scent of smoke. "Has he covered a lot of castle weddings? Are castles the new hotel ballrooms? Is it totally tired to get married at a castle?"

"A mysterious castle in the forest that no one has seen for decades?" Hildy sniffed at the improbability of such a thing. "I think not. You are the Belle au Bois Dormant, okay? A total legend. Bespoke to the max. Trust me."

Beneath the soothing smile she was giving Fiona, Hildy sent a silent *thanks a lot* to Walter for adding another bridal insecurity spiral to her to-do list. Luckily, Hildy excelled at stopping a meltdown in its tracks. It was one of the most valuable life skills she'd picked up during her sorority era, right up there with eyelash curling and planning a seated dinner for forty.

"Which I promised *you* could write about." It sounded as if Fiona was reminding herself along with everyone else.

Granted, she had a lot of details to keep track of this week; some forgetfulness was understandable. Fiona also had a wedding planner with two assistants plus staff, a wedding designer who traveled with his own retinue, and a dedicated beauty team. It wasn't like she was going to be stuffing Jordan almonds into three hundred mesh gift bags with her own hands.

Or whatever the table favors turned out to be. Hildy was thinking maybe a sachet of raw gems, judging by the lavishness of the welcome hamper that had been waiting for her at the hotel. Local wines, foie gras, a picnic blanket featuring a limited-edition toile print created specifically for the occasion (according to the glossy wedding guide)—Hildy might have never left her room again, if she didn't have a story to protect.

"I don't see why that precludes Walter from doing a piece on the castle," Maude argued. "Think of the exposure. He's an *award-winning* reporter."

Who makes out with his rivals while kissing up to potential sources, Hildy thought, flames of anger licking the sides of her face. So much for his vaunted journalistic integrity. There was probably a lot more than kissing going on between Walter and Maude. People didn't cross the Atlantic for a handshake.

"Plus he came all this way," Maude went on, adding a little whine to the sauce. "As a favor to me."

Poor Walter, forced to take a trip to the south of France! Maude might believe he was there to help, but Hildy knew the truth. He was there to help himself to *Hildy's* story.

"I know it's *your* wedding, Fiona," Mr. Prescott weighed in. "But it can't be easy for Maude."

That got Hildy's attention. Was there some hidden drama playing out in the background—and did Walter know about it? When she glanced his way, he gave her an inscrutable brow lift. Whatever. She'd figure it out soon enough.

"What are you talking about?" Fiona frowned at her father. "Maude totally supports me."

"Of course she does! But here you are settling down, and she's still alone. Think about how it feels for her to be thirty years old with no marriage prospects."

"My birthday isn't until November," Maude reminded her father.

"And who knows? Things might change by then." Mr. Prescott winked at Walter. "For now, we should all be grateful Maude found a date who's gainfully employed. And not looking for a green card."

Okay, then. It sounded like Maude had a few skeletons in her dating closet. No wonder Walter looked good by comparison, with his fancy haircut and the way he filled out that summer-weight suit.

"And she gets the castle," Fiona pointed out. "That's a pretty nice maid of honor present. Better than the pajamas Daisy gave us."

"I'm going to turn it into a retreat center and event space," Maude explained in response to Hildy's questioning look. "Which is why I need all the media hits I can get," she added, with a grateful smile for her escort.

Hildy cocked her head, beaming her own message to Walter. *Conflict of interest much?* It was one thing to charm and disarm a source to expedite the process of earning their trust, but there was a pretty clear line between friendly chitchat and sleeping together.

"Sounds like there's a story there," she said to Maude. "I don't know how familiar you are with *Life, Styled*—"

"It's a magazine."

"Thank you, Walter." Hildy bared her teeth at him. "I'm sure she's aware. Unless she's been trapped under something heavy."

"It's very popular with people my age," Fiona chimed in. "Not that you're that much older, Maude." She bit her lip, too late to keep from putting her foot in her mouth.

"We do a lot of stories in this vein," Hildy said, smoothing over the awkward moment.

"Who doesn't?" Walter murmured.

"Our coverage is distinctive. As a woman-owned-and-run

business, we bring a unique perspective, looking beyond basic news angles to explore a more personal journey."

"You can spare her the sales pitch." Walter checked his watch. "I've got everything well in hand."

Hildy lasered him with her eyes. "I'm sure you do."

"Right." Maude glanced between Walter and Hildy, who were still locked in a stare-off. "Shall we table this discussion until later? I need to get back to the castle, and Walter must be exhausted. I'm sure he'd like to rest before tonight."

What a classy way to inform the world that you were about to get horizontal with your plus-one! Some might be put off by the mustiness of air travel, but not Maude. Then again, Walter's appearance was less sweat-stained than artistically rumpled, like a high-end cologne ad. And there were always showers, so maybe they'd go vertical instead . . . Hildy pulled the plug on that line of thought before it could go any further.

"Go ahead." She kept her voice sweet, so only Walter would catch the hint of menace. "Take a nice long nap. I'll be here. Doing my job."

He scowled at her. "It won't be that long."

Too bad for Maude. Hildy buried that thought as soon as it appeared. Walter wasn't the only one who could keep a secret.

NOW

10

Hildy

ONE WEEK BEFORE THE PRESCOTT-SCHAFER WEDDING

TAMNIÈS, France—"Do you think I'm being punished?" Hildy asked Corinne. She'd already given a blow-by-blow account of her confrontation with Walter and his new girlfriend, during which Corinne had remained surprisingly calm. Hildy suspected it had something to do with the two-hour massage that had left the hotel room smelling like a field of lavender.

"Let's not make it more than it is." Corinne sipped her detoxifying lemon water. She'd turned down Hildy's offer of wine on the grounds that she planned to drink her body weight in rosé tonight.

That was the theme of this evening's welcome party: Roses and Rosé. Hildy had been planning to repaint her nails a delicate pink, but the bloody red she was currently rocking seemed more fitting under the circumstances. The goal was warrior queen, not bubblegum princess. Which Corinne would understand if she hadn't had all the stress pounded out of her.

"Walter being here is not a small thing," Hildy argued. "It's an outrage. How dare he pull a stunt like that?"

Corinne rubbed more lotion into the back of her hand. "A wedding reporter chasing the biggest wedding of the year? Shocking. Or were you talking about his other reason for being here?"

"It happens over and over," Hildy insisted, ignoring the dig about Maude. "Walter appearing out of nowhere." She made an exploding gesture with her fingers. "Poof!"

"One, I'm pretty sure the 'poofing' is mutual. And two, if you're waiting for me to say that you and Walter are connected by some deep and mysterious invisible string, don't hold your breath."

Annoyingly, Hildy had been angling for a crumb or two of acknowledgment, though she would have settled for pity. *There he goes, all up in your business again. What a conniving snake!*

"I'm talking about repeating patterns. Gradually working out the kinks in your karma until you evolve to a higher form." She hesitated. "Maybe Walter and I are trapped in some kind of loop, until we fix our mess."

Corinne slow-blinked, like she was giving it serious thought.

"You see what I'm talking about?"

"I see plenty." Corinne peeled off the eye mask she'd been using as a headband, fluffing the hair at her crown. "Like how hard it is for some people to tell the difference between destiny and dysfunction. They have so many of the same letters."

"You're hilarious."

"I know." She took another sip of her water before setting the glass aside. "I've been thinking."

"You mean like right now, during our conversation?"

Corinne pretended not to hear. "Maybe it's for the best, Walter being here."

Hildy eyed her warily. "How do you figure?"

"Because you know how important this story is for us. We have to *nail* the Prescott wedding. There's no other option." She waited for Hildy's nod of acknowledgment. "This week is going to be a pressure cooker."

"The Rolls-Royce of pressure cookers," Hildy reminded her, because they weren't exactly serving time in a penal colony.

"Still," Corinne carried on, undaunted, "the battle lines are drawn. We're on one side, and Walter is over there." She gestured at the wall. "As someone who's had a front-row seat for your whole deal with him, I'm thinking this could be the moment you settle things for good. Battle royale. To the victor go the spoils."

It wasn't an exaggeration. If everything went according to plan, snagging the Prescott wedding would be much more than a onetime circulation boost. A story this big would establish *Life, Styled* as a player on the main stage, without sacrificing any of their youthful freshness and vitality.

She didn't know what Walter stood to gain, besides a chance to show off in front of his girlfriend. And a trip to France. Maybe he'd been promised a raise, or at least a bonus, but Hildy had an entire business to run. People were depending on her.

"When you say 'settle this' do you mean this assignment or—" Hildy let the question trail off, hoping Corinne would fill in the details.

"Yes," Corinne answered. "All of the above. Break the chains of the past. Wash that man right out of your hair. Go big or go home."

Inspirational speeches were not Corinne's forte, but Hildy appreciated the sentiment. "I have no idea whether you're manipulating me or being totally sincere, but I kind of like it, so." She shrugged, accepting the kernel of truth behind the platitudes. It would feel incredible to one-up Walter in a head-to-head competition. That would silence all the lingering doubts (his, Hildy's, her family's) about whether she'd earned her place.

She tucked her hair behind her ears in the universal sign for *shit's about to get real*. "Walter's ass is mine."

"Or you could just say 'go team,'" Corinne pointed out. "Keep it nice and simple."

* * *

The site of that evening's welcome event was a walled garden adjacent to the hotel. The roses and rosé were as advertised: blush-pink bottles glistening with condensation arrayed on a long line of tables, with a twelve-foot botanical wall as a backdrop. Neon letters (F & R) added a little zing to the floral tapestry.

Hildy did a slow 360, pretending to admire the décor. No sign of Walter yet. Getting here first should have been a victory, but it almost felt too easy. Did he know something she didn't? Was there another, better angle she should be pursuing?

She reminded herself to smile as she mingled with the other guests, making a game of guessing the relatives from the acquaintances. Observing other people's domestic circles was something of a hobby for Hildy. More than one of her therapists had pointed out that this likely had to do with the unconventional structure of her own family.

Fair enough; everyone had issues, and it made sense that this would be one of hers. Hildy was also aware that she had a habit of collecting surrogate mothers (not including Corinne, who was as maternal as a vegetable peeler). There was no great mystery behind the inspiration for the magazine's Found Family feature. The important thing was that it happened to be a work of genius that regularly made people cry on public transportation. That was the definition of resourcefulness in Hildy's book: leveraging your personal baggage to make great content.

Most people didn't realize how much psychology was involved in being a magazine editor. It wasn't enough to understand what readers wanted or why a certain story mattered. You also had to have a feel for how your writers were wired, since most of them were as high-strung as racehorses.

Case in point: Walter Burns, the first reporter she'd ever managed. Hildy had intuited early on that he had a chip on his shoulder about growing up without a lot of money, so it was her job to reframe situations to keep him from getting twitchy. *We're not going out to dinner; it's just a cup of coffee. Talent writes its own ticket, so walk into that place like you own it.* That kind of thing.

It had worked well . . . until it didn't.

That was a long time ago, though. Grown-up Walter had no problem holding his own at fancy weddings. Where Hildy had to practically turn cartwheels while twirling a baton, all that was required of Walter was to fix those big brown eyes on someone and listen like his life depended on it. Which proved Hildy's point that money wasn't the only currency that mattered.

Not that Walter would be lacking in funds for long if things got serious with his Prescott heiress. International-travel-plus-family wedding didn't exactly say "casual." Interesting how he didn't have an issue with *Maude's* background. Apparently some women were allowed to come from wealthy families without it counting as a character flaw.

Fiona waved, her other hand clutching the arm of a smiling blond guy with the side part and slicked-down hair of a little boy in an old-time sitcom, though the muscles and tan were very much of the modern gym era.

Time to work. Hildy put her shoulders back, relaxing her face into a smile as she approached the happy couple.

"Hildy, this is Robbie," Fiona announced, bouncing with excitement. "I'm so glad you finally get to meet him."

Robbie offered a firm handshake and the easy grin of someone who had been described by his college roommate as "the guy most likely to sleep through having his eyebrows shaved off and not be mad about it afterward."

"Hi," he said. "Pleased to meet you. Thank you for coming."

"Hildy's the one doing the story about us," Fiona whispered, since Robbie clearly had no idea which of their many guests he was addressing.

"Sweet." Robbie blinked like he was searching for something

else to say. "Can I get you some of me and Fee's favorite pink wine? We like to drink it while we watch the sunset, because the colors kind of match. Pink sky, pink drink. And it's less sweet than a cosmo."

Hildy could picture the two of them in matching Adirondack chairs, clinking glasses. She smiled at the image, and also because it was important to get Robbie on her side.

"Thank you so much for inviting me here to help you capture your wedding memories in a glossy, full-color format you'll be able to look back at and really cherish for the rest of your lives." As opposed to finger-staining newsprint.

"Cheers to that!" he replied. "You can never have too many pictures of Fee. Especially when she dresses up."

"Aww, sweetie!" She buried her face against his shirt, nuzzling him with her nose.

"What did I miss?"

Hildy tried not to flinch. She couldn't let Walter know he'd caught her off guard, creeping up from behind like a shadow. "They're really excited about the awesome wedding story I'm going to write."

"Sounds like I got here just in time."

"Not how I'd describe it." She turned to face him, watching as he absorbed the impact of her dress, from the strapless bodice to the flirty little skirt.

Walter had changed too, into a loose button-down the color of green grapes. She couldn't remember the last time she'd seen him in short sleeves. Of course Hildy knew in theory that he had forearms, but it was different witnessing the actual shape of them, with the skin and the hair. Blah blah blah, muscles etcetera; plenty of people had them. "Where were you anyway?"

"Doing some background research." His tone was deliberately vague, as if that would keep her from digging.

"About what?"

"The wine."

She paused in case he wanted to come up with a better answer. "You have never been a bigger nerd than you are right now."

"I'm sorry, some of us didn't grow up drinking wine at every meal."

"That's too bad. It was really soothing for me as a toddler. Cheerios and Chardonnay. I took the best naps."

He frowned, but it looked less like disapproval than repressed amusement. "What if we both do it?"

"Do what?" Hildy asked.

"The story."

"About my wedding?" Fiona asked, peeling her cheek off her fiancé's shoulder.

"And the castle," Walter added, in case anyone had forgotten his first allegiance was to Maude.

"We can't work together." Hildy swung a finger between herself and Walter.

"Who said anything about working together?"

"You want to work *against* each other?" The emphasis landed a little wrong. Hildy told herself no one else had noticed, but that didn't explain Walter's flushed cheeks.

"We'll both do a story," he said, voice gruffer than usual. "Fiona can choose the one she likes best."

Hildy couldn't seem to stop shaking her head. That was how intensely she disagreed. "It's a ridiculous idea."

"I don't know," Fiona mused. "We did that with the invitations. I had to see them side by side to pick my favorite font . . ."

"You're not afraid of a little competition, are you?" Walter's face was all innocence—if you overlooked the wicked gleam in his eyes. He was manipulating her and they both knew it.

And yet she was incapable of ignoring his challenge.

"Me? Of course not." Hildy didn't want to overplay her hand with a fake laugh, so she added a bemused huff instead. "I wouldn't want Fiona to settle for less than the best."

"Looks like we're on the same page," Walter said. "For once."

"If you think you can see it to the end. Follow-through hasn't always been your strong suit."

His jaw tightened. "When *I* commit to something, I'm all in."

Robbie glanced between them, as if he was trying to puzzle out the smallest row of letters on the eye chart at the optometrist's office.

"Are you sure you don't mind?" Fiona asked Hildy, with a not-so-subtle tip of the chin in Walter's direction.

She pasted on her brightest smile. *Look at me, No-Drama Hildy!* "It's totally fine. Don't give it a second thought. I'm certainly not going to."

"Oh good!" Fiona said. "It makes me happy when people get along."

"She's a lover not a fighter," Robbie confirmed. He tapped the side of her glass. "Time for a refill?"

"I thought you'd never ask!"

While the lovebirds wended their way to the nearest wine station, Walter rounded on Hildy.

"You can stop looking so pleased with yourself," she snapped. "This doesn't change anything. It's been my story from the beginning, and it's going to stay that way."

"As long as you're sure."

"Maybe you should just give up now. Save yourself the embarrassment of being sent home empty-handed."

"Why, Hildy, it almost feels like you don't want me here."

"How perceptive. Have you been working on your communication skills?"

"Are you sulking because I outplayed you?" He leaned closer, daring her to deny it.

"The week is young." She flicked her hair, drawing his attention to her bare shoulders. Suddenly aware of how close they were standing, Hildy edged back a step. "Shouldn't you be with your girlfriend?"

"My—you mean Maude?"

The hesitation piqued her interest. "Do you have another one?"

"I just don't think of her as being defined by our relationship."

"How enlightened of you."

"She's working," Walter said, ignoring the taunt.

"So am I." It was supposed to be Hildy's exit line, but he spoiled it by following her.

"Working your way to the wine table?"

"For research."

He lowered his voice. "You're not supposed to wear perfume at a wine tasting."

"Stop sniffing me, Burns."

"I'm not."

"And I'm not wearing perfume." Scented body oil didn't count. She held her arms out, wrists together. "Want to make a citizen's arrest? I assume you travel with handcuffs." Hildy let her raised brows paint the rest of the picture.

Walter cleared his throat. "Shouldn't you be asking people who they're wearing? Or did you already do the brand-name census?"

"Yes, because my goal has always been to make *Life, Styled* the print equivalent of QVC. One product placement after another."

"Heeeey." Corinne came to a stop in front of them, arms wide. "What are you two numbskulls doing together?"

"Nothing." Hildy answered too quickly, like a kid with her hand in the cookie jar. "I'm going to taste some wines."

"Me too," Walter announced.

Corinne shook her head. "I don't think so, kids. We've been down this road before, and we all know where it leads. How about we call it a night?"

"I'll go to bed when *he* goes to bed." Hildy jerked a thumb at Walter, who snorted.

"I appreciate the offer, but I'm going to have to pass."

"Unbelievable," Hildy groaned, watching him saunter toward a group of bridesmaids with the smugness of someone who'd just gotten the last word. "Where does he get off?"

"Not something you need to worry about," Corinne said, dragging her in the opposite direction.

THEN

11

Walter

EIGHTEEN MONTHS AGO

NEW YORK—According to the map on his phone, Walter had reached his destination. The security gate looked like any other industrial storefront in Brooklyn, until he spotted the metal DG logo above the buzzer, as in Domaine Gabby. The proprietor must not want random hipsters stopping by in search of wholesale sparkling wine.

Walter had a different target in mind.

The assistant he'd spoken to on the phone buzzed Walter into the building and introduced himself as Duri. "Gabby's in back. Should I let her know you're here?"

"I'm good. Thanks for your help."

"Write nice things," Duri said before heading back to what Walter presumed to be his office.

The light at the end of the corridor suggested daylight, so Walter was only partly surprised to step through a heavy steel door and into a glass-roofed atrium. A bar lined one wall, and there were a handful of high tables made from wine barrels.

"You have got to be kidding me," Hildy said, setting down her glass of champagne. She was seated at the bar, glaring at Walter as if he'd just stolen her parking spot.

"Hello to you too." Had she really thought he was going to let her last performance go unanswered? Walter wasn't that big of a sucker. Not anymore, anyway.

He turned to the woman in a floral jumpsuit with waist-length box braids. Even without the context clues, he would have recognized Gabby from her online bio. "Walter Burns," he said, extending a hand.

"You write the wedding column." She had a firm handshake. "Bells and Whistles."

He nodded, never sure how to respond when people recognized his professional affiliation. *I'm sorry? It's harder than it looks? No, I don't get to eat the cake?*

"There's no personal connection between us," Hildy preemptively declared. "Just to be clear on that point."

Gabby's eyes slid between them. "I have no idea what's going on here, so this is me making an informed decision to move on."

Smart of her. Walter should have made the same call a long time ago. "Duri said it would be okay if I stopped by."

"Actually, we're kind of in the middle of something." Hildy made a flicking motion with one hand.

"The more coverage the better, as far as I'm concerned. You're not going to make me choose, are you?" Gabby laughed at that, missing the venomous scowl Hildy shot Walter.

"I'm all about supporting woman-owned businesses. Believe me, I know how hard it is to launch a start-up in this economy." The only thing missing from Hildy's performance was a violin.

"Interesting." Walter let Hildy sweat a little, since they both knew he could expose the truth about her background any time. "Are you getting hazard pay for day drinking on a Tuesday afternoon?"

"I should," she sniffed, looking him up and down.

Walter did the same to Hildy, taking in the silky sheen of her shirt and the crisp pinstripes of her tailored skirt. "That must be your working-the-salt-mines outfit?"

"Is fashion part of your beat now?" Hildy fluttered her lashes at him. "I didn't realize you were branching out."

For a shot fired at random, that one stung. It was a question Walter had been asking himself more and more lately: Should I want more? And if so, what? Maybe he needed to push himself harder, try his hand at politics or public health reporting. What if he was stagnating on the wedding beat? He tucked those fears away before Hildy caught a whiff of them. She was the last person to understand career angst, or any other form of self-doubt. Must be nice to be born into money *and* a professional destiny.

Gabby turned to Hildy with a frown. "Did he run over your dog or something?"

"Not my dog, no." Hildy added a pensive tip of the head, as if Walter had done something much worse.

"You don't want to hear about us," Walter assured Gabby. "That's old news."

"Snoozeville," Hildy agreed, more emphatically than strictly required.

He kept his eyes on their hostess. "I want to know more about you."

"I'm not the story." Gabby edged behind the bar as if she could physically evade his question. "This is the heart of what we do." Ice sloshed as she lifted an open bottle of Domaine Gabby Demi Sec from the bucket on the counter. "Can I pour you a glass?"

Hildy made a show of sipping from her flute of bubbly, in case Walter needed a reminder she'd gotten there first.

He wondered if Hildy knew how true that was, considering Walter had learned about Domaine Gabby from a *Life, Styled* stringer he'd overheard talking to the bartender at a wedding in the Hudson Valley.

It was a good story: the fresh-out-of-college business major convincing a vineyard in France to partner with her to bring high-quality champagne to an unexpected corner of Brooklyn. There weren't a lot of women in the wine industry, much less women of color. When he ran into Corinne coming out of a coffee shop this morning and casually asked what she'd done with her partner in crime, her vague reply about fizzing it up in Brooklyn had been enough of a clue to rearrange Walter's plans for the day. Why not combine an interview with a little light torture? Two birds, one stone.

Ignoring Hildy's eye roll, he slid onto the stool next to hers.

* * *

Fifteen minutes later, Hildy kneed him in the thigh for the sixth time. Or was it the seventh? The shape of her kneecap was going to be imprinted on his leg.

"Oops," she said, swiveling in the other direction. "I keep forgetting you're there."

It would have been more convincing if she hadn't waited until he was mid-sip every single time.

"Do you sharpen those things?"

"Only my tongue." She stuck it out at him when Gabby wasn't looking.

"What do you think of this one?" their host asked, wiping the condensation off a new bottle.

"Juicy," Walter said on autopilot, yanking his gaze from Hildy's mouth.

"I'm not sure he's a champagne person," Hildy sighed, as if his lack of savoir faire caused her personal distress.

"It's true I grew up in more of a Diet Dr Pepper household."

"Not what I was saying." Hildy took a sip of her drink. "Champagne is the beverage of joy. It's pure *effervescence*, sparkling on your tongue. Hope and excitement and giddiness. Whereas Walter has always struck me as more of a . . . hmm." She pretended to think it over, glossy nails drumming the bar. "Glass half empty kind of guy."

"I do prefer a little substance with my bubbles." He locked eyes with Hildy. "Solid fundamentals that stand the test of time, as opposed to empty promises that trick you into making bad decisions."

Gabby looked worried.

"But this has all the complexity and nuance anyone could want." Walter angled his glass to catch the light. "It's like eating a piece of homemade sourdough bread with Irish butter and just a hint of orange blossom honey, and yet light as air."

Gabby held up a finger. "I can use that. Hold on." She reached under the counter for a spiral-bound notebook. While she was writing, Duri stuck his head in.

"Sorry to interrupt. You have a call." His eyebrow choreography suggested time was of the essence, though the crisis apparently wasn't serious enough to stop him from winking at Hildy. Another day, another conquest. Did she ever get tired of keeping so many hearts on a string?

Gabby excused herself, Duri hot on her heels.

"You are such a suck-up. *Irish butter and an orange grove, blah blah blah*," Hildy mocked as soon as they were alone. "Maybe you should go into PR."

"Think you can do better?"

"Shhh!" Her eyes narrowed in concentration. She'd always had the curiosity of a cat. It was one of the things that fooled Walter into thinking they were cut from the same cloth.

"Can you hear what they're saying?"

"Not with you breathing like that." Hildy tried to pinch his nostrils, but he ducked out of the way, grabbing her by the wrist.

Neither of them heard the door open.

"Oh good. You two fools plus alcohol. What could possibly go wrong?"

Walter recognized the dryness of Corinne's delivery before he turned to see her standing in the doorway.

"Gabby got called away." He tried not to look guilty, which should have been easy since he wasn't technically doing anything wrong. Anyway, Hildy started it. "We're sitting here very quietly waiting for her."

Corinne's sniff was laden with disbelief. "Fancy meeting you here, Burns."

A flustered Gabby hurried back into the tasting room.

"See?" Hildy said to Corinne. "There she is."

Walter got a rare glimpse of Corinne's softer side as she introduced herself to the proprietress. Her expression conveyed the unmistakable blend of bashful and eager that said *I find you attractive*. Judging by the prolonged eye contact that accompanied Gabby's lingering handshake, the feeling was mutual.

"I'm so sorry." Gabby's apology was mostly directed at Corinne. "I need to run ten cases up to the Bronx. The sommelier at Batista is freaking out, because she's a total diva, but they also move a ton of bubbles, so I have to stay on her good side." She broke off, remembering that she was talking to three journalists. "Off the record."

"Need a hand?" Corinne offered, already tightening the belt of her coat.

Gabby looked surprised, but not in a bad way. "I mean, I wouldn't say no." She grabbed a canvas tote and a water bottle, and Corinne followed her out the door.

"They ditched us," Hildy observed after silence had settled over the tasting room.

"Pretty much," Walter agreed.

The toes of her shoes tapped the underside of the bar. "You can go, you know."

"So can you."

"I think I'll stick around."

"Me too."

"It's probably going to be a while."

Walter shrugged. It wasn't like he was bored. He lifted one of the open bottles from the ice bucket, angling it toward Hildy's glass in a silent question.

"It would be a shame to waste it." She nudged her flute a little closer, watching him divide the champagne between them until the bottle was empty.

Since Hildy didn't seem inclined to talk, he flipped to a clean page in his notebook, jotting down his thoughts about the setting. A light rain pattered against the glass roof. Walter tipped more champagne into his mouth. It wasn't the worst place he'd spent an afternoon.

"See anything you like?" he asked. Hildy practically had her nose pressed against the open page.

"Like I can read your handwriting." It had been a joke between them once, but those days were long gone.

"Are you going to the Martell wedding?" he asked, not wanting to dwell on the past.

"No, I'm sending someone."

The booze must have loosened his tongue, because he blurted out the first reason that came to mind. "Hot date?"

"Wouldn't you like to know."

This time he kept his mouth shut. It was none of his business.

"It's not like I make a habit of blowing off work for my social life," she said.

"Did I say that?"

"You were thinking it."

"I didn't realize you'd added mind reading to your long list of skills." Walter was utterly cooked, if so.

Her nostrils flared, and he felt a rush of anticipation. What kind of tongue-lashing would she give him this time? He was so focused on waiting for her lips to move, it blindsided him when her arm shot out and grabbed his notebook. Before Walter could process what was happening, Hildy ripped out a page, wadded it up, and shoved it down the front of her blouse.

She crossed her arms, grinning as if she'd checkmated him. He let his gaze stray slowly over her mouth and chin before dropping to the telltale lump under her shirt. If that was how she wanted to play it, he was more than willing to call her bluff.

Hildy must have read the intention in his face. He'd barely started to lean in that direction when she fished the crumpled paper out of her bra and crammed it into her mouth. Her jaw worked, up and down.

"Blah," she complained, spitting the damp wad onto her palm.

Walter raised both hands when she tried to give it back to him. "I'm not touching that."

"Don't be a baby."

"Says the person who ate paper."

"I didn't *eat* it." Hildy shook her head, like he was the ridiculous one. "It's totally intact. Go on. You can have it back," she said, flapping it at him.

"No thank you."

"It'll dry out."

"I don't want your regurgitated paper."

"Give me a break. I barely chewed it." Wincing, she reached into her mouth. "Thought I might have missed a piece. That flavor really lingers."

"Where are you going?" he asked when she stood.

She swished the last of the champagne from cheek to cheek before setting down her glass. "Home."

"We could share a ride," he suggested, when she was halfway to the door.

After a pause, she turned back to face him. "Why?"

"To be sure you make it there safely?" Walter didn't know why he phrased it as a question. As if there were any other possible motive for following her home.

"Save the knight in shining armor routine for someone who doesn't know better." The door slammed behind her with an echoing clang.

Walter picked up the damp scrap of paper, intending to bank a shot at the trash can behind the bar. Somehow, he wound up tucking it into his pocket instead.

NOW

12

Hildy

SIX DAYS BEFORE THE PRESCOTT-SCHAFER WEDDING

VÉZAC, France—If she had to describe the overall vibe of the prewedding festivities to a friend (as opposed to her magazine's readers) Hildy would have said that it had the luxurious yet lightly educational ambience of a Viking River Cruise. Although Hildy considered herself several decades too young to embark on a cruise geared toward PBS-viewing retirees, she had a thorough understanding of the experience from Corinne, who had gone on several with Gabby. The fact that both were sixty-five at heart seemed to be the glue that cemented their ongoing, if nonexclusive, relationship.

As on a fancy cruise, wedding guests who didn't want to lounge by the hotel pool could join a daily cultural excursion to add some enrichment to their stay in France. Since this didn't necessarily seem like Fiona and Robbie's style, Hildy assumed the destination had been chosen by an outside consultant—until Fiona explained that her late mother had spent a year in this part of the world as an exchange student, and always talked about it as one of the happiest times of her life.

That was an undeniably sweet tribute to Fiona's mom. Hildy was less moved by the itinerary for Day One, which bore the fingerprints of a different member of the Prescott clan.

Explore the cutting edge of horticultural design at this unforgettable art garden, where the grounds of a stately manor play host to a lush tapestry of sculptural boxwood forms infused with whimsy and mystery. A private tour will be followed by lunch amidst the greenery.

"Imagine that, a garden tour," Hildy grumbled. "I wonder whose idea that was?"

"Not that you're jealous," Corinne said around a mouthful of croissant.

Hildy raised her sunglasses to give Corinne the full impact of her disdain. "For your information, I'm not always thinking about Walter."

"Who said anything about him?" Corinne slugged her fresh-squeezed juice. "Let's go, one-track mind. Try not to piss off any of our sources. Or their sisters."

As if! Most people found Hildy charming and fun—and the exception to that rule wouldn't be joining them today.

* * *

While the other guests posed in front of hedges that looked like extras in a surreal European production of *Little Shop of Horrors*, Hildy wandered ahead. She wanted to check out the maze on her own, because what was the point of a maze if you couldn't pretend you were lost, or on your way to a romantic assignation?

If that also meant avoiding Maude, Hildy was happy to file that under the fringe benefit column.

The gravel crunched under her wedge heels as she ambled along, turning and twisting among the sculpted boxwoods. It would have been more atmospheric with a long dress, but Hildy didn't have the height to pull off a maxi skirt.

According to the map, there was a tearoom on the other end of the maze. Hildy could set herself up at a table and wait for other guests to wander by so she could ply them with refreshments while collecting quotes about Fiona and Robbie. Until then, it was nice to have a little breathing room. She needed a minute to remind herself that nothing had really changed, despite Walter's absurd idea of competing for a story that was already hers. Her mandate was the same today as it had been yesterday: Knock this story out of the park, and all good things would follow.

There was no reason to expect anything but success. Weddings were her playground . . . although some would argue that Walter was equally experienced on these monkey bars.

But Hildy had the whole *Life, Styled* team behind her. And she wasn't juggling a romance with her professional duties. Clear eyes and free hands!

Her footsteps slowed as she registered the hushed voices coming from somewhere ahead. A bass rumble, then a soft reply. Whoever they were, they sounded . . . intimate. A man and a woman, judging by the burst of laughter that was quickly silenced. Had they realized Hildy could hear them? She started to back away, placing each foot as silently as possible, when a low moan caught her ear.

Well, well, well. Someone was starting their day with a bang. And since the gardens were currently closed to the public, it had to be members of their group. She walked more quickly in the opposite direction, trying to give them privacy. Despite covering her ears, Hildy couldn't help registering that the muffled gasps and grunts were escalating to a definite climax.

An alarm went off, right around the same time as the unseen woman. Hildy cursed under her breath before realizing it wasn't *her* phone. The amorous couple was scrambling now, their whispers growing frantic. It hit Hildy in a sickening rush: They were panicking like they were late, and *that* meant they were almost certainly about to hurry around the corner.

The maze felt a lot less whimsical now that she needed a quick escape. After tiptoeing around the next bend, Hildy spotted an opening in the hedge. It was a false turn that dead-ended after a few paces. If she flattened herself against the prickly wall, it might give her just enough cover—assuming they sped past without glancing to the left.

Hildy had about ten seconds to get her breathing under control before the first set of footsteps raced through the maze, sending gravel flying. Her first instinct was to close her eyes, but she quickly realized that would not make her invisible. Plus she kind of wanted to know which of the wedding guests were having a *really* good day.

Oh, shit.

It was Maude.

Who was supposed to be leading a tour of the gardens in five minutes.

Hildy listened for several beats before risking a glance down the path. They must have decided to stagger their departures so no one would question their disheveled state. Did she have time to run away before Walter got here? She didn't trust him not to sense her presence.

I can't believe I just heard Walter Burns having sex.

It was like something out of the Brothers Grimm: *Don't go into the maze, little girl! You'll regret it.*

She took a tentative step onto the path, jerking out of sight when she heard someone coming. These footsteps were slower. Was that how Walter walked? Hildy wasn't aware of having studied his gait, but something seemed off. Maybe a sensitive part of his anatomy had come into contact with the poky shrubs.

Not that she would wish that on him.

Much.

Hildy held her breath as he passed her hiding place. *Keep walking*, she silently urged. *Nothing to see here!* For once, he did as she wished.

She stared at the back of his head for several breaths before her brain caught up.

It wasn't Walter.

* * *

If she'd paused to think, Hildy would have realized it *couldn't* be Walter, but she'd been too busy freaking out to apply logic to the situation. Now that she was back in her right mind, Hildy wasted no time tracking down a likely source of intel.

"Hey," she said to Fiona, who was lingering near the back of the group with Robbie. "Quick question about one of the guests. I'm trying to get a sense of who's who, for the story, and I saw a guy with dark curly hair, fairly tall, leather bracelet on his wrist?"

That alone would have been enough of a clue that it wasn't Walter. Hildy would bet good money her nemesis had never owned a bracelet, much less worn one.

"He looked a little old to be one of the groomsmen," Hildy added, in case that narrowed it down.

"Did he have an accent?" Robbie asked.

"Um." Hildy wasn't sure whether people moaned with an accent.

"Better question," Fiona said. "Was he bothering Maude?"

"I guess you could say that," Hildy allowed.

"Then I know *exactly* who it was." Fiona's tone hinted at drama, like maybe she was aware of Maude's extracurricular activities. "He's the historic preservation guy. Every time Maude wants to do something at the castle, she has to ask him for permission. We're pretty sure he's deliberately making things harder. Here, jump through this hoop! Now go dive through that one over there."

"And some of the hoops are *on fire*," Robbie added.

Fiona leaned closer to Hildy, lowering her voice. "They've been going at it for months. Maude is usually super calm, but he really gets to her."

"Yeah," Hildy said, a little too emphatically. "I mean, I can imagine."

"Those two are like *rawr*! *Woof woof*!" Robbie pretended each of his hands was a mouth, snarling and barking at each other.

"Something a lot of people don't know about Robbie is that he was in the Puppeteering Club in college," Fiona informed Hildy with obvious pride.

"We did really gentle stuff," he assured Hildy. "Nothing hard-core."

Maybe it was time to take another look at the wild world of marionettes. But first, Hildy had another interview to conduct.

* * *

She cornered Maude later that morning, on a shaded gravel path bordered by waist-high boxwoods. It was clear from the other woman's body language that she didn't welcome the interruption but was going to do her duty as hostess anyway.

"Are you enjoying the gardens?"

Not as much as you. Hildy kept that thought to herself. "They're incredible."

"This was one of my inspirations for the grounds at Château Fiona. Though obviously not on this scale."

"How is that going? With the castle." Hildy casually brushed her palm over the bristly surface of the nearest hedge. "Everything coming together to your satisfaction?"

Maude narrowed her eyes. "Why do you ask?"

"I heard there were some issues. With the historic preservation person? What was his name again?"

"Loïc," Maude replied, taking her time with it. "He's the archaeologist supervising the excavation of a troglodytic habitation in the caves underneath the castle. There may be even older cultural remains on-site."

"Like . . . dead people?"

"Art," Maude corrected. "Engravings. Considering the area, it wouldn't be surprising." Hildy nodded like she got it, while making a mental note to listen more carefully the next time Corinne went on one of her Travel Channel spiels.

"Are you going to be based in France, going forward? Since you'll have a business here."

"It depends," Maude said, obscurely. As if picking up on the unspoken part of Hildy's question, she glanced behind her. "Have you seen Walter?"

"I'm sure he's fine." This was not a guess on Hildy's part. She had personally sent Walter on a completely different outing, going so far as to slip a revised itinerary under his door and hire a car to pick him up an hour before the bus departed for the gardens. The goal was to dispatch him on a wild-goose chase while she covered the actual excursion. Only now it appeared she had unwittingly given Maude an opportunity to cheat.

"So," Hildy said, watching Maude's expression for any hint of guilt. "You and Walter."

"Shouldn't we be talking about Fiona's love life?" Maude pushed back. "I'm not sure how this is relevant."

Under other circumstances, Hildy would have enjoyed the sass. She could picture inviting Maude to brunch, maybe downing a pitcher of mimosas. A tiny voice whispered that maybe this was why Walter liked Maude enough to violate his principles by fraternizing with a source. That was better than supposing he'd been seduced by her millions . . . and yet Hildy's annoyance spiked.

Dicking him around is my *job.* And in her case, it was consensual. Or at least reciprocal. One of those.

"Just collecting background detail. For the story."

"I like Walter. He's very easy to be around."

Hildy's exhale carried a whiff of *yeah, right*.

"You disagree?"

"No comment." Which was its own comment, as Maude well knew. "Whatever I think or don't think about Walter, I hate to see anyone in a situation where there's an imbalance of power."

"And which of us do you see as having the upper hand in this scenario?"

"Here's what I know," Hildy said, in lieu of answering. "It doesn't end well when one person is way more into his romantic partner than she's into him. Especially if he decides a baby will fix everything, only it backfires because the woman is even more determined not to be tied down, so she takes off and publishes an academic paper about how monogamy is a primitive system, and we could learn a lot from non-Western cultures about more enlightened and fluid attitudes toward sexual partnerships. Meanwhile, he's stuck at home with a newborn, pining. Just to choose an example at random."

At some point in her preteen years, it had occurred to Hildy that she might not even be a biological Johnson, if her mother was that big on bucking traditional family structures. That added some extra salt to the wound when people made assumptions about Hildy's cushy background. Were you really a nepo baby if you didn't have the right DNA?

Maude blinked at her. "That does sound . . . complicated."

"It's okay. I have a pretty great life. But it would have been nice if my mother had figured out her shit before other people got dragged into it."

Maude hesitated, looking torn. It might have been one of those *I am about to lie to you* microexpressions. Then again, it could also mean *I am about to confess something meaningful.* People were tricky like that.

"Walter and I have been very honest with each other."

Hildy's claim to the moral high ground was shaky on that front, so she accepted this with a curt nod. She'd delivered her coded warning, for reasons she didn't fully understand. And now she had a job to do, regardless of other people's messy lives.

"Let's talk more about plants," Hildy said, opening her voice recording app.

THEN

13

Walter

TWO YEARS AGO

NEW YORK—Aside from the Venus flytrap, which he knew mostly from time-lapse nature videos, Walter had never felt menaced by greenery. That changed when he walked into the "Beyond Bouquets: (Un)Natural Art" expo at the Javits Center.

The atmosphere was closer to the reptile house at a zoo (creepy things watching you from all sides) than your average florist. Instead of pink-and-white, the preferred palette ranged from bloodred to gothic black, with plenty of swampy green and midnight purple in between. Walter had the distinct impression that if he touched one of the stabby-looking arrangements, he would lose a finger—but not before the poison took him out.

So this was where the race to make your wedding utterly unique led. Maybe the next hot trend would be cakes that weren't sweet, or flat champagne. Although that would just be wine, so possibly it wasn't avant-garde enough. When Walter told his editor he wanted to expand his horizons, he should have been more specific. Sinister wedding décor was not the departure from the norm he had in mind.

He wandered down the center aisle, waiting for something to catch his eye. There was always a choice with trend pieces: Go with the most outrageous example to get people talking, or give a more balanced view? According to the paper's market research, the majority of Walter's readers were in it for the voyeuristic thrills, so he felt less of an obligation to focus on practical centerpieces people might actually choose for their wedding.

At the next booth, a stark white tablecloth was completely bare. Walter assumed they were still setting up, until a woman in a black suit rose from her stool to greet him.

"Striking, isn't it?" She gestured at the table. "Did you notice the monogramming?"

"No," Walter admitted.

"White on white," the designer said, as if she were sharing a secret. "Nothing to distract the eye or destroy the harmony of the whole. It's a place for the mind to rest. I call it Tabula Rasa."

Walter had questions—many of them—but before he could ask, another voice caught his ear.

"Yes, we were hoping for something that really says 'raw' and 'danger.' When you think about it, marriage is a pretty big risk. And who doesn't love feathers?"

A few booths farther down the aisle, Hildy was chatting up an exhibitor whose display featured a life-size peacock constructed of melon halves, eggplants, and purple fingerling potatoes. He nodded his thanks at the minimalist designer, tucking a business card into his pocket as he turned to go.

"My fiancé's favorite color is puce," Hildy was saying as Walter came to stand behind her. "I'd like to honor that if possible."

She had to be joking, and not just about the puce. He leaned closer, trying to peer over her shoulder. No press credentials that Walter could see. Hildy's dress was soft and swishy, but he had no idea whether that qualified as a work outfit. Could she have gotten engaged since the last time he saw her? His gut said no. Forcefully.

"He's also fascinated by cryptids," Hildy continued. "If that sparks—" She broke off mid-sentence, slowly turning to face Walter.

"Nice," the floral designer purred, lifting his oversized pink glasses to give Walter a once-over. "Are we talking Nessie? Bigfoot? El Chupacabra?"

"That's not my fiancé." Hildy gave a theatrical shudder, as if the idea of being engaged to Walter was too horrifying to contemplate.

The designer's lips plumped in disappointment. "I could have sworn I was picking up an energy."

"We do know each other," Walter admitted. "But it's more of a professional relationship."

"'Relationship' is a strong word." Hildy leaned forward. "He mostly just follows me around."

"I had a stalker once," the designer informed them. "It didn't go anywhere."

It was unclear whether he expected condolences. "I'm paid to be here," Walter said, before Hildy could sell him down the river.

"Don't tell me." The designer gave him another head-to-toe examination. "Not a driver. Or an assistant." His voice dropped. "Private security?"

"Yes!" Hildy clasped her hands together as if she'd been hoping he'd guess. "You wouldn't know it to look at him, but he's lethal in three separate martial arts." She tipped her head back to smile up at Walter, one hand lightly caressing his arm. "Do you want to demonstrate?"

"Demonstrate what?"

"One of your deadly moves." She turned back to the designer. "He can snap someone's neck with his quads."

The designer's hand flew to his cravat. "How exciting! I read a book like that." He leaned across the front of the booth for a better look at Walter's thighs.

"I'm not her bodyguard," Walter said.

Hildy winked at the designer. "That's what he's supposed to say. Keeping a low profile is important in his line of work. He's probably thinking about a dozen different ways he could off someone right now."

"How did you guess?" Walter locked eyes with her, making all kinds of silent promises. "Actually," he told their new friend, "I'm part of her wedding team."

"Hair?" the designer guessed.

"Yes, Walter." Hildy crossed her arms, her smile razor-sharp. "Tell him exactly what you do for me."

"I'm her . . . handler." The word popped into his head straight from the police procedural he'd binged over the weekend. Because what could be more appropriate to a floral expo than undercover cops and their morally gray informants?

"Please. Like you could handle me."

"She's a little sensitive about needing supervision," Walter explained to their rapt audience.

"I handle myself just fine."

Walter widened his eyes, waiting for her to replay that last bit in her head. She shot him a look of defiance. Far be it from Hildy to admit to a mistake.

"What services do you provide?" Pink Glasses asked.

"Whatever she needs." It was possible that sounded more suggestive than he'd intended; the designer fanned himself. Walter hoped Hildy was enjoying this heaping serving of her own medicine. "Keeping her on task, mostly. She has a tendency to lose focus."

A battle played out behind Hildy's eyes. Walter witnessed the exact moment the urge to argue gave way to her instinct for drama.

"That's me." Hildy knocked her knuckles against her forehead. "Brain like a sieve."

"There's a lot riding on this wedding," Walter continued as if she hadn't spoken. "It's more of a corporate merger, really." Lowering his voice, he delivered a final salvo. "She's marrying into the mob."

"I told you not to use that word in public," Hildy chided, smacking him in the arm.

"My bad."

"I'll punish you when we get home."

Walter realized he was still looming over Hildy at extremely close range and eased back a few inches.

The designer drummed his fingertips together. "You know, if I were the fiancé, I'd worry this one"—he jerked a thumb at Walter—"might get a little *too* committed to his job."

"It's not a problem." Hildy threw Walter a dismissive glance. "He's barely adequate."

"And I never mix business with pleasure," Walter retorted. "Once burned, twice shy, as they say."

Hildy rolled her eyes. "If you'd been burned by me, you'd know."

"I guess some people are more memorable than others."

He swallowed a yelp at the sudden pressure on his shoe. There was no need to look down to know that Hildy was standing on his foot.

She smiled up at him. Walter bared his teeth right back. He wasn't sure which of them was the bigger bullshitter.

* * *

"What the hell was that?" he asked, when he'd tugged Hildy free of the flow of human traffic.

She shook off his grip. "Why are you asking me? You're the quote-unquote handler. What was *that* about?"

"Why were you pretending to be engaged?"

"Who says I was pretending?"

"Are you?"

"Pretending?"

"Engaged."

"What's it to you?"

Walter closed the distance between them. She was toying with him, but he refused to be sidetracked. He locked eyes with her, daring Hildy to lie to him.

"Fine," she sighed, looking away. "I'm not engaged. But it's easier to let everyone assume I'm a bride-to-be. People expect to see a bride at a wedding expo, so they just start yapping."

Walter felt some of the tension ease from his shoulders.

"You think I should flirt instead?" She tapped her bottom lip, pretending to think it over. "Maybe I could ask them to dance? Put my hand low on their back and whisper sweet nothings?" Hildy rose onto her toes to bring her mouth closer to his ear. "I hear you're very popular on the bridesmaid circuit."

It shouldn't have surprised him that Hildy knew he'd been pressed into service as a dance partner at a wedding in Connecticut last month. There was very little that escaped her notice. And yes, the bridesmaids had passed him around once they figured out that he could lead, after which assorted relatives had gotten in on the action. What was he going to do, say no to the groom's grandmother?

"Why does it matter how many bridesmaids I'm sleeping with? Last time I checked, I wasn't married. Or fake engaged."

"Wait, are you serious?" she burst out, forgetting to act nonchalant. "I assumed it was gossip. That is so—" She broke off with a huff of disgust.

"It's so what?" he prompted.

"Unethical. As a journalist."

It didn't seem to matter how long they'd been at odds. Somehow, it still bothered Walter that she thought so little of him. "I don't get involved with my sources, Hildy. Give me that much credit at least."

NOW

14

Hildy

FIVE DAYS BEFORE THE PRESCOTT-SCHAFER WEDDING

TAMNIÈS, France—Walter had the audacity to act surprised when Hildy climbed onto the bus the next morning for that day's signature activity, a local gastronomy tour and tasting.

"You made it," he said, as if Hildy were known for blowing off scheduled events to play Baldur's Gate with her buddies.

"It takes more than a canceled wake-up call to stop me." Especially since she always set two extra alarms. Jet lag was no joke.

"Who would be so diabolical?" Walter asked, with a frown of fake concern. "At least it wasn't kidnapping."

"Nobody got kidnapped. You went there of your own free will. And it wasn't exactly a gulag."

"On the contrary. I found it inspiring."

"Really?"

"Oh yeah. Great background for my story. There's nothing like historical context to give a piece of reporting depth, don't you agree? And Josephine Baker was such an icon. Another American expat, finding her castle in France—the story practically writes itself." He smiled at Hildy, all smugness and good hair. "You must have had that in mind when you so generously sent me there."

"Of course. Every step I take is meticulously planned." She

managed a thin smile of her own. "You're welcome, by the way." Hildy made a show of looking around the empty bus. "Where's Maude?"

"She's meeting us there."

"Castle stuff?" Hildy guessed, wrinkling her nose in sympathy.

Walter's eyes narrowed, as if he sensed a trap. "Yes."

Never one to pass up an opportunity to grill someone about their private life, Hildy dropped into the seat next to his. "I have a question. About the two of you."

"The two of who?"

"You and Maude." Was it strange he had to ask? A little. But then he seemed distracted, blinking a few extra times as he focused on Hildy's face.

"Okay," he said, with visible reluctance.

Hildy took a deep breath. She could do this. "You probably know what I'm going to say."

"Almost never."

Was he for real right now? "It should be pretty obvious in this case."

"Can I get a hint?"

"Sure. It starts with 'were you dating her' and ends in 'when you had your tongue in my mouth behind the coatrack.'"

He had the nerve to blush, as if he was a sweet, innocent schoolboy. Ha! Schoolboys didn't kiss like that.

"I seem to recall your tongue in my mouth too."

Seem to recall? Like it was a faint memory? Hildy could still feel the ghostly echo of his hand cupping her ass at inconvenient moments, such as right now. The idea that she was doing involuntary Kegels over something that was barely a blip on Walter's radar made her want to sharpen her claws on his shoulder. "Since *I* wasn't dating Maude at the time, my conscience is clear."

Walter's mouth fell open, as if it had finally dawned on him what she was getting at. "No—me neither. There's no overlap.

Zero connection between the two." He shook his head, in case the double denial wasn't emphatic enough.

Hildy did the math in her head. "Then this is a recent development. Like, *really,* really recent. You figured what the hell, third date, let's go to her sister's wedding in France?"

More head shaking. "It's not what it looks like."

"Huh." She pursed her lips, pretending to think it over. "Because it *looks* like you're getting ready to write about someone you're also dating. Even though you allegedly don't do that."

"I can't really talk to you about this," Walter said after an uncomfortably long pause. He was staring at his hands, avoiding eye contact.

"Fine. Have it your way." Springing out of her seat, she headed for the back of the bus.

"Hildy," he said.

She tuned him out. It was none of her business if Maude cheated on Walter and they went through a big messy breakup that meant he had to leave before the wedding. *Life, Styled* would be there to pick up the exclusive and run with it. And what could be more important to Hildy than the future of her magazine?

* * *

The destination for today's outing was a small agribusiness nestled among the rolling green hills outside the medieval city of Sarlat. The Fauvard family had been producing foie gras and other duck-based delicacies for generations. The actual food preparation took place behind the scenes, far from the tourist-facing tasting room inside a charmingly rustic converted barn.

While the proprietors described the delicacies they would be sampling today, Mr. Prescott beckoned at Walter to join him.

With the grace of a panther, Hildy prowled into eavesdropping range. It sounded like standard male bonding about all the meat they were about to eat, because God forbid anyone subsist on cheese and bread. Clearly Mr. Prescott was clueless about the magnificence of Girl Dinner.

Possibly she was being too harsh, but Fiona's father had rubbed her the wrong way from the beginning, when he'd dropped several sledgehammer hints about his familiarity with her business. Circulation growth (steady, if not astronomical); chief competitors; who among his "friends" had deigned to advertise in the pages of *Life, Styled.* It could have been the mark of a polite host who studies up on his guests so he can make small talk, but to Hildy it smelled like a power play. Mr. Prescott wanted her to know he had her number, in case she was thinking of printing something less than glowing about his daughter's wedding.

She wondered if Walter had gotten a similar speech, or if his connection to Maude was enough of an insurance policy.

"Listen, I wanted to touch base about the wedding coverage," Mr. Prescott was saying now. That was her cue.

Hildy deftly inserted herself between them. "I'm right here. Go ahead."

"Good," Mr. Prescott said, as if he'd summoned her. "Just making sure we're all on the same page."

"In what sense?" Walter asked.

"There's no need to mention any of the fuss with this historic preservation person. Loke or whatever his name is. About the castle."

Walter shot Hildy a look that said *your turn*.

"Which fuss would that be?" Hildy tried to sound like she already knew everything and was merely narrowing down the list.

"Red tape." Mr. Prescott waved this off as if it were a gnat circling his lunch. "You know how these European bureaucracies operate."

From the gravity of his *hmm*, you would have thought Walter routinely contemplated that very thing. Imports, exports. Embargoes. Shipping lanes. More business words.

"Are you worried it's going to interfere with the ceremony?" Hildy asked.

"If it does, I know who to blame." Mr. Prescott scowled through the open doors of the barn, shooting eye lasers at a mud-spattered car from which Loïc had just emerged. "He's given poor Maude a hell of a time. Not to mention the money he's cost me." He clapped a hand onto Walter's shoulder. "I'm glad she has you to lean on."

"Yes," Hildy cooed, burying the sarcasm under a layer of sugar. "Isn't she just so lucky? To have such a dependable and unwavering source of support."

Fortunately, Mr. Prescott was oblivious to tone. Probably a survival mechanism, as the father of two daughters. With a vague farewell, he wandered off to hobnob with his other guests.

Meanwhile, Maude and her handsome history expert had joined the rest of the party in the tasting room. Loïc struck up an animated conversation with one of the staff members, who handed him a heaping taste of foie gras. That would have been a fifty-dollar dollop stateside, but he didn't hesitate to feed it to Maude, one hand cupped under her chin as he watched her lips close around the spoon.

Talk about gourmet foreplay. Get a plate, people. Maude dabbed at the corner of her mouth, which was still glossy and pink. Perks of being fed like a baby bird.

Hildy glanced at Walter to see if he'd noticed, but he was looking at her.

"What do you think it is?" he asked.

Unbridled sexual tension, Hildy almost said in response. "What do I think what is?"

Walter frowned, as if Hildy was the one missing the obvious. "The issue with the castle."

"Roof or plumbing, if I had to guess." She couldn't quite read his expression. "Are you digging? Even though your girlfriend's dad asked you to hush it up?"

He tried to disguise his flinch by scratching his neck. "It's not a cover-up."

"It's a little bit of a cover-up."

"Maybe it'll be a moot point, if everything goes smoothly."

In wedding-adjusted terms, "smoothly" translated to "nothing is messed up enough for guests to notice." There was almost always a minor disaster behind the scenes. The lighter ones—like choosing your wedding day to switch to a natural deodorant—made it into *Life, Styled* under the heading, "Psst! Letter to My Past Self." A sewage-related disaster would be harder to laugh off.

"What will you do if the wedding doesn't happen?" Hildy had an impulse to cross her fingers or toss salt over her shoulder to ward off the bad luck of saying the words out loud, but Walter seemed unperturbed by the question.

"Move on to the next extreme wedding." His eyes flicked in her direction. "What about you?"

"Continue to thrive," she lied.

No way was she going to tell Walter how much was riding on this story. If Hildy couldn't deliver on the promises she'd made to advertisers, a lot of them would walk, tanking the magazine's budget for the entire quarter and possibly beyond. So basically the wedding had to happen, even if Hildy needed to climb up there and hammer some roof beams herself.

Maybe if the person in charge of restoring the castle wasn't distracted by a certain Frenchman, things would be progressing more rapidly. Oh brother, now Maude was brushing crumbs off the front of Loïc's shirt. Unless they were stuck on with superglue, she really didn't need to rub that hard.

When Walter started to turn in that direction, Hildy grabbed his arm without thinking, spinning him to face the back of the barn. "Is that a hayloft? Have you ever thought about how hay is like beef jerky for horses?"

He gave her a funny look. "I have not."

"A little less handsy with the sister-of-the-bride's boyfriend." Corinne hooked her elbow around Hildy's, towing her to a table in the corner. "What do we have here?" she asked an aproned staff member.

"Magret de canard fumé."

"Like prosciutto, but it's duck," Hildy translated.

Corinne accepted a thin slice on a round of crusty bread. "Oh shit. Sorry! I meant 'merde.' This is incredible."

The magret maker laughed.

"Try it," Corinne urged. "You need to find a different object for your lustful thoughts. A foodgasm will make you forget—"

"Thank you," Hildy interrupted, turning to make sure Walter wasn't in hearing range. For once, he and Maude were together, though her gaze kept flitting to Loïc, who was looking right back at her from his post near the door.

"What's he even doing here?" Hildy wondered out loud. "Are they expecting a rock art emergency at the duck farm?"

"I think he gave her a ride."

"I bet he did."

"In his *car*."

"I hope the seats recline."

"Not our problem," Corinne reminded her.

Hildy knew she was talking about more than ergonomics. "I like knowing people's business."

"Some more than others." Corinne accepted a glass of walnut liqueur from another member of the staff. "Fuck me, that's good. No idea how to translate that to French."

"Seems like something they'd say." German was the go-to language for depressing one-word put-downs, but the French were the MVPs of making everything about sex.

Corinne took another sip of her drink. "Not going to lie, I was afraid it would taste like furniture polish."

Hildy frowned at her. "Why?"

"The color, I guess. Where are you going?"

"To say hi to Fiona and Robbie."

Corinne gave a grudging nod of approval, but not before checking the distance between the bride and groom's table and Walter.

"How's it going?" Hildy asked Fiona, who was glowing with either love, whatever facial treatment she'd had at the spa, or the oxytocin rush from eating all those fat-filled French delicacies.

"So great," Fiona enthused, dropping another slice of duck breast into her mouth. "Is it just me, or is everything here delicious?"

Robbie sighed, casting a forlorn glance at his plate, where four slices of bread had been denuded of their toppings.

Walter slid into the empty fourth chair. "What's happening, kids? Are we doing an interview?"

"No." Hildy kicked him under the table, semi-accidentally. "We're being sociable. I mean, I am. And letting these two lovebirds enjoy their delicious, artisanal duck. And figs, which I happen to know are an aphrodisiac. A famous chef told me that," she added for Walter's benefit. "He takes a very sensual approach to food."

"You might want to fact-check that claim," Walter said.

"About the figs?"

"All of it."

Hildy turned to address Fiona and Robbie. "Have you talked about the cake?"

Walter made a sound of disbelief. "You don't know about the wedding cake?"

"I know *everything* about the cake," Hildy retorted. "Ask me about the passion fruit gelée."

"I don't need to ask." He let her stew for a few seconds. "I've already tasted it."

Damn it. Hildy's fist clenched, hopefully out of Walter's line of sight. She forced a smile. "I meant whether they're going to feed each other the first bite. And if so, are they going for smash and grab or something more restrained."

Fiona flapped her hands at chest level, showing off her perfect nails and massive diamond. "So it's actually going to be really cute. We have these meringue mushrooms on top of the cake that we're going to feed each other. Perfect bite-size morsels."

"Also, meringues are gluten free," Robbie added. "And egg whites are high protein."

"Yes," Hildy said slowly. She hadn't pegged Fiona's husband-to-be as a keto warrior.

"We should practice!" Fiona picked up a piece of bread and held it out to her fiancé.

"I don't know, Fee—"

"Come on, babe. What are you waiting for?"

"Here, we'll all do it," Hildy said, in case having an audience was making Robbie twitchy. "Ready?" she asked Walter, holding up a slice of bread.

He gave her a wary look. "Try not to poke my eye out."

"I did have a lot of coffee this morning, so I'm feeling a teensy bit shaky." She jerked her arm like she was drawing a Z in the air.

"That's how we used to feed my baby cousin." Robbie smiled at the memory. "Either the airplane or the choo-choo, depending on his mood."

"Do you want the choo-choo, Walter?" Hildy batted her lashes at him.

His hand closed around her wrist, holding it in place. Before Hildy could react, Walter bent to sink his teeth into the bread. When his lips brushed her fingers, she almost dropped it.

He sat back, taking the bread with him. Hildy watched him chew, eventually remembering to close her own mouth.

"See, Robbie?" Fiona said encouragingly. "We can put our own spin on it. Just relax," she half sang, bringing the bread to his lips.

At the last second, he jerked sideways, and the baguette poked him in the cheek.

"Oh my gosh." Fiona placed the hand not holding a hunk of bread over Robbie's. "Thank goodness we're doing this now. Can you imagine if that happened at the wedding? I'll come in more slowly this time."

"It's not you, Fee." Robbie's face twisted. "I'm worried about getting a wheat belly. You know what they say—carbs are the silent killer."

"It's called Spanx, Robbie. Everybody uses them."

"But I want to be shredded on our honeymoon! You're so beautiful, I don't want people looking at us and thinking, 'She should be with somebody like that Aquaman guy.'"

Fiona looked utterly perplexed. "But I love your body."

"I love *your* body."

Hildy started to make a *maybe let's lower our voices* gesture, but they were too far gone.

"If you really loved me, then you would love what I love," Fiona insisted. "Which I just said is your body!"

"I already had my final fitting. I don't want to mess up the lines." Robbie gestured at his stomach.

Fiona threw up her hands. "We're never even going to wear clothes in Bali."

"That's why I want to look good naked!"

Yelling the word "naked" was a surefire way to get everyone in hearing distance to tune in. Fiona shifted uneasily, aware they were attracting attention. "Who cares how you look if you're going to be hangry all the time?" she asked in a lower voice.

"Try the foie gras," Hildy suggested. "It's totally low carb."

Robbie turned to her with the wide, innocent eyes of a cartoon bunny. "Is that the mean one? Where they force the ducks to eat too much?"

"Good question," Hildy stalled. "I'm sure Walter knows."

He put a hand to his ear. "Sounds like Maude's calling me."

"She's definitely not," Hildy said through gritted teeth.

Apparently Walter only had ears for his beloved, because Hildy's voice made no impression.

"So," she said into the silence that followed Walter's escape. "Anybody want dessert?"

Robbie whimpered.

Hildy could have slapped herself. She blamed the lingering effects of having her fingers licked. Walter had probably been trying to bite one off.

Fiona shoved the foie gras into her own mouth. "There," she told Robbie. "I saved you."

It seemed the crisis had been averted, until Fiona abruptly stood.

"Where are you going?" Robbie asked. "Fee?" He hurried to catch up with his fleeing fiancée.

Corinne strolled up, licking the back of a spoon. "Should I be worried?"

"They're fine," Hildy replied, with more confidence than she felt. "Or they will be, once Robbie has a snack."

"Maybe he needs a juice box and a nap too."

Don't we all, Hildy thought, watching Walter smile at something Maude said. He'd probably let *her* choo-choo him all day long.

"I'm sure it's just normal prewedding nerves." Behind her back, Hildy crossed her fingers. "Lots of couples get them."

"As long as we don't make it worse." Corinne reached for the last piece of bread. "And by 'we' I mean 'you.' And Walter."

THEN

15

Walter

TWO YEARS AND THREE MONTHS AGO

NEW YORK—It wasn't the first interview Walter had bombed, but the feeling never got more pleasant. And considering how many strings he'd pulled to get a sit-down with the hottest chef in New York, returning to the office empty-handed was not an option. Although if worse came to worst, they could run a photo spread instead, since Stellan Cubillo's reputation for hotness seemed to owe as much to the young Swedish-Spanish chef's looks as it did to his cooking.

You'd think a celebrity pâtissier who was also one of the town's most eligible bachelors would be primed to talk about his process, his vision, his fitness regimen, what he had for breakfast, and so on. Unfortunately, Stellan appeared to be the tortured-artist type, who preferred to keep his thoughts to himself. Walter pitched him a softball about learning to cook in his grandmother's kitchen—a subject on which he had written an entire cookbook—and all he got was a mumbled, "She was a special woman."

Okay, then. Another few minutes of this and they'd be reduced to playing word association games. Walter looked down at his notebook, hoping for inspiration. So far he'd written the date and the location.

The door to the kitchen swung open, bringing the welcome promise of an interruption.

"There you are!"

Walter stiffened at the sound of Hildy's voice. By the time he turned his head, she'd swept across the room like a miniature tornado, making a beeline for Stellan. If the trailing edge of her presence was enough to make Walter unsteady, he could hardly blame the chef for looking dazed.

"I'm Hildy," she said, arm extended.

"Enchanted," Stellan murmured. Was he playing up the accent, or had he just been too monosyllabic for it to register before?

"What are you doing here?" Walter asked Hildy, when it looked like the chef was going to keep holding her hand indefinitely.

"Did you think I'd let you tackle something this important alone? Don't be silly." She extricated herself from Stellan's grip, using that hand to boop Walter on the nose.

They absolutely were not on booping terms, but since when did Hildy care about boundaries? She looked delighted with herself for making Walter scowl.

"The two of you are together?" Stellan asked, not bothering to mask his disappointment.

Hildy gave an understanding nod. "It surprises a lot of people. We've got sort of a grumpy-sunshine thing going." She waggled the fingers of her left hand. "I thought we might be getting our hands dirty, so I didn't wear my ring."

She was an astonishingly smooth liar, as Walter knew better than most.

"Scoot." After knocking him out of the way with a swing of her hips, Hildy propped her elbows on the counter. "What did I miss? Are we sampling yet?"

"I would be happy to feed you," the chef rumbled. "Perhaps a coffee first?"

Funny. He hadn't offered Walter a beverage.

Hildy gave a gasp of delight. "I'd love to try your coffee."

"Are you sure that's a good idea?" Walter feigned concern. "You know how you get."

"I think I'm capable of choosing what I put into my body," she replied, with equally false sweetness.

After an appreciative look at the body in question, Stellan busied himself with the espresso machine. As soon as his back was turned, Walter widened his eyes at Hildy, who narrowed hers back at him.

"Mmmm," she sighed at the first sip from the tiny white cup. It was an annoyingly over-the-top reaction that nevertheless managed to spike Walter's pulse. "Could you get a coffee flavor this rich in a cake?"

"I have, yes. But it was not easy." As if she'd flipped his talkative switch, suddenly Stellan was Mr. Chatty, telling Hildy all about his experiments with roasting his own beans, complete with detailed descriptions of the different flavor profiles, processing methods, tips for proper storage . . . Walter's eyes were starting to glaze over when Stellan switched tacks.

"It is a dream of mine to visit the places the beans are grown."

"I would love that," Hildy said at once. "Waking up with the sunrise and watching the mist burn off the distant peaks, surrounded by nature."

Walter snorted, doing his best to pass it off as a cough. He could tell from Stellan's rapt expression that he was imagining cozy campfire scenarios with Hildy, whose yearbook superlative had probably been "Least Likely to Rough It."

"How long have you been engaged?" Stellan asked, a furrow forming above his dramatic nose.

"Oh goodness." Hildy pretended to think it over. "It feels like an eternity. And then some."

"I thought it must be a long time," the chef said. "Because you are not very physical together."

"That's Walter," Hildy said at once. "He's extremely buttoned up. I have to rein myself in, bring it down to his level."

"That must be difficult." Stellan's eyelids seemed to be getting heavier by the second. Maybe he needed a coffee too, before he smoldered himself into a pile of ashes.

"Watch this," Hildy instructed, before swooping in to press a quick kiss against Walter's cheek. "Did you see that flinch? For one little kiss on the cheek?"

"I didn't flinch." Walter wondered how Hildy would react if he kissed *her* out of the blue. Maybe somewhere other than her cheek.

"It looked like a flinch to me," Stellan said.

"Enough about him. Tell me about you." Hildy gazed at Stellan as if he was the star attraction in a sculpture gallery. "How did you get into the wedding cake business?"

"My sisters," the chef confided, with none of the reluctance he'd shown Walter. "I have four, and for each wedding, they asked me to bake the cake. If you have sisters, you know it must be a different cake every time. I asked myself, what cake is the essence of Marie, and Birgitta, and Lola, and Ebba. Everyone wants a cake just for them, yes?"

Hildy nodded as if he'd said something profound. "The universal desire to be seen."

"But make it cake," Walter muttered. Hildy patted him between the shoulder blades as if she was burping an infant, a *there there* that felt more like *shut up*. He took the opportunity to snake an arm around her waist, tugging her close. Purely for revenge purposes.

Hildy stiffened for an instant before registering Stellan's attention—at which point she melted against Walter's side, resting her head on his shoulder.

A timer sounded, and Stellan excused himself.

"Stop touching my stomach," Hildy hissed.

"Oh, so you're allowed to poke me in the nose, but I can't lightly rest my hand on your abdomen?"

"That's where all my vital organs are. Have you ever met a cat? You're lucky you still have two arms." She beamed as the chef rejoined them, twisting free of Walter's grip under the guise of examining the plate in Stellan's hand. "What do we have here?"

"This is a fig and cardamom cake. You know what they say about figs?"

"We both know," Walter interjected. Not that either of them paid any attention to him.

Hildy rocked forward on the balls of her feet, staring at the cake like she was ready to dive in.

Stellan sliced a thin wedge, the knife sinking into the golden sponge. "Do you want to feed each other?" he asked Hildy. "You can use the fingers if you like. To me, food is an experience of the whole body, not just mouth or tongue."

"I think probably a fork. Walter's kind of a germaphobe."

"What will you do at the wedding?" Stellan asked him.

"Great question." Hildy nodded her approval. "What do you think, Walter? You would never smash a dessert this magnificent in my face, would you?"

"It's cake," Walter reminded her. "Not a Ming vase."

"You see what I'm dealing with?" Hildy stage-whispered.

Stellan smiled in understanding. "Please. Allow me." He sliced off a bite of cake with the side of the fork before holding it out to Hildy.

"Aw, that's so sweet of you!" She leaned over the counter, mouth open. As her lips closed around the fork, her eyes drifted shut.

Walter aggressively cleared his throat when the chef's gaze strayed to the neckline of Hildy's blouse.

"I think I just died and came back to life. You're not just an artist," a wide-eyed Hildy told Stellan. "You're a wizard."

The chef inclined his head, accepting this as his due.

"Now I'm even more curious." She lowered her voice like she was about to confess her deepest secret. "What kind of cake would you make for us?"

"For you, the richest dark chocolate with a hint of spice," he told Hildy. "And for him, something astringent and dry."

"Like arsenic?" Hildy pressed her hands to Walter's cheeks, squeezing his face into a pout. "Kidding! Though I have always wanted to try the hot young widow aesthetic." She took the fork from Stellan, helping herself to another bite without offering any to Walter.

The chef brought out more cakes for Hildy to taste, followed by an array of ganaches and glazes. From his preening, you would have thought he was a panther dragging carcasses back to his lair to impress a mate, instead of a guy whose main weapon was a stand mixer.

"Do you think you'll make your own cake?" Hildy asked, setting down her fork. "When you get married."

"Who can say? Alone, I am only half the flavors." Stellan cast a pained look at the window, showing off his profile.

"Have you ever been tempted? By marriage, I mean?"

Even Walter couldn't tell whether Hildy's question was part of the interview or driven by personal interest.

"I have yet to meet the right woman. Or when I do, it's too late." His gaze flicked to Hildy.

Subtle, Walter thought.

"You never know," she said, consolingly. "Life is full of twists and turns."

"I hope so," Stellan agreed. He jotted something on a slip of paper, sliding it across the counter. "Give me a call if you have more questions . . . or want to try something new. I make a very good breakfast," he added, in case anyone had missed the insinuation slithering through the room.

"Thank you." She tucked his number into her purse.

"You have something, just there," the chef said, not quite touching her face. "May I?"

She lifted her chin, and Stellan gently dabbed at the corner of her mouth with his thumb.

"Caramel," he reported, after licking his finger.

"I think we're done here." Walter grabbed Hildy by the elbow. "Thank you for a fascinating morning."

"Until next time," Hildy called over her shoulder, allowing Walter to herd her to the door.

"What the hell was that?" he asked when they were outside.

"Which part? When I saved your cratering interview?"

"Yes, I'm sure you had my best interests at heart." Although it was true that he'd gotten more out of Stellan *with* Hildy than without her. "I'm not sure I want to give the guy more publicity."

"Go ahead and walk away. I'll be happy to take over."

"I bet he'd love that."

"What can I say? He has good taste."

"How is it tasteful to proposition someone's fiancée while he's standing right there?"

"Oh please. Anyone with half a brain could see our issues from space." Hildy pulled out a lip gloss, reapplying without a mirror before popping an Altoid. "He knows we're never going to make it to the altar."

NOW

16

Hildy

FOUR DAYS BEFORE THE PRESCOTT-SCHAFER WEDDING

BEYNAC, France—The Château de Beynac came into view long before they reached the village that shared its name. The massive stone fortress towered above the surrounding landscape like a giant gargoyle. You'd have to be a lunatic to storm those walls, Hildy reflected, hanging back as the rest of the group started their trek up the steep and twisting cobbled streets. Talk about picking your battles.

When she reached the castle, Hildy wandered past the wooden entrance gates to a grassy quadrangle bordered by watchtowers. A low stone wall marked the edge of the precipice, beyond which the landscape unfurled with a dramatic plunge. The view of the valley was even more spectacular from up here.

She was taking pictures for reference when someone approached, clearing his throat to alert her to his presence. Hildy knew it was Walter before she turned around. He'd obviously followed her; the only question was why.

"If you're thinking of pushing me over the edge, fair warning. I will take you down with me," she said, preemptively.

He came to stand beside her. Their eyes met, Hildy using hers to transmit a silent, *well?*

"Now why would I want to do that?"

"Eliminate the competition."

"That would be cheating. I'd rather beat you on an even playing field."

Hildy had other questions. *Since when? Have you forgotten I know the real you? How does sucking up to Maude qualify as fair?* But she contented herself with a small snort. "Okay, Mr. Honorable."

She rubbed the spot between her eyebrows where she *might* be developing a matched set of wrinkles. It was too soon for Botox, but Hildy would not have said no to a magical plumping serum. Especially if she was going to be standing in bright natural light next to Walter Burns.

"Headache?"

"I'm fine. Just getting the lay of the land." She moved away, pretending to read a placard explaining some significant historical event.

"I never thought I'd be in a place Richard the Lionheart visited," Walter said, joining her.

"Is that what you're going to write in your story?"

"I don't know." He sounded cagey, like he was regretting mentioning it. "Is that what *you're* going to write?"

"No, I'm going to do a Freudian analysis of the male need to erect giant phallic towers all over the landscape." There she went again, talking to Walter about dicks. Speaking of Freudian. Hildy took a cleansing breath. "It's nice of Fiona and her family to plan all of this. The excursions."

Walter didn't respond right away. "Do you remember Carlee and Carlton's wedding?"

Hildy considered denying it, but it was as much her memory as his. "Yep."

"I always thought that's the kind of ceremony I'd want."

"Disney-themed?" she asked, distracted by the effort not to yell, *Why are you thinking about weddings?* He couldn't marry Maude. Because of the cheating, obviously. Which Hildy still hadn't told him about.

"I didn't mean the costumes."

She shrugged, out of guesses. It was too hard to think over the chorus of worry in her head. What if I tell him and he doesn't believe me? What if I tell him and it turns out I'm wrong? What if I don't tell him and it ruins his life? What does it mean that I don't want that to happen? What kind of nemesis am I?

"Sincere," Walter said, oblivious to her spiraling. "Down-to-earth. More about the people than the trappings."

"I don't know. These trappings are pretty sweet." She gestured at the panoramic view, as if she could physically redirect their conversation onto safer ground. "Not your average beach resort. It's so cool how there's another castle everywhere you turn."

"Very cool," he agreed, looking ever so slightly suspicious of her sudden interest in architecture.

"You'd think they'd want privacy," Hildy continued. "To rule over their own little domain."

"Probably they were more worried about controlling water access and trade routes." He pointed at the confluence of two rivers in the valley below. "Since they weren't building these places as vacation homes."

Right. God forbid ye olden times people have an appreciation for leisure. "It's still weird they could stare into each other's windows. Or shoot a flaming arrow." She pretended to hold a bow, adding a whooshing sound effect as her imaginary projectile took flight.

"Maybe that was the point. Keeping tabs on each other."

"Like helicopter parents," she suggested. "Before they had AirTags and social media."

"A medieval mother-in-law."

"Crazy stalker ex."

An uncomfortable silence descended. *Way to make it awkward*, Hildy silently congratulated herself. You couldn't just riff a little; it had to be a record scratch.

"I'd build a castle next to yours," he said, as if that were a casual thing to drop into a conversation.

"To spy on me? Steal my shipments of grain? Launch a sneak attack when I least expect it?"

"Or maybe it would just be a mind game."

"Then I'd build a moat. Filled with piranhas."

"I'd get a catapult," he countered.

Unfortunately, Hildy had exhausted her knowledge of siege tactics. But she wasn't about to let him win. "You can't arrange your whole life around me."

"It's a little late for that."

Speaking of catapults! What kind of remark was that to launch at someone? "What are you talking about?"

"Forget it." His jaw tightened, but she'd always had a knack for sneaking past Walter's defenses.

"That's why you started writing about weddings, isn't it? You knew it was one of our top-performing features and you wanted to steal my thunder."

"No, I started writing about weddings because *you* told me they made great stories. And I wanted to get out of tabloids because I could tell you thought I was a gutter crawler!"

"You can't be serious!" She preferred not to think about how many choices she'd made over the years with Walter's voice in the back of her mind.

"Yes, I can! It's—" He broke off without finishing.

"Were you about to say, 'it's a free country'? But then you remembered we were in a different country?"

"France is also a free country," he grumbled, which was not a denial.

Weird how she could read his mind sometimes and at others find herself totally in the dark about what he was thinking.

His mouth twitched in what looked like a reluctant smile. An answering expression started to bloom on her face, but luckily a gust of wind blew her hair forward before he could see. Or maybe it wasn't lucky, because now Walter was smoothing her curls away from her eyes.

"We should go find them," she chirped, pivoting away from his searching gaze.

"Who?"

"Our people. The rest of the group. Fiona and Robbie."

Walter looked puzzled at this change in Hildy's MO. It wasn't like her to cut their alone time short. She'd always been Team Prolong the Agony, but not anymore. She was evolving so hard right now. Boss Mode activated.

"You got what you needed?" He took a step back, gesturing at their surroundings, and Hildy remembered she was supposed to be doing research.

"Yes." She hoped it sounded more convincing to his ears. "You?"

Walter hesitated. "I'm not sure there's anything more to get."

She refused to give him the satisfaction of asking what he meant.

* * *

"I don't see why we can't have the wedding here," Mr. Prescott was saying to Fiona as Hildy approached. He had selected an even higher spot on the battlements, where the chest-high stone walls were topped with square bricks that protruded like jack-o'-lantern teeth. "Or over there." He pointed across the river. "There are plenty of castles."

"Daddy," Fiona chided, "those are other people's castles. We can't just barge in and ask to get married. Besides, Maude put so much work into *her* castle. I don't want to ruin her big reveal."

"I'm just saying this is a real fortress." Mr. Prescott made a fist, like he too was a pillar of strength. "You don't hear anyone making a fuss about historic preservation here."

"I think Fiona is looking for something more subtle," Hildy said, in the soothing tone she'd perfected over a lifetime of managing her uncle. "Arboreal. Secluded. Romantic. Bewitching."

At some point during her speech, Walter must have snuck up behind her. His voice was practically in her ear when he felt the need to comment, "That's a lot of words."

"I know some other ones," she replied, matching his confidential murmur. "Overbearing. Busybody. Buttinski."

"What do you think of it?" Mr. Prescott asked Walter. "Our castle."

"I haven't seen it yet," Walter admitted.

That had to hurt. Hildy made a pouty face of mock sympathy, even though she was tap-dancing on the inside. Walter pretended not to notice.

"But I have full faith in Maude's abilities," he told her father.

"Good answer." Mr. Prescott nodded his approval. "Do you think this place has a dungeon?" It was clearly an invitation. To Hildy's surprise, Walter gave a sigh of regret.

"I should stick with the bride and groom. Duty calls."

"Fair enough." After a manly pat on the shoulder for his favorite reporter, Mr. Prescott headed back inside.

Hildy sidled over to Fiona and Robbie before Walter could get there. "How's your day going?"

"Majestic!" Robbie said. "I wish I had a pet eagle."

"But you'd want it to be free," Fiona pointed out.

"That's true, babe. You think of everything."

They really were well suited. Hildy felt a stab of envy. It must be nice to find someone you really and truly clicked with, as opposed to a fair-weather faux-boyfriend. "I don't think I've ever heard the story of how you two met."

"Believe it or not, we are actual childhood sweethearts." Fiona beamed at Robbie. "Met at tennis camp when we were kids, didn't find each other again until the summer after college."

Hildy did the math a couple of times to make sure she had it right. "So . . . last year?"

"When you know, you know," Robbie said, as if it were that simple.

Far be it from Hildy to argue with a besotted groom, but she had her doubts on that front. Sometimes what you thought you knew turned out to be a delusion that you spent the next decade trying to shake.

"It's like the best of both worlds." Fiona sounded like a real estate agent trying to sell Hildy a timeshare. "All the newness of falling in love, but with this built-in comfort, like you've known each other forever."

"Because you have!" Robbie held up his hand for a high five, which somehow transitioned to rubbing their noses together while whispering endearments.

Corinne joined them in time to hear the end of the story. "Don't get weird and spoil their moment."

"Why would she get weird?" Fiona asked, pulling away from her fiancé.

"About the childhood sweethearts thing." Corinne looked like she wanted to take a flamethrower to the words as soon as they were out, but it was too late.

Fiona turned wide eyes on Hildy. "You don't believe in it?"

"She's had some issues in that area," Corinne replied for her.

"Did you break up?" Fiona pressed. "With your childhood sweetheart? Is it hard for you to be here right now?"

Hildy double-checked to make sure Walter was out of hearing range. "I'm thrilled to be here! Loving every minute. And I wouldn't say *childhood*."

"Emotionally they were children," Corinne translated. "But it was a very different scenario."

"Nothing like you and Robbie," Hildy assured her. "You guys are golden."

"Oh, good." Fiona exhaled in relief. "I was afraid you were going to say it wasn't real. That there's no such thing as a bond that can last your whole life, even if you don't see each other for years."

"Hildy is the last person who would tell you that." Corinne clapped Hildy on the shoulder, reminding her to smile.

Fiona shook herself. "That sounded super insecure, didn't it? Sometimes it feels like this wedding is a highway with cars zooming everywhere and Robbie and me are trying to walk across it, you know?"

"Totally normal. I've seen a lot of weddings and there is always a ton of pressure on the couple. You're doing great." Hildy squeezed Fiona's right hand so as not to impale herself on the massive engagement ring.

Fiona blushed prettily. "That's nice of you to say. But you could tell me if there was something you know that I don't. It's better than getting hit with a nasty surprise, you know?"

"Of course," Hildy assured her, with what she hoped was a wise nod.

The words "nasty surprise" played over and over in her head, as if Fiona had stepped on a reverb pedal.

She had to tell Walter the truth. It would almost certainly blow up in her face, considering how poorly frank conversations had worked out for them in the past, but at least her conscience would be clear.

Clear-ish, anyway.

THEN

17

Hildy

TWO AND A HALF YEARS AGO

NEW YORK—The phone on Hildy's desk buzzed. She pressed the intercom button.

"What's up, Olive?"

"There's someone here to see you. A *man*." Her intern's normally chirpy voice was subdued.

"Is it a *police*man?"

"No!" There was a rustling in the background. The next words were barely above a whisper. "It's *Walter Burns*."

Corinne must have tipped off the front office staff. Which was honestly insulting, because Hildy wasn't going to make a scene at her own place of work. She saved that for other venues. *Life, Styled* was a serious enterprise, while also being fun and full of creative zing!

Hopefully, that would be evident to Walter from the reception area. Maybe they needed a funkier front desk? Or a really cool floor lamp. They could probably afford a few modest upgrades. According to their financial analyst, now that the magazine had survived its first year, the odds of the whole thing collapsing around them would drop every quarter. Surely that was cause for an extremely cautious celebration. Prosecco if not champagne.

"Hildy?" Olive whispered. "Do I need to call Corinne?"

"No! Tell Walter I'll be with him in three minutes. I'm just finishing something up."

"What are you—"

"Olive." Hildy generally applauded her intern's curiosity, but they had already had several conversations about when to ask follow-up questions and when to deliver a line as written. No one needed to know Hildy's bathroom schedule.

"Right. Sorry."

Hildy set down the phone. How would her office look to someone seeing it for the first time? She didn't have any plants, the biggest piece of wall art was a whiteboard, and the couch in the corner had been chosen more for comfort than aesthetics, since both Hildy and Corinne had been known to use it for the occasional power nap when they were at the office late.

But maybe it was okay that she didn't have a designer showplace for an office, since she wasn't a figurehead editor. Walter, of all people, should appreciate a more democratic approach to office space. This was a room where actual work happened, hence the clutter. Instead of trying to straighten the mess, Hildy decided to use her remaining two minutes to check her hair and reapply her lipstick—and then blot it off so it didn't look like she was trying too hard. She was a journalist, not an actress playing the part. Though there was no reason an editor couldn't also be hot, as Meryl Streep had demonstrated in *The Devil Wears Prada*.

Dropping her mirror back into her purse, Hildy kicked the desk drawer shut. What else? She'd been on the phone all morning, trying to get access to a temperamental young chef they were hoping to profile, but it wasn't the kind of work that left a visible trace, and she needed Walter to know she wasn't just counting the minutes until she could enjoy an expensive lunch on the company dime.

Footsteps approached her door. Olive was extremely literal about time, which was great for punctuality but less awesome when Hildy could have used a more generous definition of three minutes. Grabbing one of the old proofs she used as scratch paper, Hildy flipped it over and started drawing red lines through the text at random.

There was a brief knock—Hildy was pretty sure she didn't jump—and then the door swung open.

"That bad?" a much deeper voice than her intern's asked.

Hildy's head jerked up. She wondered what he'd told Olive to convince her he didn't need an escort. *It's okay. We're old friends. I've seen her half naked.*

Her expression must have been confused, because Walter nodded at the page on her desk, now striped like a candy cane. "I didn't realize you could read upside down."

Damn. It took her a half second to rally. "And backward, but who's counting?"

"Maybe you should just set it on fire. Hand back the burnt remains."

"I'm not that kind of editor." She slid the stack of papers that strongly suggested otherwise into a drawer. "What can I do for you, Walter?"

Did that sound suggestive, or was her imagination playing tricks? Hildy had once had an elaborate sex dream about Walter involving this very office, but that was a secret she'd take to the grave.

This Walter was a lot more polished than the imaginary version, and not just because Dream Walter's pants had been around his ankles. Had he dressed up to see her, or was this his new normal? Because that was an expensive suit, and the fit suggested custom tailoring—thankfully not in the too-snug style popular among some guys her age. The line between dress pants and leggings should be crystal clear, in Hildy's opinion. It was much classier to leave something to the imagination.

The drape of Walter's navy wool trousers gave only the barest hint at what was underneath. Then again, Hildy had already been up close and personal with everything his pants concealed, so she didn't need a preview of coming attractions. Although teen Walter had been a different animal than the man whose presence seemed to be sucking all the air out of the room.

"Take a seat," she said, attempting to regain control of the situation.

He scooted the chair a little closer to her desk before sinking into it. "How are you?"

"Fine." If he wanted to go through the charade of making small talk, she could play along. "You?"

"Same." Walter white-knuckled the arms of his chair before deliberately placing his hands on his lap.

Hildy was burning with curiosity but equally desperate to hide that fact from Walter. "Can I help you with something?"

"Maybe."

The plot thickened. "I assume there's a reason for this visit?" she hinted, when he failed to elaborate.

"Call it a professional courtesy."

She let the skepticism flash across her face like a neon sign. "You? Are being courteous? And professional?"

"Off to a great start," he muttered, fiddling with his watchband.

"I'm just surprised. Did a trio of holiday ghosts recently visit you?"

"A job is a job, Hildy."

"Keep telling yourself that."

"I don't have to."

That brought her up short. "What's that supposed to mean?"

"I gave my notice."

"Really?"

He shrugged, not quite managing to sell it as a casual gesture. "It was time for a change."

Hildy turned the words over in her mind, searching for a hidden meaning. "Tired of spreading scurrilous gossip?"

When he didn't bite, she moved down the list of possibilities. "Are you dying? For the record, if this is a tragic-yet-vague deathbed confession, I will murder you myself. Although you don't look sick. Or like you're having a breakdown."

"Try not to sound so disappointed."

She hit him with her most penetrating stare. "You know I'm going to figure it out. Why don't you save us both time and fess up now?" It came to her in a skin-tightening rush, like an allergic reaction. "Did you write a book?"

He shook his head.

The relief was short-lived, as a horrifying new possibility occurred to her. "Did someone poach you?"

He had the talent and the name recognition. Hildy would have tried to hire him herself if their history were less fraught. As things stood, Walter would assume she was recruiting him purely for the pleasure of laying him off the following week. Also, Corinne would have her committed the second Hildy floated the idea of bringing Walter Burns on staff.

Weird how she couldn't stop gnawing on an idea that was so clearly a nonstarter.

"Yes," he admitted. "I got a new job."

She watched him stand, gripping the back of his chair before pacing to the bookshelf, as if he had a sudden urgent need to inspect the framed picture of Hildy at her friends' wedding on Oahu.

"Food service?" she guessed. "You'd rock a hairnet."

"Journalism."

She should have known he wouldn't leave the news biz until they wheeled him out on a gurney. Hildy picked up a stack of sticky notes, ruffling the edges with her thumb as she waited for

Walter to spill. When he stayed stubbornly silent, her annoyance levels climbed. "How exactly is that relevant to me?"

"I thought you'd appreciate a heads-up. We might be seeing more of each other."

Surely he didn't mean that the way it sounded. "If you started a lifestyle magazine just to spite me—"

"I didn't," he cut in. "Not sure how you think I would have bankrolled that."

"Whereas I just fished the loose change out of my couch." She brushed her palms together as if it had been that easy, as opposed to a yearslong campaign of pitching their business plan to potential backers. "I guess I should be happy you won't be spying on me from the shadows and following me around town anymore. Or digging through my trash."

Walter sighed. "I never went through your trash, Hildy."

"So you admit to the rest?"

"No, I—" He stopped himself there. "The attention doesn't seem to have done you any harm." Walter made a show of looking around her office.

She stifled the urge to throw a pen at him. How dare he suggest that Hildy owed even a fraction of her success to him? "Because I made it work. But that was never plan A. You forced me to play the game that way."

"Sure. I'm the bad guy." He dug a hand into his thick hair, rumpling the careful styling. "This was a bad idea."

"Not your first."

"Yeah, well, let's hope it's my last." He paused in the doorway. "Sorry for wasting your time."

"Wait, what's the job?"

"I changed my mind."

"About the job?"

"About telling you. Why spoil the surprise?"

"That's not funny. Walter!" she yelled when he didn't turn back. Leaping from her chair, Hildy ran after him, garnering a curious look from Olive.

The stairwell was empty. Hildy let the door clang behind her as she hurried to the elevator. According to the light-up display, Walter was halfway to the ground floor.

Fine. If the universe didn't want her to catch him, Hildy wasn't going to embarrass herself by tearing down the stairs barefoot, shrieking his name. This was probably just Walter's way of psyching her out—showing up at her magazine to act all mysterious and broody. Hildy could do the same back at him . . . as soon as she figured out where he worked.

"Why are you running around like your hair's on fire?" Corinne asked, stepping out of the break room with a bag of microwave popcorn.

Hildy stomped into her office, collapsing onto the couch. It felt like she'd just finished a ninety-minute barre workout. "Walter was here."

Corinne bent to peer under Hildy's desk.

"What are you doing?"

"Checking for blood and body parts. Or your underwear."

Hildy rolled her eyes. "Allegedly he stopped by as a professional courtesy."

"What did he really want?"

"To get in my head."

Corinne huffed at that. "Waste of time."

"I know, right? Like I'm going to let him mess with me again. Fool me once, etcetera."

"It was a waste of time because he already lives there rent-free." She tapped her temple for emphasis.

"I think I know why he showed up," Hildy said, ignoring the unsolicited commentary. She frowned at her co-worker's gargoyle impression. "What is that face?"

"Inside me there are two wolves." Corinne pressed her fingertips to her sternum. "One doesn't want to encourage this weird obsession, but the other knows she needs to be ready to stage an intervention. Let's hear it."

"Maybe it was a cry for help."

"You think Walter Burns came to *you* for help? Out of all the millions of people in this city?"

"Yes, Corinne." She needed to revisit the idea of getting a KEEP UP, PEOPLE T-shirt. "Of a certain kind. That only I can provide."

"You know sexual healing is not a real thing, right?"

"I'm talking about forgiveness. What if he came to apologize?"

"Did he apologize?"

Hildy shook her head.

"Then that kind of undermines your theory."

"It's possible he was distracted." Hildy brushed a stray crumb off the couch so she wouldn't have to see Corinne's expression.

"Listen. I'm all for the two of you sorting out your shit, but if it hasn't happened by now, maybe it's time to let go of that—" She paused, circling a hand as she searched for the right word.

"Vendetta?" Hildy guessed.

"I was going to say 'dream,' but sure. Let's go with your version."

Hildy knew when she was being humored, but decided to let it ride. She had always preferred her tough love in very small and occasional doses, like a vitamin C supplement for her common sense.

Maybe Walter was like chicken pox: one of those viruses that never really go away once they get into your bloodstream. The important thing was to remember she'd been inoculated against him a long time ago.

NOW

18

Hildy

THREE DAYS BEFORE THE PRESCOTT-SCHAFER WEDDING

TAMNIÈS, France—According to an *aww*-inducing note in the wedding program, today's entertainment, *Un Jour à la Campagne*, was an homage to Robbie's favorite elementary school event, a daylong celebration of physical challenges in the great outdoors. Instead of Popsicles and water balloons and three-legged races, the wedding guests would take part in slightly more elevated activities that paid homage to local culture.

Hildy thought it was nice they'd carved out a little time on the itinerary for something Robbie-centric, even if grown-up Field Day wouldn't have been her first choice so soon after washing her hair. A lot of weddings gave the groom less airtime than the DJ. The fact that Fiona was willing to share the spotlight tracked with her observations about the two of them as a genuinely sweet couple. Reason number infinity she needed to nail this story—once she established *Life, Styled*'s exclusive coverage rights.

A frisson of unease tried to hijack her thoughts, but Hildy kicked it aside. She had a plan for the day, and she was going to follow it. Step one: a little first-person immersion in current events.

When the bus delivered them to the open pasture outside the hotel village where most of the games would take place, she immediately looked for the archery area. Due to a mild Robin Hood fixation in childhood, Hildy had always suspected she might be a secret prodigy with a bow and arrow.

"Are you picturing me with an apple on my head?" Walter asked when she was standing in line for her turn.

"I wasn't thinking about you at all." For once it was true. Her thoughts had been fully occupied with a vision of herself in head-to-toe leather, supple and fawn-brown, not shiny and black like a divorced dad in a bomber jacket psyching himself up to "get back out there" on the dating scene.

"Bold choice," Walter continued his unsolicited commentary.

Her first thought was that he was questioning her ability to pull off leather pants. Then she remembered he couldn't actually read her mind, despite how often it felt that way. She executed a slow turn, like she was barely interested enough to spare the energy. "What is?"

"You. Shooting a bow."

"You don't think I can do it?" Her temper was at a low simmer, standing by to see how far he pushed it.

Walter rubbed the pads of his fingers together. "You might get blisters. Especially with those soft hands."

"I'm touched by your concern." Even though the soft hands bit was almost certainly a dig about her background.

"Don't let me stop you. It's no skin off my nose if you can't type."

"Since when are you an archery expert?"

"Is that so hard to believe?"

Hildy took her time looking him over, focusing on Walter's upper body. Her memories of the coatroom incident were a mix of foggy and blade-sharp, but she did recall the firmness of his shoulders, and how easily he'd supported her weight while simultaneously crushing her against him.

"Not really," she admitted.

Walter seemed surprised, as if he'd been bracing for a fight. Some of the tension left his posture. "I covered the MacCormack-McKissack wedding. Medieval theme. You weren't at that one."

"No. We did the Manion-O'Neills that weekend. In Newport."

"With the regatta?"

"Yep."

"Nice."

"It was." Look at her, agreeing with Walter Burns! For a moment, they were two colleagues talking shop. It was a dynamic Hildy had never imagined—neutral, casual, *mild*—instead of their usual all or nothing. She tried to picture the two of them as polite acquaintances. The prospect was strangely deflating.

Hildy stepped out of line. "I changed my mind." She glanced at her manicure as if that was the issue. Better for Walter to think she was a prima donna than watch her try something she might not be good at.

With a smile that was supposed to mean *buh-bye*, she headed toward the paint-your-own-pottery station. That was a skill Hildy knew she could perform even after several glasses of pinot.

"Can I help you?" she asked, when Walter fell in beside her.

"I was going to ask if you wanted to try canoeing."

"You really think we could paddle in sync?" Hildy had a vivid mental picture of the two of them turning in circles for hours until they finally capsized from exhaustion. She stopped walking in order to glare more effectively. "Are you planning to follow me all day?"

"Yes, Hildy. I'm trying to copy off your paper."

A person who didn't know Walter well might have missed the undercurrent of snark, but to Hildy it was like a metal snap fastening into place. They were back in alignment.

"I thought you might be hoping for one last score," she volleyed. "Déjà vu all over again."

"Here?" He made a show of looking around. "In this field full of people?"

"You wish. A score as in selling a story about my private life to your former tabloid overlord. For old time's sake."

He took a step closer. "And what exactly would I report?"

"You want me to give you the headline? Way to phone it in, Burns." Hildy surveyed the nearest cluster of wedding guests. "Maybe I'm dating him. In the pink shorts." She indicated a group of Robbie's college buddies on their way to the lake.

"You're going to have to be more specific."

"Rugby thighs."

"I have no idea what that means."

"Yes, you do." Hildy sent a flirty little wave at her hypothetical vacation boyfriend. He pointed at himself, brow creased.

"Do you even know that guy?"

"Does it matter? I'm sure you can get someone to take a picture of me standing near him. Voila! Instant relationship."

To his credit, Walter took that one on the chin, lowering his head as if to say *touché*.

"I guess I could ask him out," Hildy mused, staring at the sporty stranger as if giving the idea serious consideration. "Add a little meat to the story. As it were. Maybe it'll turn into something. That would be a great anecdote to tell our grandchildren."

Hildy's imaginary paramour took a step in their direction, until Walter's glare stopped him in his tracks.

"I don't see it," Walter said. "A guy like that—he's not going to give you what you need."

"Which is what?" It was foolish to allow Walter that kind of opening, but Hildy's curiosity outweighed her sense of self-preservation.

"Someone who can go toe to toe with you." Walter turned to face her. "Otherwise you'll get bored."

That was an uncannily accurate summation of her dating history. Hildy pretended not to care. "Well, let me know if you run across someone who has what it takes."

"I will." His inflection was just ambiguous enough to give her pause.

"Is that why you're nipping at my heels, Walter? You think I require a chaperone?"

"Most of this stuff is for pairs, and I don't really know anyone else. Except Corinne, and she went back to the hotel to meet Gabby's shuttle."

Hildy waited for Walter to correct himself. "And Maude," she prompted when he appeared to have been struck by girlfriend amnesia.

"Oh. Right." His slow nod was the definition of unconvincing.

"You know, don't you?" A wave of guilt made Hildy's skin prickle, like it was a size too small for her body. She should have said something sooner.

"Know what?"

Shit. Maybe he didn't know. "Something about Maude?" she hinted, keeping it vague.

"Are you trying to trick me into revealing something about the wedding?"

"No! This isn't about work." Unless Walter disappeared to lick his wounds when the situation with Maude blew up. It was not a thought that brought any satisfaction. If anyone was going to make him run away crying when he got his ass handed to him at this wedding, it should be Hildy. *After* she told him the truth about his girlfriend, because if their positions were reversed, Hildy would want to know. And there was a difference between pranking someone and neglecting to mention the ticking time bomb under their bed.

"I know the timing isn't great, and I'm probably the last person you want to hear this from, but I think Maude . . . might be involved with that Loïc guy." She braced herself for denial or even anger, but Walter just blinked at her, like he'd temporarily gone offline.

After waiting a few more seconds, Hildy's patience ran out. "Are you doing some kind of man thing where you act like you don't have feelings, or do you not believe me? Because I swear, I'm only trying to dominate you professionally. I wouldn't mess with your personal life."

"Good to know."

"You don't seem that upset."

"I'm not."

She studied his face for signs that he was crying on the inside before accepting that Walter was telling her the truth. Which meant . . . well, she wasn't sure what exactly, except that she'd just embarrassed herself. "I should have listened to Corinne. She said you probably had an open relationship."

"It's not that."

"Throuple?"

Walter sighed. "We're friends."

There was an audible pause before she asked, "Who?"

"Me and Maude. Who did you think I meant?"

"That. What you said." She cleared her throat. "Explain."

"We hung out a few times. It was obvious to both of us it wasn't going to go any further, but she needed a date to her sister's wedding, and figured I might want to cover it. It was a mutually beneficial arrangement."

"When you say, 'mutually beneficial,' does that mean sex?"

"No. I told you—it's not like that. At all."

"Damn it!"

"You're mad I'm not sleeping with Maude?"

"No! I'm upset that you fooled me. Here I am, a past master of the fake-dating form, and I totally fell for it. I must be losing my touch." She shook her head. "And to think I was worried about your feelings. No wonder you don't care whether she's making l'amour with another dude. I thought you were just clueless."

"You have a lot of faith in my observational skills. Considering how not subtle those two have been."

"People see what they want to see." Surely he'd been to enough weddings to realize that. "Love is blind, etcetera."

Walter looked like he wanted to keep arguing, but a buzzing electric hum announced the arrival of Mr. Prescott aboard a tricked-out golf cart with garlands of flowers draped around the sides.

"If it isn't the press pool," he said, gliding to a stop beside them. "Enjoying yourselves?"

As with most of her conversations with their host, there were multiple layers to what sounded like a simple question. *Are you impressed with the scale of this production? Can you believe someone as important as yours truly is taking the time to be friendly with the help? I trust your publication will pay suitable tribute to the majesty of this wedding?*

"Yes." Hildy widened her eyes just enough to appear sweet and innocent without looking like a dope.

"Very much so," Walter chimed in.

"We were pleased to be able to get Scudro. He did the landscape art piece you'll see on the helicopter tour. You know, a lot of people think Banksy has gone bougie."

Hildy nodded as if she'd heard the same thing, while privately wondering if Mr. Prescott had seriously attempted to hire the famously anonymous guerilla artist as a party clown for his daughter's wedding week.

"Have you tried the life-size Settlers of Catan?"

"It's on our list." Walter didn't specify which list.

"Good, good." Mr. Prescott was already scanning the horizon. "You haven't seen Maude, have you?"

Hildy stared at the grass as if she was searching for a four-leaf clover. There was no chance she could talk about Maude right now without giving away the game.

"She's working on something at the castle," Walter replied.

Mr. Prescott sighed. "Poor Maude is going to need a vacation when all this is over." In case that wasn't enough of a hint, he added, "I know she's been wanting to visit the Maldives."

That part was clearly directed at Walter, who managed to maintain an expression of casual interest. Because what this conversation needed was more layers of awkward. *Wrong guy*, Hildy wanted to say, preferably while giving the golf cart a nice hard shove from behind. There was just enough of an incline for it to roll away.

She forced herself to stand still as Mr. Prescott waved at someone standing near one of the food tents.

"There's Philippe," he informed them. "Do you know him?"

"I'm afraid not," Hildy said, after sliding Walter a quick look to make sure he wasn't nodding.

"Philippe Vasseur. Of Papier Propre. The largest supplier of paper products in western Europe," he added when neither of them responded.

"Of course," Walter murmured, as if that guess had been on the tip of his tongue. Hildy would have kicked him if she wasn't wearing sandals.

"We're like a family in this business," Mr. Prescott continued, as though they'd requested an impromptu soliloquy about his corporate BFFs. "If you tallied up all the guests at this wedding, you'd be looking at near-total control of the global paper industry."

If he was suggesting she work that tidbit into her story, Mr. Prescott was higher than a kite.

"Hard to put out a newspaper without paper, eh? Or a magazine." He slapped his thigh a few times, which apparently signaled that the conversation was over. The golf cart lurched into motion, trundling slowly over the grass.

They watched in silence until he was out of hearing range.

"Some people watch too much TV," Hildy said as the hum of the engine faded. As if scheming billionaires needed more negative role models. "I take it he doesn't know. About you and Maude?"

Walter shook his head.

"He's going to be so bummed."

"I doubt it. I don't exactly fit in with this crowd."

"They're not Hapsburgs, Walter. It's the twenty-first century."

"Like calls to like. Look at Robbie and Fiona."

"You think money is what they have in common?"

"It doesn't hurt."

Hildy wanted to tell him that he was wrong about that. Money could hurt as easily as anything else people used against you.

"You could tell him," Walter pointed out. "Maude's father. About me. He might be pissed enough to send me packing."

Did he really think she would stoop that low? Maybe his opinion of her would always be in the gutter. What was the French expression, "plus ça change"? She flashed him her fakest smile.

"No, thanks. *I'm* not in the business of selling secrets."

THEN

19

Walter

FOUR AND A HALF YEARS AGO

NEW YORK—Walter wasn't prepared for the yelling.

Watching clips of red carpet arrivals didn't capture the dizzying volume of so many voices clamoring for attention. *Hey, famous person, over here!* A cacophony of voices calling out again and again, as if they were casting lures. *Look this way. No, this way! Give us a smile!*

It wasn't catcalling, exactly—the celebrity/press ecosystem was a symbiotic relationship—but in practice, it didn't feel different enough to ease his conscience. There was something predatory about lying in wait, even in a setting this public, with prey that had plenty of warning. He felt like part of a mob, a seething, barely civilized mass. Walter wondered if the glitterati ever got used to the onslaught of flashbulbs. Would *he* get used to being on the other side of the firing line, jostled by his more ambitious colleagues?

He hoped not—unless he was kidding himself about this being a temporary gig. Walter checked his phone for the twentieth time. No need to push to the front of the scrum until she arrived.

His pulse spiked. After a three-week trial run repackaging content from other sources and manning the tip line, he had been liberated from desk duty for the night. It was an audition of sorts, if not the kind the performers arriving for this evening's benefit would recognize. Walter had asked if he needed to research any of the actors and musicians and dancers who were supposed to be in attendance tonight, but his boss had told him to focus on what—or rather, who—he already knew.

As if that would make his job simple.

She's not a world-famous pop star, he reminded himself. The competition for her time would be less fierce. All he had to do was get her attention and make sure they got a clear shot of her face, preferably in the same frame as her date. For bonus points, Walter could try to get a sound bite.

"What do we want to know?" *If she'll talk to me*, he silently added. The surprise of seeing him might be enough to make her stop. After that, he had no idea what to expect.

"Keep it simple," his boss told him. "'Who are you with? Are you having a good time?' Don't try to discuss anything serious. Or ask what she's wearing. We care about people, not brands. If some designer wants free advertising, they can pay for it."

It was an embarrassingly pedestrian assignment—not at all the type of thing Walter had gone to J-school for. Then again, pride didn't pay the bills and his student loan deferment would expire in a few short months.

That was the stark economic reality of his life, yet for some reason Walter felt as though he was making excuses. Maybe it was the background hum he'd been feeling all day. Not just dread or nerves or resignation, though there was some of that mixed in, but a distinct buzz of anticipation as the hours trickled past, bringing him closer to this moment.

A car door slammed. Walter used every inch of his height to peer over the heads of the surrounding reporters and photographers. Standing on the curb as her town car slowly pulled away was a woman in a sky-blue dress with a head full of curls.

"Excuse me," he said, already pushing toward the temporary barrier that had been erected to keep the press and other peons away from the VIPs. As the crowd around him shifted, she came in and out of view. He glimpsed a sliver of profile, the flutter of a delicate sleeve, a bangle sliding over a slender wrist. How was it that she looked like a different person, and yet Walter would have recognized her anywhere?

He pushed harder, worried she'd pass his vantage point before he reached the front. When he was two bodies back, he decided to seize his chance.

"Hildy!"

Somehow she heard his voice amid the chaos of the red carpet. Walter felt a thrill of satisfaction when she abruptly stopped, glancing behind her before turning to search the throngs on the other side of the partition. He shoved past the last person standing between him and Hildy.

She blinked several times, polished smile faltering for an instant before she lifted her chin to a photo-ready angle. *Well?* her dark eyes seemed to say. *What now?*

Rational thought fled, leaving Walter with a single resounding impression.

It's Hildy.

She was almost close enough to touch.

A dark-haired man in a sleek midnight-blue suit placed a hand at Hildy's waist. Had he been there this whole time? Maybe Walter didn't have the chops for this job if he hadn't even noticed she wasn't alone.

Other people—other *couples*—were backing up behind them. Walter felt his window closing. He forced his lips to move.

"Who are you with?"

It was more of a croak than the confident shout he'd practiced in his head, but Hildy heard him just fine. Her brows drew down in a look of confusion as she took in his press badge. Had she assumed he was there as a starstruck civilian, eager to gaze upon her magnificence from a distance?

"David Wong," her date supplied with a polished smile. "New York City Ballet." He paused, waiting for Walter's belated nod of acknowledgment before continuing. "Hildy and I are happy to be here supporting the arts—and each other."

While Walter fumbled with his recorder, the handsome ballet dancer pulled Hildy closer. She turned to gaze into his eyes, their posture giving the unmistakable suggestion of intimacy.

"Got it," Walter's photographer said, nodding at Hildy and her companion, who took that as their cue to stroll onward, hand in hand.

Hildy shot Walter one last burning look before disappearing into the theater, because of course he was still standing there staring after her like a stray dog. If he had to name her expression, Walter would have said she looked almost angry. But what did Hildy have to be mad about? Young, rich, and beautiful, with the world on a string—including her obviously smitten date.

As he walked back to the subway, Walter told himself the evening had been a success. Crucially, he had something to file (*Media heiress Hildy Johnson has a new dance partner!*). Perhaps more importantly, he'd found the answer to a personal question, one that had plagued him for years.

Had there been something special between them?

Seeing her on the red carpet confirmed his suspicion that the Hildy Effect wasn't unique to him. Her charisma had always been weaponized. It was just Walter's bad luck to get caught in her blast radius when he was too young to know better.

NOW

20

Hildy

THREE DAYS BEFORE THE PRESCOTT-SCHAFER WEDDING

TAMNIÈS, France—"*That's* the joust?" Hildy meant the question rhetorically, but it didn't stop Walter from getting his two cents in. "You were expecting horses?"

He was still following her. Either that or he also felt the need to hit something, and the damp *thwacks* and raucous cheering would have drawn him in that direction with or without her.

She charged onward toward the large rectangular inflatable with a rope draped across the middle. If she'd thought about it, Hildy would have realized this was going to be an unconventional joust. You couldn't hand actual weapons to a bunch of wedding guests. The obvious solution was to have one barely dressed person ride their partner's shoulders while wielding a fearsome pool noodle.

She watched with no small amount of awe as one of the bridesmaids bludgeoned another again and again, barely pausing between blows.

"Keep it below the shoulders," a guy in a black-and-white striped jersey said into a megaphone. "No head shots. That's a penalty for the green team."

The bloodthirsty bridesmaid holding the green pool noodle

looked like she was ready to throw down. While she was yelling at the umpire, the pink team struck, knocking the opposing pair's noodle into the water.

Hildy and Walter were close enough now to join in the applause.

"Does that mean they win?" Hildy asked the man standing next to her.

"Not until the bottom half goes down."

"I like this game," she told Walter. She was envisioning the two of them ducking and weaving as they wielded their pool noodles. Walter was stronger, but he'd be handicapped by his fear of beating on a woman. She was pretty sure she could take him.

"Why are you looking at me like that?"

"How am I looking at you?"

Walter thought about it for a second. "Like you're going to grind my bones to make your bread."

"To the victor go the spoils."

"What?"

"Trash talk. I'm getting my head in the game."

He looked from the pool to Hildy, eyes lingering on her face. "*You're* going to play?"

"Why? Are you questioning my skills?"

"At pool noodle jousting?"

She ignored the sarcasm. "Five dollars says you go down first."

"Wow. Big talk for somebody who's afraid to get her hair wet."

Rude of him to know her weaknesses. "I guess we'll find out which one of us has the killer instinct."

"I'm not dueling you, Hildy."

"*Bawk bawk*," she clucked, flapping her arms.

Walter rolled his eyes. "Very mature. It's the bride and groom's turn anyway."

Sure enough, Fiona and Robbie were standing in front of the referee, beaming with excitement.

"Let's hear it for the future Mr. and Mrs.," the referee barked.

"Do we have a challenger? Anyone?" he prompted, when no one stepped forward.

"Come on, guys!" Robbie sent a hopeful smile at the milling crowd. "We'll go easy on you."

Fiona beckoned to one of her bridesmaids, who mimed drinking something. It must be mimosa time. Hildy's heart squeezed at the forlorn look on Fiona's face. People assumed brides were the center of attention, with everyone dancing attendance on them. In reality, there was often an invisible wall separating the leading lady from the rest of the wedding party, because even if they were all doing the same activities, no one else was on the same journey. However it looked from the outside, getting married was not a group activity.

The groomsmen seemed to have the same idea as the bridesmaids, waving Robbie off with talk of lunch. Fiona's fiancé looked hopefully at one of his uncles, who had to be at least sixty.

"Change of plans." Hildy grabbed Walter by the wrist, lifting his arm as high as she could reach. "We'll play," she called, hopping a little to sell it.

"What are you doing?" Walter gritted out.

"Look at those poor babies," she said through her smile. "It's like they're getting picked last for kickball. At their own wedding! We have to help them."

"Are you sure that's . . ." He trailed off mid-thought as Hildy shrugged her arms free of her cover-up.

"It's a brilliant idea," she finished for him, shimmying the dress down her legs until she could step out of it. Her bathing suit was not exactly sporty, but it wasn't a G-string either. Not that Walter could tell, with his eyes locked on the grass.

"Your turn." She clapped her hands like a coach, two quick *get moving* slaps. "Unless you're planning to wear your shirt in the pool?"

"It might be better." His fingers twisted the hem. "For you to hold on to."

"I need both arms to whack people." She was a little concerned by his limited grasp of battle tactics. "Your job is to hold on to me. And not fall over."

"That's not what I'm worried about."

Something was obviously weighing on him, so it was time for one of her legendary pep talks. "Listen. It's like kickboxing, only in the water and with more props. Plus the piggyback element. And I could really use the workout. Bottom line, it'll make Fiona and Robbie happy, so suck it up."

He gave a slow nod, falling in beside her as she walked over to the referee's chair. It would have been cooler if there was one of those movie sequences where everyone geared up and checked their weapons like they were going to war, but a pool noodle was a pool noodle. It didn't make cool sound effects. Hildy let Fiona choose first, and was only mildly surprised when she took the neon green one.

"Robbie's favorite color," Fiona explained.

"That works out, because Walter loves pink." Hildy grabbed the other noodle, tapping it against Fiona's in a quick salute, one warrior to another.

"No hits to the face," the ref reminded them.

"Everything else is fair game though, right?" Hildy asked.

"Glad you're on my team," Walter murmured behind her.

She turned to stick her tongue out at him, but that plan flew out the window when she registered his shirtlessness. There was no time to process the discovery now, so she took a mental snapshot of his naked torso for future contemplation. Maybe she could paste it on a dartboard, with the bull's-eye in that delicious valley between his pecs.

"I guess we should do it in the pool," Walter said.

Hildy blinked at him.

"You getting on my shoulders," he clarified, red-faced.

"That's what I thought you meant," she lied, waving at him to go first.

Sighing like he was about to walk the plank, Walter climbed the short flight of steps and lowered himself into the water on the other side. Hildy started to ask if it was cold, then realized that would sound weak. Also, she could just check his nipples.

That was a yes, then.

She had a brief out-of-body experience during the . . . mounting, for lack of a better word. Walter hunched down, Hildy attempted to climb onto his back with dignity and poise, there was some slipping and sliding involving her inner thigh and parts of his face, as well as boob-to-back contact (but who was counting?), and then finally she was sitting on him.

His shoulders. She was sitting on his shoulders, with her legs dangling down his chest.

"Is this okay?" Walter asked, taking a tentative hold of her shins as he straightened from a crouch.

She wiggled her hips, worried she might slip backward and take them both down. "I'm not humping the back of your head, FYI."

"I appreciate the clarification."

"We just need a nice, tight fit," Hildy continued, as if overexplaining would make it less awkward. "Meaning your grip."

"That's exactly where my mind went."

"Walter."

"Hmm?"

"You're going to have to hold on a lot harder than that."

"I don't want to hurt you."

Too late. The words floated into Hildy's head, sharpening her resolve. "I can take it."

He slid his hands a little higher, abandoning the knees after a brief clench. When his palms finally settled on her upper thighs, he huffed as if she'd just kicked over his sandcastle.

"Are you wearing sunscreen?" He sounded judgy, as if he couldn't believe she'd made such a rookie mistake. Poor Walter, tortured by her naked quads.

"I'm sorry for caring about skin cancer."

"It's slippery."

"Squeeze harder." Hildy ignored the corresponding clench in her stomach muscles when his fingers flexed.

When Fiona and Robbie lined up on the opposite end of the pool, Hildy sent Walter a silent cue that it was time to move.

"Did you just steer me with your thighs or are you trying to strangle me?"

"Be glad I don't have a whip. Assume the position, Seabiscuit." She made clip-clop sounds with her tongue.

While the referee reminded them of the rules, Hildy took practice swings with her pink pool noodle. The poke, the slash, sideways sweep, the thumper—

"It's much more intimidating when you give them a name," Walter said, cluing Hildy in that her monologue had gone audible. He let go of her right thigh long enough to give her an encouraging pat.

The crowd gasped as Hildy wobbled, weight shifting to one side. She slid halfway down Walter's arm before he managed to arrest her momentum with a firm shove in the other direction. The only problem was that she was now draped horizontally across his face and neck, clinging to his opposite shoulder while he anchored her ass with the crook of his elbow. It probably looked like a figure skating lift gone horribly wrong.

He laughed, and Hildy felt the heat of it from her stomach down. She couldn't even writhe away for fear of dunking herself before the match even started.

"You guys okay over there?" Robbie yelled.

Hildy raised her thumb.

"The joust starts on my whistle," the ref announced.

"Let's do this." Hildy reached down to pat Walter's stomach.

Under other circumstances, she would have asked about his core workout. "As soon as you turn me around."

By some miracle, they managed to slip and scramble her body back into position by the time the whistle blew, though they'd probably both need physical therapy later. And maybe the other kind of therapy. Shaking off those memories, Hildy gripped the pool noodle with both hands, ready to enter the fray.

"Can you go any faster?" she asked, several shuffling paces later. "More gallop, less stagger?"

"I'm trying not to drop you."

Hildy bucked her hips, urging him forward.

"Not helping," Walter grunted.

When they finally reached the midpoint, Fiona surprised her with a swipe to the ribs.

"Hiyah!" she bride cried out.

"Nice one, babe!" Robbie held up a hand for a high five.

"I thought she might be ticklish," Fiona confessed.

"Not there," Walter said under his breath.

Hildy pretended not to hear. She was too busy being miffed their opponents had drawn first blood.

They traded blows for a while, one dull smack after another. When the whistle signaled the end of the first round, the two teams retreated to opposite ends of the pool. Hildy's arms were rubbery, so she could only imagine how Walter felt.

"How are you holding up?" she asked him, after someone dressed like a medieval page squirted Gatorade into their mouths.

"I'm fine."

Hildy eyed their opponents, hoping to see signs of flagging energy. Unfortunately, Robbie and Fiona were as bouncy as ever. "We should probably end this."

"I would nod but—"

"My pelvic bone is in the way, I know. I'll assume you agree."

"With what?"

"The plan."

Walter tilted his head in an attempt to look up at her. "Are you going to let me in on it?"

"Just hold on really tight."

"So . . . the same thing I've been doing?"

"Correct. Now get me back over there." She tensed her thighs. "Giddyup, partner."

"I live to serve."

"Good boy. There's a lump of sugar with your name on it back at the stable."

When the whistle blew for the second round, Hildy waited until Fiona raised her arms to strike before making her move.

"Hildy, what are you doing?" Walter sounded panicked, possibly because she'd leaned so far forward to poke Fiona's underarm he was no longer entirely vertical.

"Letting her have it," she replied, waiting for Fiona to seize this golden opportunity to steal their pool noodle.

"Don't!" Walter jerked back.

The chain reaction kicked off when Hildy let go of their pool noodle to grab two handfuls of his hair before she went flying. Fiona lunged for the pink noodle, only to feel her own weapon slipping away. She swayed, arms windmilling.

Just drop it, Hildy thought at her. Without a noodle of their own, she and Walter would be sitting ducks—which was the whole point of letting herself be disarmed.

Instead, Fiona lunged after the falling foam sticks.

"Fee!" Robbie screamed, as his bride-to-be threw her weight sideways. When she hit the water, he plunged after her like a kid bobbing for apples.

Meanwhile, Hildy had let go of Walter to grab for Fiona's arm. The movement must have caught him off guard, because the next thing Hildy knew, she and Walter were a tangle of limbs at the bottom of the pool.

She came up spluttering, largely due to the arm locked around her midsection.

"Let go," she told Walter, wriggling free before he could give her the Heimlich. Hildy waded over to where the bridesmaids were fluttering around the edge of the pool.

"What if she drowns?" one of them said. "Can you imagine? Literal *days* before her wedding!"

"She's not going to drown," someone else countered. "Fiona's a really strong swimmer. Remember that spring break in Cabo?"

"That was a lazy river, Christine. She had an inner tube!"

"What's she doing down there?" another bridesmaid asked.

Hildy was wondering the same thing. After briefly surfacing for more air, both Fiona and Robbie had gone back under.

"Looks like she lost something," one of Fiona's attendants said. It sounded like they were calling plays on ESPN.

"Oh my God. What if it was her ring?" The bridesmaid with the fishtail braid cupped her hands around her mouth as she yelled, "Was it your ring, Fiona?"

Hildy felt a squeeze of panic. Had Fiona been wearing her epically expensive ring to pool-noodle joust? Surely she wouldn't . . . okay maybe she would. But this wasn't the Atlantic Ocean. All they had to do was find it. She was thinking about joining the search when Fiona popped up again, followed a second later by Robbie.

"What is it, Fee?" her bridesmaids chorused.

Fiona silently held up her left hand.

There were several gasps of "No!" Others were too shocked to do anything but press a hand to their mouths.

"What are you going to do?" a bridesmaid wailed.

Walter edged closer to Hildy, keeping his voice pitched low. "Was it the ring?"

She shook her head. "Fingernail."

"She lost a fingernail?" He sounded more confused than alarmed. "Is she bleeding?"

Hildy shushed him. She didn't have time to explain the art and science of acrylics right now.

"Isn't that bad luck?" one of the bridesmaids stage-whispered.

"What about the pictures?" another of them gasped. "She can't do close-ups like that!"

"Don't worry, Fee! You can use a hand model," the bridesmaid with the braid assured her. "No one will know."

Hildy raised both hands, urging everyone to chill. "It's going to be okay. Someone here is bound to have nail glue. We'll get through this."

Fiona shook her head. "I should have known better than to get them wet. I just wanted to have fun with you," she told a dripping Robbie.

"It was fun," he assured her. "Until the end."

No one pointed accusingly at Hildy, but she felt the heat of unspoken condemnation. "Sorry about that."

"She gets carried away," Walter said. "With the competitive spirit."

Hildy rounded on him. "Or maybe it's because my little pony got spooked and started running away?"

Walter made a show of clearing his throat, as if she'd just proven his point.

"Can we focus on what's important here?" Hildy said.

Robbie nodded, his expression resolute. "Does anyone have a scuba mask? I am going back in. I won't rest until I find that nail for you, Fee!"

"I'll help." Walter slipped under the rope to join the underwater rescue mission.

Hildy turned to Fiona, ready to apologize again or reassure her about the wonders of nail technology, but she was being pulled out of the pool by a gaggle of sympathetic bridesmaids.

"Let's go back to the hotel," one murmured, while another announced that she had already alerted Fiona's beauty team.

"I'll order champagne from room service," a third promised.

Hildy wasn't sure her presence would be welcome just now, so she watched them depart, followed by a triumphant Robbie holding his beloved's fingernail aloft like a pale pink Excalibur.

Walter joined her on the grass, tugging his shirt back on. "That could have gone better."

"You think?"

"Unless this was your plan?" He gestured at the bridal party leaving their own event early.

"For your information, I was *trying* to let them win. If you hadn't panicked—"

"I was saving you from yourself!"

"I didn't need saving. My self-control is legendary." *Except around you*, she added silently. He really was a menace to her reputation.

"I guess it just happens." His voice was muffled as he bent to slide on his shoes, but the words wormed their way under Hildy's skin.

"What happens?"

He straightened. "You. Making a splash."

She ignored the terrible pun. "And you're an innocent bystander?"

He shrugged. "I'm just a reporter. I don't make news."

"You think I want to be the center of attention?"

Walter didn't deny it.

"Here's a PSA for you. I'm part of the story whether I want to be or not. So yeah, I know how to shape the narrative. Better than letting other people use me." She let that sink in for a second before turning her back on him and walking away.

THEN

21

Walter

FIVE YEARS AGO

COLUMBIA, Mo.—“Burns!”

Will Wineke, city editor for the campus paper, was an old-school newshound with a graying walrus mustache who didn’t believe in coddling student reporters.

“In my office,” he barked, not waiting to see if Walter would respond to the summons. When Wineke called, the newspaper staff jumped.

“What can I do for you?” Walter asked from the doorway, notebook and pen at the ready.

“Still looking for a job?” He lowered his voice slightly from full roar, but it was still loud enough to alert half of Walter’s colleagues to the fact that he had yet to find postgraduation work.

“Correct,” Walter replied, ignoring the clench of anxiety in his gut. On top of a stagnant job market, he’d further narrowed his options by ruling out any and all outlets owned by Johnson Media. Waiting and hoping for however many months it took to find paying work might be an option for someone with no student loans (or unlimited access to the Bank of Mom and Dad), but Walter didn’t have that cushion. He thought back for the umpteenth time to the decisions that had brought him to this pass.

How different would his life be right now if he hadn't walked away from that fellowship?

At least he still had his principles—if not much else.

Wineke eyed him like he was waiting for Walter to crack and change his story. Before Walter could break into a sweat, his boss grunted.

"Hildy Johnson."

Walter choked on his own spit. "What?"

"That answers that." It sounded like Wineke was talking to himself more than Walter.

Walter shook his head, lost.

"You know her."

It wasn't phrased as a question, but Walter felt compelled to nod anyway. Maybe that was going to be his claim to fame for the rest of his life. The first line of his obit would be: *Once spent a week in Hildy Johnson's orbit*. Had she mentioned him to someone? Could Hildy possibly be thinking of offering him a job? That would be preposterous . . . unless her conscience had finally kicked in.

"You're a good reporter." The heavy exhale that followed clued Walter in that there was an asterisk after that compliment. "Ordinarily I wouldn't mention this, but I know you need the work. And you have that connection with the Johnson girl."

Had a connection, Walter silently corrected. *Past tense*. But he was too curious to interrupt.

"Might be a stepping stone to something better." It sounded like Wineke was trying to convince himself. He fixed Walter with a penetrating look. "You follow any of the gossip sites? Celebrity news, who's dating who, that kind of thing."

It had to be a trick question. If Walter said yes, he'd look frivolous for wasting time that would have been better spent on hard news. But if he said no, would he disqualify himself from whatever job-adjacent possibility might be in the offing?

"I'm aware of them," Walter replied, trying to thread the needle.

Another grunt. "Derek Gratz is looking for a stringer."

It took Walter a second to connect the dots. Derek Gratz as in *Gratz on That*, an online tabloid with enough clout that even mainstream news outlets paid attention to their feed.

"And you thought of me?" Walter wasn't sure whether to be flattered or offended.

"It's about the Johnson kid."

Ah. He should have realized Hildy wouldn't come looking for him. This was a case of her life crashing into his, again, like an asteroid. "How did you know? That I knew her."

"Old friend at the Pachner Institute. He told me the two of you worked together a couple summers ago."

Walter nodded. It was technically true.

"You want to talk to this Gratz guy?" Wineke asked, clearly ready for this conversation to be over.

"Okay."

His editor slid a piece of paper across the desk. "Call him at this number."

* * *

It had never occurred to Walter that the founder of *Gratz on That* might look like someone's dad. He'd expected a pitchfork or devil horns, but when they met via Zoom, Walter's laptop displayed a grainy image of a pasty forty-something with wire-rimmed glasses. He could have gone undercover at any midsize IT department.

"Think of it as a chance to catch up with an old friend," his potential employer said, several minutes into their call. To hear him tell it, spying on Hildy would be easy, totally legal, and fun—as if Walter was joining a new gym.

He hesitated. It wasn't that the work sounded shady—though it did. Or at least, it wasn't only that. Yet even as he asked follow-up questions to show he cared about things like journalistic ethics, he was mostly thinking about Hildy. A sense of inevitability settled over him. Walter had never fully believed their story was over. All these years, part of him had been waiting for some kind of postscript.

In the face of her silence, he could only assume that summer had been a joke to her, a silly exercise she put up with because her family expected it. Like sailing lessons and horseback riding, or whatever else her type of people considered basic life skills. She certainly hadn't cared about Walter, except as a means to an end.

Which should have made it easy to forget her.

Except it still hurt. He had questions only she could answer. How was it possible to like someone so much when she represented everything he was against? Big money, class privilege, nepotism—Hildy had the cheat codes to life. And what did it say about Walter that he'd swallowed her act hook, line, and sinker? Of course she wanted to write an uplifting story about a wedding. Struggle had no place in Hildy's life. She probably thought the world worked that way for everyone.

He wondered if she was still majoring in journalism, or if that had been a passing fancy.

If he took this job, Walter supposed he would find out. *When* he took this job.

The trick would be thinking of her as an assignment rather than a person he'd once known. It helped that she looked like a stranger these days, according to the pictures he'd seen online of Hildy cruising the party circuit. High school Hildy had been pretty enough to fluster him, but still in the realm of normal. Version 2.0 gleamed with money and polish. Everything about her had a faint sheen, from her curls to her clothes. He would never have dreamed of befriending this Hildy, any more than he'd approach a movie star on the street and ask them to hang out.

And now a celebrity was what she'd become—someone whose comings and goings were of interest to total strangers. He should have found it validating to see her living that high-society life: more proof he'd been right. She wasn't serious about the work because she didn't have to be. Hildy's first allegiance would always be to people like her, with money and connections. So why did he feel so disappointed?

Except *disappointment* wasn't quite right. He wasn't sitting on a mountaintop, judging her behavior. This touched Walter too, an acid prickling in his stomach that tasted more like regret or embarrassment. Maybe he was still kicking himself for believing in a different Hildy. Or maybe he was ashamed of the part of him that still felt pathetically excluded from her world.

Because the assignment wasn't just Hildy. Derek Gratz wanted someone to report on what he described as the "junior C-suite set," the pampered and hard-partying young offspring of corporate titans. Find out where they are and who they're with. Name names, because apparently there were people out there who desperately wanted to know how trust funders were spending their parents' money. Walter would have called it ridiculous if he wasn't just as curious—in this one instance.

For him, it would be like pressing his nose to the glass of a fancy department store, staring at all the luxury items he could never afford—although it wasn't *things* he coveted so much as access. A foot in the door. He wanted to be someone you wouldn't easily ignore because a more important person came along.

As opposed to a nobody.

If that meant playing the hanger-on, lurking in the shadows just beyond the spotlight, he could check his ego for a chance to work his way up the ladder. It wasn't how he'd imagined starting his career, but it was a chance. *Gratz on That* drew more traffic than all but the biggest metropolitan dailies, and Walter wouldn't have to wait years to see his byline.

Plus he needed money for rent and groceries.

And was it really any worse than what Hildy had done to him?

Even as he told himself these things, the thrum of excitement in his blood said *liar*.

He thought of the last time he'd seen her, when she walked out of a room as soon as he entered, as if she didn't want to breathe the same air. Walter had been too afraid to follow, choosing instead to torture himself with what-ifs. This time, he wouldn't back down.

"I'll do it," he said.

NOW

22

Hildy

THREE DAYS BEFORE THE PRESCOTT-SCHAFER WEDDING

TAMNIÈS, France—While the other guests napped, worked on their tans, or paid an emergency visit to their nail tech, Hildy and Corinne strategized damage control. It wasn't the fingernail itself so much as the overall harmony of the proceedings that had them on edge.

The good news was that Hildy had a plan to smooth things over. The bad was that it required Walter's participation.

"Do whatever you have to do to guarantee buy-in," Corinne advised. "If that means banging it out, no judgment. Although I reserve the right to say I told you so."

"Sure. I'll take one for the team."

"Try not to suffer too much," she deadpanned, sending Hildy off with an ironic salute.

As usual, when Hildy wanted Walter there was no sign of him. She had no choice but to confront him in his room. If only the walk were longer, so she'd have more time to pump herself up. Her enthusiasm ebbed even further when she ran into Maude in the covered passage outside his door.

"He's in there," Maude helpfully volunteered, before Hildy could trot out an excuse. "I'm sorry I misled you about the situation with the two of us."

"Trust me, I get it." Sometimes a fake relationship was the shortest distance between two points. "And you were right about it not being any of my business."

"That's not how Walter made it sound."

"Oh?" Speaking of phony, Hildy was not quite selling nonchalance. It was generous of Maude to overlook the bad acting and answer in good faith.

"He told me a little about your history. I didn't realize the two of you were so—"

During the epic pause that followed, Hildy tried to guess where Maude was heading. Rude? Immature? Fucked up?

"Entangled," she finally said.

"I suppose that's accurate." Hildy Johnson, queen of understatement. "How much did he share?"

"Not much. Reading between the lines, I gather there's been . . . conflict."

"That's one word for it." A memory struck, of running into Walter outside a theater. She'd been seized by a rush of pleasure—*there he is!*—as if her nervous system had forgotten they didn't like each other anymore.

And then he said, "Who are you with?" and a flash burst in her eyes. That was how she found out he was working for a tabloid.

The worst part wasn't that he'd used her life as a professional foothold. Hildy had made a deliberate choice to be seen with high-profile dates in public places to keep her name out there while she got ready to launch *Life, Styled*. The problem wasn't the press; it was Walter. He'd made her feel silly and forgettable, as if their time together meant nothing to him. She was an assignment, not a friend or a fellow journalist—much less anything more.

"But you were close? At one point?" Maude asked.

Hildy shrugged, as if that was a stretch. Maude didn't need to know about the brief interlude during which Hildy would have shouted from the rooftops that she liked Walter more than anyone she'd ever met. Trusted him, admired him, wanted to kiss him—the whole enchilada.

"Maybe you could talk to him—"

"How's Loïc?" Hildy interrupted.

"Fine, I assume." Maude looked down, fiddling with her earring, but she could take a hint. Which was good, because it was past time to set aside the Walter of it all and get down to business.

"Listen, I'm sorry we upset your sister. I'm going to fix this. Not just the fingernail but the whole thing. I know that wasn't how she wanted the day to go."

Maude tipped her head, acknowledging the apology with surprising equanimity. "Fee is stronger than she looks. Yes, she's invested in this idea of making everything perfect and shiny and beautiful, but that doesn't mean she's in denial about the fact that life doesn't always work that way."

"Of course not," Hildy murmured. Wanting your world to be aesthetically and spiritually harmonious didn't mean you were a superficial person. Or that you were trying too hard to give reality a glow-up because of your fundamental immaturity and unwillingness to grapple with hard truths. No matter what people said in the comments.

"I think she hoped her wedding would be an exception, but Fee will bounce back." Maude gave a rueful shrug. "Walter tells me chaos is part of the process."

He'd know. Hildy kept that thought to herself.

"About Walter . . . and me," she began. "I appreciate you trying to help, but this is one of those situations where you get shot with an arrow and it can't be removed without doing more damage. The only solution is to break off the sticking-out part and get on with your life." Hildy was pretty sure she'd seen that in a movie.

"Or it could be a splinter," Maude pointed out. "You need to get it out so you can heal."

It wasn't the argument that struck Hildy so much as the tone. "Are you big-sistering me?"

"Sorry. Is that annoying?"

"I like it, actually." That didn't change the fact that despite what Maude or Corinne or anyone else might believe, Hildy and Walter weren't going to kiss and make up. Flowers didn't spring from the ashes if you'd spent years sprinkling salt all over them. And napalm. "Fiona's lucky to have you."

"On that note, I'd better go check on her." Maude's smile was guarded, like she didn't want to get Hildy's hopes up. "Good luck."

* * *

As soon as Walter opened the door to her knock, Hildy slipped past him, noting very casually with her keen observational skills as a journalist that his hair was still damp from the shower, and he smelled like honey and thyme. That would be the body wash from the wedding guest welcome hamper, though she didn't remember the scent being quite that mouthwatering straight from the bottle.

While Walter closed the door behind her, Hildy took the opportunity to snoop. His room wasn't identical to hers in the soulless copycat fashion of an American hotel chain, but the décor had a similar weathered coziness: reading chair, thick rug, painted wardrobe, big fluffy bed. She took all of this in at a glance, because Walter was apparently the kind of neat freak who used actual hangers and drawers instead of scattering his personal items over every surface. A total bust on the espionage front, but then that wasn't the main purpose of this visit.

"You have an idea," Walter guessed, before she could launch into her preamble.

Hildy felt compelled to disagree, because it was rude to see through someone as though they were dressed in head-to-toe plastic wrap. "I wouldn't call it an *idea*. This is more of an agenda. Or—a plan of attack."

"I'm all ears." He gestured for her to take the chair.

"We need to table this." She circled a hand between them.

He copied the gesture, brows lifting in question. "This?"

"The fighting. Friction. Occasionally immature behavior. Our whole deal. Just until the wedding's over," she added, in case he thought this was a permanent ceasefire.

Walter didn't answer right away. She would have given a lot to be able to unscrew a panel on the side of his head and spy on his thought process.

"Do you really think that's possible?" he finally asked.

"What I think is that it doesn't look good for either of our brands to derail the wedding of the century."

"Is that your main concern?"

Her heart beat a little faster, sensing danger. "As opposed to what?"

"Fiona and Robbie's personal happiness."

"What am I, Lady Macbeth? Of course I care about them. My plans have layers. It's a hallmark of my style."

"How do you see this playing out?" he asked, after another loaded silence.

"We declare a truce. Right now, tonight, just the two of us. Grab a pair of your tightie-whities and wave them around like a flag."

"Nice try. I'm not showing you my underwear. Which are not white, by the way."

"Have you tried OxyClean?"

"Why Hildy, don't tell me you've started doing your own laundry?"

"There's a lot you don't know about me, Mr. Judgmental."

"There's a lot you don't know about *me*."

"Great," she said through a strained smile. "Glad to hear it."

"Do you need an antacid?"

She bit back a retort. One of them had to set an example. "We can't just pretend not to hate each other. If we're going to sell this, we have to take it to the next level."

"Mild distaste?"

Hildy started to roll her eyes before catching herself. "We need to be—cordial. Pleasant."

"Like maiden aunts? Should I also take up crochet?"

"Sure, Walter. Whatever floats your boat." Hildy blew out a breath, hoping it would take the sarcasm with it. "We need to act like we like each other, and any conflict people may have observed between us was just . . . the way people talk to each other when they're—you know."

"Friends?" he guessed.

She shrugged. Close enough. "No more egging each other on, okay?"

Walter held up a finger, like this was a press conference and he was waiting for her to call on him.

"Yes?" Hildy said, with what she felt to be remarkable forbearance.

"How much are we pretending to like each other?"

She gave a thoughtful *hmm*. "I figure if we have sex on one of the lounge chairs by the pool, preferably in broad daylight, that should cover it."

He made a wheezing sound.

"Any more questions?" she asked sweetly.

"I'll follow your lead."

"You have plenty of experience at that."

"It was a job, Hildy."

"I'm sure hitmen tell themselves the same thing." She started for the door, before changing her mind and strolling up to Walter, who was still hovering awkwardly in the middle of the carpet. "Corinne had a suggestion, but I'm not sure you'll like it."

At this distance, she didn't have to raise her voice above a whisper.

He swallowed roughly. "What was it?"

"Have you heard of a sexorcism?"

"What?"

"Sounds fake, right? We should just shake on it. Like professionals." She held out her hand.

Walter stared at it for several breaths before pressing his palm to hers. They stayed like that, watching each other. The shower gel smelled even better at close range.

"It's not very French," he said at last. "A handshake."

"Go ahead. French it up." She offered him her cheek.

He leaned in slowly, giving her plenty of time to change her mind before he pressed his lips to the side of her face. It wasn't too long or too wet, but it sure as hell wasn't an air kiss. She started to turn, thinking to give him the other cheek, but Walter didn't pull away. As her face moved against his, their mouths brushed.

Hildy angled her head slightly, lips easing apart as they met Walter's. It was barely a conscious decision.

Bad idea, her better self whispered. *Shhh*, her body replied. *Let us have this.*

Why did the feel of his tongue in her mouth unravel her more than another man's mouth between her thighs? She'd never gotten this hot this quickly from kissing anyone else. As Hildy sagged, boneless, he wrapped an arm around her waist to draw her up and against him.

"Is that French enough for you?" she whispered.

He breathed a ragged "no" against her earlobe.

She twisted to meet his mouth again, hardly realizing they were moving until she felt the edge of his mattress against the back of her legs. That jarred her enough to register the insistent buzzing of her phone, which snapped Hildy out of her trance. Sanity returned with a vengeance. Hildy used the heel of her hand to shove him back a step.

"For reference, that was taking it too far."

"I guess we overcorrected." His breathing was still uneven.

Hildy gave a decisive nod. "It's good we had this time to practice." She checked her phone, only half surprised to see a series of texts from Corinne. Most were variations on the theme of a stop-sign emoji.

Were she and Walter that predictable? How annoying. Hildy preferred to think of herself as a force of nature, shifting and changing like the wind.

"I'll see you at breakfast," she told him, hurrying for the door.

"I'll be on my best behavior," Walter promised.

Whatever that meant.

NOW

23

Hildy

TWO DAYS BEFORE THE PRESCOTT-SCHAFER WEDDING

TAMNIÈS, France—"I've been thinking," Walter said when he joined Hildy at breakfast the next morning. "If we're really going to make this work, we need to lock in."

The smile Hildy had practiced in the mirror last night faded. "We're having breakfast together. You don't have a fork sticking out of the back of your hand. I'd call that a win."

"I think we need to go deeper."

"Is that supposed to be a double entendre?"

"No, Hildy."

"Good, because I haven't had enough coffee for that. I'm not sure there's enough coffee in the world." She gazed thoughtfully into the distance. The lack of eye contact made it easier to pretend last night had never happened.

"I'm talking about having an honest and open conversation," he persisted.

"About?"

"Us."

"You're going to have to be more specific."

"Our relationship."

She raised her sunglasses so he could see her brows arch.

"Whatever you want to call it. The past. Our history."

"And you think that's going to smooth out the kinks? Also not a double entendre," she added, before he could ask.

"I'm hopeful, yes."

Hildy shook her head. She'd never pegged Walter as a wide-eyed idealist. Maybe he was on new meds.

"I disagree," she said with great restraint and maturity. Had he met the two of them? Giving airtime to all their grievances would be like bringing two toddlers and a box of Sharpies to the Museum of Modern Art.

He reached past her for the sugar, keeping both his expression and his tone perfectly pleasant. "It's not a one-woman show, Hildy."

"It's not Wrestlemania either. We haven't even gotten through one breakfast, and you want to do freestyle couple's therapy?"

"Interesting."

She narrowed her eyes. "What is?"

"That you used the word 'couple.'"

"Let me guess. Your amateur psychoanalysis is also going to help us pretend to get along?"

Walter shrugged. "It might."

"Alternative proposal."

He gestured for her to proceed.

"Act like we just met. Blank slate." Hildy pinched the rim of her white plate, angling it toward Walter as a visual aid. It would have been more effective without the crumbs, scrapes of butter, and smears of purple-red jam, but presumably he got the point.

"I don't know."

"Tell you what. While you think about it, I'll fix you some breakfast." She pushed back her chair, ignoring Walter's wary expression. On her way to the buffet, Hildy bent to whisper in his ear. "Don't worry. I'm not going to spit on it."

She took her time selecting an assortment of fresh fruit and pastries. When she returned to the table, Hildy presented it to him with a flourish.

"Ta-da!"

He frowned at the plate. "Are those raisins?"

"It's a pain aux raisins, yes."

Walter looked up. "I hate raisins."

"Really?" She pursed her lips, pretending to be surprised. "That's too bad."

"And pineapple makes my tongue itch."

"I didn't realize you were such a delicate flower. I guess that's what comes from being total strangers who just met at this destination wedding."

"That's funny."

"What is?"

"For someone who just met me, you have an uncanny knack for choosing all my least favorite foods."

"That *is* funny."

Walter nodded. "Fuzzy apricots, no thank you. Pineapple and raisins, we've covered. What's this?" He pointed at a white blob.

"Plain yogurt."

"Sour dairy. Yum. Definitely wouldn't want to put any honey on that to make it more palatable."

She beamed at him. "You have to admit, it's kind of impressive."

"For sure," he agreed. "Who knew you were this obsessed with me?"

"I have no idea what you're talking about. It was a prank."

"And yet to know my tastes that well, you'd have to be paying extremely close attention."

Hildy concentrated on breathing in and out through her nose while she scrambled for a response. "It's like they say. Keep your enemies close."

He smiled to show he wasn't fooled. "You're a big girl. I'm sure you can admit when you've been outplayed."

"Fine. Whatever. You win."

"For my prize—"

"Who said anything about prizes?"

"I did." He studied her face, like he was gauging how much he could get away with. Hildy felt heat bloom beneath her skin. Was he going to kiss her again? She supposed she could allow it on the grounds that it would help sell the story of their shiny, happy reconciliation. Assuming they didn't get carried away and wind up tearing each other's clothes off on this wrought-iron table.

"For my prize," he repeated, "I get to ask you one question."

"What? No. I'd rather let you trim my bangs."

"Just truth, no dares. You're not scared, are you?"

"Of you? Ha." She dragged his plate to her side of the table so she could eat the offending pineapple. "Go ahead. Bring up something awkward and upsetting from our past. What could possibly go wrong?"

Walter didn't waste any time. "I'll start with an easy one. Why didn't you call me after we . . . ran into each other at the awards banquet?"

"Uh, because I was embarrassed."

"That you kissed me?" He asked like it was a foregone conclusion.

"That I kissed anyone! It wasn't spring break in Daytona. We were at a work event, and I have a reputation to uphold." She huffed at his presumption. "Way to make it about you."

Though of course it was a thousand times worse that she'd thrown herself at *Walter*. She needed to be in full fighting form around him, not floppy and half naked like a lust-crazed snail without its shell. "Why didn't *you* call *me*, Mr. Hard-Hitting Questions?"

"You made it pretty clear you were done with me."

She would have argued the point, but Hildy's memory was not 100 percent clear on that front. The fog of war and all that. "What time is it?"

Walter glanced at his watch, the actual ticking kind with a leather strap and no smart features. It looked annoyingly good on his stupidly masculine wrist. "Apparently it's avoiding the subject o'clock."

"We have a big day ahead, Walter. I don't want to inconvenience our hosts by being late. Speaking of which, there's Fiona and Robbie now."

Walter rolled his eyes like he couldn't believe she'd resorted to such a weak evasion, but the joke was on him because the happy couple really were standing behind him.

"Look," Fiona announced, wiggling her left hand to show off a matching set of blush-pink acrylics. "Good as new!"

Hildy put a hand to her heart, deeply relieved the damage wasn't permanent. "All's well that ends well!"

Fiona nodded. "And the fact that it was my ring finger is a total coincidence that doesn't mean anything bad. So there's no need to worry it was a sign from the cosmos or anything."

"Only good vibes." Robbie held up his hand for a high five before thinking better of it and gently pressing a kiss to Fiona's knuckles instead.

"Aww, babe," Fiona cooed. "That's so sweet."

"Didn't want to mess up your nails."

Hildy lowered her eyes to let them have their little moment, but it was a wasted effort. Elsewhere on the terrace, a table full of wedding guests were tapping their silverware against their coffee cups. Fiona and Robbie obliged with another kiss.

"It's like we're dogs," Robbie said, keeping his voice low. "Everybody wants us to show off our one trick."

"Next they'll be asking us to fetch," Fiona jumped in.

"I wish! More like 'sit.' 'Stay.' 'Good boy.'" Robbie huffed at the ridiculousness of the idea, but he wasn't far off. Between the ceremony, the pictures, and the reception, there was quite a bit of enforced stillness in his future. Hildy opted not to bring that to his attention, since being the bearer of bad news didn't really suit the sunshiny mood she was supposed to be selling.

"At least we get to go on an adventure first," Fiona reminded Robbie. "Deep underground in a spooky cave!"

Hildy set down the pastry she'd just stolen from Walter's plate. "How deep are we talking?"

"What she really wants to know is how spooky," Walter translated, while filching one of Hildy's strawberries.

Annoyance flickered faintly, both for the strawberry and his casual *I-know-things-about-Hildy* flex. She could have gotten over that phobia years ago. Maybe catacombs and crypts and other subterranean spaces less directly associated with death were totally her scene now. Walter had no business acting like—

Except he does, she reminded herself, because they were buddies now. At least while other people were watching.

"It's totally safe," Fiona assured her. "Little kids can do it. You ride a cute little train. It's not like ropes and crawling through tight spots and 'oh my God, is there enough oxygen down here?' Remember Belize?" she asked Robbie.

Hildy stared while the two of them had a good laugh at what sounded like a near-death experience. "What about bats?"

"Worried about your hair?" Walter teased, as if Hildy were being irrational. She'd like to see his reaction if a flying rodent crapped on his head.

"The only thing you have to worry about is getting cold," Fiona said. "It's a lot cooler underground, so definitely bring a light sweater."

"Or a *cardigan*." Robbie looked proud of himself for knowing the word, beaming at all of them as he slung an arm around his fiancée's shoulders. "You're a really good hostess, Fee. Everyone is having a great time."

"You think?" she asked hopefully.

He squeezed her closer to his side. "No doubt."

"I was afraid the situation with who's doing the story might be causing some tension." Fiona wrinkled her nose in a silent apology. "Yesterday it seemed like maybe you two were a little grumpy with each other."

Hildy felt like a jerk for assuming Fiona was only concerned about her manicure. "Don't worry about *that*. The story is the least of our problems."

"Competing for a great scoop is what we do," Walter agreed. "It gives spice to our lives."

"In a professional sense," Hildy added.

They reached for the last strawberry at the same time. Walter's hand settled over hers, a warm weight.

"Go ahead," he said.

"That's okay. You can have it." Before she could withdraw her hand, the pads of his fingers skimmed her knuckles.

"Thanks, Hildycakes." He stared into her eyes as he took a bite. "You're so good to me. I don't know where I'd be without you."

Clearly he was messing with her. First the unsanctioned pet name, then the suggestive fruit eating, and now the final twist of the knife. Even Hildy would have a hard time arguing that she'd been a positive presence in his life. She stood so abruptly the dishes rattled on the table.

"I'm going to grab something for the cave." Like a Xanax. "I'll meet you at the bus."

"I'll save you a seat," Walter promised.

Hildy had a feeling he would have blown her a kiss if she hadn't kept her eyes down as she tucked in her chair and turned away, trying not to look like she was fleeing the scene.

NOW

24

Walter

TWO DAYS BEFORE THE PRESCOTT-SCHAFER WEDDING

FLEURAC, France—Walter spent the bus ride listening to Corinne explain the differences between the cave art at Lascaux, Font-de-Gaume, and today's destination, Rouffignac, to a distracted Hildy, who kept glancing back to see if he was eavesdropping. The notes he pretended to take were mostly scribbles, with the express purpose of winding her up.

The friendship between Hildy and Corinne had always intrigued him. At first, he assumed it was a purely business relationship, but that didn't account for their sibling-like bickering: quick with an insult but unmistakably bonded by loyalty. He'd tried asking Corinne about it once, but she immediately shut him down.

"The last thing you fools need is a go-between. Talk to her yourself."

It had taken a few years for Walter to realize she was right. Better late than never—or so he hoped. And now that Hildy had to pretend they were chummy, the opportunity seemed ripe for a semiprivate conversation.

Walter let the rest of the group filter past while he waited for Hildy. She seemed to be stuck on the pavement outside the stone overhang that marked the entrance to the cave. He suspected she needed a little encouragement to take the final few steps into the dark.

"Do you want to hold my hand?"

"In your dreams." She marched past him, not stopping until they reached the mostly full open-air train waiting to carry them deeper into the cave.

"Looks like we're in the back row." Walter didn't pretend to be disappointed.

"How convenient." Her smile said *hip hip hooray!* The look in her eyes added a silent *I know you planned this.*

He climbed in after her, sliding across the bench seat until he was in whispering distance. "Read any good books lately?"

"We don't need to chitchat," she hissed. "This is an important cultural attraction."

"Yeah, I got the rundown on the bus."

"I knew you were spying!"

"Somebody had to pay attention. Corinne put a lot of work into that PowerPoint."

"I was listening." She cleared her throat, as though the lie left a bad taste in her mouth. "Mostly."

"Then you know we're going to be stuck here a while."

"What do you mean, stuck? Is something wrong?" Her shoulder bumped his as she whipped around, trying to see into the darkness behind them. "Does this thing not reverse?"

He put a hand on her arm. "We're fine. I just meant the tour is going to last a while. We don't have to sit here in silence."

"You really want to know about my reading habits?"

"Not necessarily." He was playing it cool, when the truth was that Walter was hungry for any scraps of information Hildy might choose to share. Was she in a book club? Did she have a preferred genre? "I figured I should ease into the heavy stuff."

"What heavy stuff?" she asked, suspicion dripping from every word.

"Just—mature and honest grown-up talk. Since you can't run away this time."

"What's that supposed to mean?"

"The last time I tried to have a serious conversation, you panicked."

"Nope," she said, after a pointed pause. "Still not getting it."

"When I came to your office."

Her huff of disbelief fanned the side of his face. "That is *not* what happened."

"Explain it to me then."

"You showed up at my place of work to taunt me about your fancy new job—"

"No, I came to tell you about it," he interrupted. "I thought we could go to dinner and clear the air."

There was a thinking silence. "What do you mean, go to dinner? Like a business dinner?"

"No, like *Lady and the Tramp*, nudging a meatball back and forth with our noses while someone plays violin."

"Are you calling me a tramp?"

"Uh, no. Obviously you're Lady."

"That's a little reductive."

"Fine. You can be the tramp. Happy now?"

"Ecstatic. Never better."

The guide chose that moment to speak over the PA system in heavily accented English. "We are entering one of the longest cave systems in the region. You will be traveling more than one kilometer deep into the center of the cave."

Hildy elbowed him. "How far is that? I'm too freaked out to do metric conversions."

"Think of it like . . . a walk in the park," Walter replied, evading the question.

"But what if the train breaks down? This thing is a relic."

"Then we'll walk out."

She paused as if he'd said something so outrageous it defied belief. "In the dark?"

"We have our phones."

"Until the battery dies. Maybe I should have had the drugs," she muttered, as the train resumed its forward crawl.

"I missed that station at breakfast."

"Like the shamans used to do back in the day. Get high and imagine they were visiting an alternate dimension with their trippy art. As opposed to being buried under tons of rock in the pitch blackness."

"Want me to distract you?"

"Maybe," she said following a wary silence. "What did you have in mind?"

"The offer of conversation is still on the table."

"Is that the best you can do?"

"Unless you have a better idea?" They were practically invisible here in the back row, after all. He could be quiet if the occasion demanded.

"Do you see those lines?" their guide asked. The beam of a flashlight illuminated the stone wall. "Cave bears left those scratches with their claws. It's like a map for them, to find their way back to the place where they spend each winter." The pool of light panned down to the ground. "Regard the depression in the earth. That is left from a cave bear doing hibernation there."

They passed a campground's worth of prehistoric sleeping spots, beneath walls scored with deep vertical grooves that looked surprisingly fresh, as if the bears might return any day now.

"That's what you did to me." The thought traveled from Walter's brain to his lips before he could censor himself.

"Flattened you with my huge ass?"

"Carved a permanent hollow." He touched his chest, where the damage had been done. "A Hildy-shaped hole." It seemed so clear to him now, that he'd never gotten over the impact of their first meeting.

"Are you drunk?"

He shook his head, then remembered she couldn't see him. "No."

"Then why would you say something like that?"

Because it's dark, and we're far away from everything we know, and I can't stop thinking about kissing you, and I'm enough of a chump to convince myself our problems could be solved here and now, even though they're littered like landmines across the last decade.

That about summed it up.

It seemed fitting to seize this moment, on a train that was literally taking them back in time. He'd always been a sucker for a metaphor. It was an occupational hazard when your entire career was devoted to seeking out the narrative arcs in other people's lives.

"I think I might be having a revelation," he said.

"Right now?"

"I didn't schedule it in advance."

"We're in a *cave*, Walter."

"So? Maybe it's like a sensory deprivation chamber, focusing my understanding."

She shoved him in the arm. "You do read my magazine! I knew it."

"Occasionally." Once a month, to be exact. From cover to cover.

"What is this so-called revelation about?"

"I'm not sure I should tell you."

"If you can handle it, I can handle it."

That was the rub: Walter wasn't sure he *could* handle exposing his tender insides to Hildy, without any clue how she was going to respond. He'd always known his anger with her was like a potholder he'd grabbed to keep from getting burned. It made a flimsy barrier between his conscious mind and a deeper truth, which was that his feelings about Hildy were more complicated than rivalry and resentment. Those other emotions had spilled over behind the coatrack, making Walter think he and Hildy might be on the same page, if they dug deep enough.

Only now, when it was too late to salvage his dignity, did it occur to him that he could have been deluding himself. Maybe for Hildy it was simple: Walter was a stone in her path, to be stepped on or kicked aside as the occasion required. What was the saying? When someone shows you who they are, believe them.

The problem was that he didn't know which Hildy was real. Was she the impossibly charming girl who'd wrapped him around her little finger from their first hello, or the schemer who'd stabbed him in the back without a second thought? Talk about being in the dark.

"Just—forget it," he mumbled.

"Oh, sure. No problem. You can lob a grenade at me, and I'll pretend it never happened. That seems fair." She shifted away from him. "I don't understand you."

"Join the club." He could almost hear her frowning as she puzzled over that remark.

"Is this about the story?"

"What are you talking about?"

"Are you trying to soften me up?" she hissed, as if he were being deliberately obtuse.

"Soften you up for what?"

"Maybe you think I'll just give it to you. The article," she added, as if realizing how easily her words could be misconstrued.

"That would be a turnaround."

"Excuse me?" Her tone made the chilly temperature inside the cave feel like a sauna. "What are you trying to do right now, Walter?"

It was a valid question. He wasn't sure he had a good answer. "Turn back time?"

"Hate to break it to you, Cher, but that's not possible. Take it from a woman who runs a lifestyle magazine. I am fully versed in all things antiaging."

She was right, of course. They could never be that innocent again. Maybe the best he could hope for was to draw a curtain over the thornier parts of their past. Instead of forgiving and forgetting they could repress and compartmentalize. That sounded healthy.

The train trundled on, traveling deeper into the damp darkness. Between the sensory deprivation and the strangeness of the experience—the closest comparison Walter could think of was Space Mountain meets *The Flintstones*—there was a loopy unreality to the experience. France, the cave, a rickety retro train, the blanketing darkness, a silence broken only by the occasional contribution from their guide. It turned out you didn't need the drugs to cut loose.

"You warned me about Maude and Loïc," he said, because why stop now? But it was something he'd thought about afterward: the fact that she hadn't tried to leverage a humiliating piece of information.

"That was basic human decency. And also *irrelevant*, as it turned out."

"It's the thought that counts."

"Okay, Hallmark."

"I'm being serious."

"I know. It's freaking me out."

"Sorry."

"See? That's even worse." She poked him in the side. "Snap out of it. Oh shit!" Her stabby finger was replaced with a two-handed death grip on his arm. "The train is *stopping*."

"On purpose," Walter pointed out, keeping his voice level.

"We're not breaking down." He started to move before noticing Hildy's stiffness. "Are you coming?"

"I don't think that's a good idea. I'll just stay here."

"I'm sure it's perfectly safe."

"Out there? In the cave? What if I get lost—or fall into a hole?"

He didn't point out that they were parked in a circular chamber slightly larger than a living room, with a single point of egress. "You know I would find you, Hildy."

She sniffed. "So you could brag about your superior caving skills."

"Exactly." He reached for her hand before he could talk himself out of it.

She let him take it, which told Walter . . . something. Like maybe the distance between them wasn't all scorched earth and broken trust.

They moved away from the train, shuffling carefully across the dirt floor while listening to their guide describe the prehistoric images of animals that covered the ceiling like constellations. It was a primitive cathedral, full of art that was both spectacular and mysterious. Still holding Hildy's hand, Walter led them to a quiet spot away from the others where they could crane their necks upward without being trampled.

This is the coolest thing I will ever see. That thought was followed immediately by a sneaky postscript. *And I'm seeing it with Hildy.*

As if that meant something—like their initials were now carved into the rock, to last a thousand years. He wondered if she felt it too.

"It kind of reminds me of tattoos, only for rocks instead of skin. I've been meaning to commission a piece on changing attitudes to body art as a social signifier." She paused, as if suddenly remembering she wasn't talking to herself. "Don't even think about stealing that idea."

It was so far from the direction of his thoughts, Walter had to pull a mental U-turn, brakes squealing. "I can't believe you're worrying about work right now."

"What should I be thinking about—being trapped under miles of earth? In the dark? With *you*?"

"Good to know I make the short list of your phobias."

"What are *you* thinking about?" It was clearly a challenge, like she expected him to say Art or Death or Free Jazz so she could skewer him for being pretentious.

"You," he admitted. "And me."

There was a beat of silence before she replied. "I don't believe you."

"Okay."

He felt her lean closer, not quite making contact with his chest. "What's your angle?"

"Who says I have one?" Walter heard the edge in his own voice. "Why are we arguing?"

"Because that's what we do. We even argue about arguing!"

"You are wondering if it is a goat?" their guide interjected from the darkness, pointing his flashlight at a murky spot on the wall. Either he was trained in stealth or they had been too busy bickering to notice his approach.

"Walter wasn't sure," Hildy volunteered. "He has a lot less experience with goats than I do."

"Ibex," the guide informed Walter. "Not goat. Or sheep."

"Merci for settling the argument." Hildy waited until the guide had rejoined the other guests to take several steps in the opposite direction.

"You know what's crazy?" she hissed at Walter, because of course he was still following her. "This is like my longest relationship—and it's not even a relationship. I might as well be my uncle, but instead of divorcing a bunch of different people, it's always you."

A throat cleared nearby.

"Sorry," Hildy said.

Despite her fear of the dark, she moved farther from the rest of the group, as if her anger outweighed the anxiety. Walter thought about giving her space, but he couldn't let the conversation end there. He wanted to break their pattern of getting mad and giving up—or at least find out if such a thing was possible.

"We're not divorced, Hildy." He spoke quietly, so she wouldn't think he was baiting her.

"Yeah, well. Somebody should give us a prize for not letting it get that far." Her frustration wafted toward him like a rain cloud. "Maybe I'm not cut out for commitment. Maybe no one is. You can't tell me you believe most relationships are headed for a happily ever after."

"It's not like you to be this cynical."

"I guess that's why I don't let myself go to the dark side. Because when I do, I go all the way down. You want realism? How about this. People lie to themselves all the time—almost as much as they lie to each other! Calling something 'love' when it's really hormones or pheromones or whatever. You think you know a person but it's just an image you made up in your head."

The rustle of fabric alerted them that someone was approaching. He reached for Hildy, fingers brushing her arm. When she didn't jerk out of his grasp, he gently led her away.

"Are you talking about us?" he whispered, when they were alone again.

"I'm talking about human beings. All of us! We buy into these illusions, like we've never even met ourselves. Maybe we should go back to having big orgies in a cave instead of pretending monogamy has a snowball's chance in hell of working out. At least that would be honest! Maybe my mother was right. We should chew our own foot off before we step in the trap. Better to be one-legged but free."

Walter almost hushed her, thinking he'd heard someone, but

when he strained his ears there was nothing but the distant murmur of the guide pointing out a prehistoric horse on the far side of the cave. "Your mom told you that?"

Hildy gave a bitter huff. "She didn't stick around long enough to tell me personally. But she wrote it all down."

"Um." Walter was treading carefully. "That is a lot to unpack."

"That's probably why I've been in such deep denial. Isn't that how it goes? You reject everything your parents stand for until one day you're like, 'wait, maybe they were onto something.'" She didn't give Walter time to answer, too caught up in the tide of her outrage to slow down. "I mean, seriously, what's the point of this whole circus? It's like thinking you can be young forever. Hate to break it to you, but we're all going to die, no matter what your abs look like now. And the two of us are the worst!"

"Why do you say that?" He was having trouble making the jump from stomach muscles to mortality.

"Because we perpetuate the fairy tale. Shine it up and sell it to the masses, when we know relationships are a trap. We're the poster children for 'that was a mistake!' The truth is, most romantic relationships are a distraction at best—if not a straight-up liability. They can throw your whole life off course! And then what?"

"Is that what you think? Our relationship ruined your life?"

"What relationship? We're like . . . bumper cars in the night! An iceberg and the *Titanic.* The rift that keeps on rifting. Maybe that's what happens if you meet someone when you're too young. It freezes you at that stage of emotional maturity and you never grow up."

Walter suspected she would have gone on if the beam of a flashlight hadn't caught them both in the eyes.

"Could you two please put a sock in it?" The normally affable Robbie sounded like he was ready to drop-kick them down the nearest crevasse. "You're upsetting Fiona!"

"I didn't know you were there." Hildy's voice was faint, barely a scrape of sound in the silence. Too bad she hadn't located that volume setting a few minutes earlier.

"We thought we were alone," Walter said.

"So did we," Robbie shot back. "Me and Fee snuck over here to have a quiet moment together in this amazing place and contemplate time and eternity, but no! It had to turn into a horror show."

There was a gasping hiccup from the corner, where Walter could just make out the shadowy figure of a sobbing Fiona being consoled by her sister.

"Shit," Hildy whispered.

"It's not what it sounded like," Walter started to say, but Robbie held up a hand.

"Fee's the one you need to talk to. Not right now," he added, when Hildy took a step in that direction. "She needs time to heal from having her dreams stomped on."

"Corinne's going to kill me," Hildy groaned, after Robbie rejoined his fiancée. "*I'm* going to kill me." There was a slight pause, during which he sensed her gaze sliding his way. "You'll have to take a number."

"I don't want to kill you, Hildy."

She grunted at that. "Doesn't really matter, since I'll probably murder you first, before I off myself."

"So this is my fault?"

"No. This is on me, because I was stupid enough to let my guard down. Even though I *know* it's always going to end like this."

It was a bit of a stretch to claim she could have predicted this exact scenario, but Walter knew better than to push back.

"I can't believe I lost my shit *again*." It sounded like she was talking to herself. "How many times can I make the same mistake before I get a clue? But that's it. I'm really done. No more screwing around."

"Hildy—"

"Don't," she warned, cutting him off. "You can't change the past. There's no point pretending anymore."

They were the last words she spoke to him for the rest of the long, chilly trip back to the surface.

THEN

25

Hildy

SEVEN YEARS AGO

SAN DIEGO, Calif.—There should really be a licensing process before people were allowed to give advice. *Go to the Associated Collegiate Press conference*, Hildy's professor had insisted at their last meeting. *It's a good time. And you might learn something.*

Ha!

Halfway through the first day of panels and workshops, Hildy's main takeaway was that the journalism world was suffocatingly small. Or maybe the real lesson was that the past always came back to bite you in the ass at the worst possible moment.

Exhibit A: The session Hildy was most excited about—Making Tracks: Finding Your Footing in the New Media Landscape—turned out to be a total bust. So much for attaining desperately needed clarity about her future in the industry. It was hard to apply strategies you hadn't heard because you were forced to flee thirty seconds into the introductory remarks when your sworn enemy walked into the room.

In hindsight, Hildy realized she should have brazened it out. If anyone was going to turn tail and run, it ought to have been Walter. But Hildy's brain had gone AWOL, leaving her central nervous system to hit the panic button. Her body reacted as if his presence was a lethal poison: churning gut, skin blazing hot and then clammy, a suspicious heaviness in her bladder.

Hildy had just enough presence of mind to fake a phone call. It didn't matter how much she wanted to look at Walter to see if he'd changed in the last two years. Aside from the bombshell of a first glimpse, Hildy couldn't risk acknowledging his presence. They weren't supposed to meet again until she had a plan—and a comprehensive makeover. Ideally there would also be a ridiculously hot love interest to follow her around making adoring remarks. *See, Walter? Some people aren't desperate to get away from me.*

Instead she was having a bad hair day, her complexion was a wreck, and everyone she knew from school had chosen other morning sessions, leaving Hildy looking like a rejected loser.

Maybe he didn't see me. It was a big space, and there had been rows and rows of full seats between them, not to mention Hildy's cat burglar–style half crouch on the way out.

She hightailed it to the nearest restroom. Her stomach was still complaining, a dull throbbing ache that seemed to be spreading through her lower body. And now a sharper twinge that reminded her of . . . oh no. Hildy latched the stall door, staring in dismay at her formerly pristine underwear. Just to make the day a little more awesome, her period was early.

"Shit fucking fuckers," she muttered, checking her purse and coming up empty. A vague memory of using her last emergency pad surfaced, followed by the mental note she'd made (and promptly forgotten) to replenish her supply. Time to swaddle herself in cheap toilet paper.

A hand reached under the wall from the adjacent stall with a wrapped pad between two fingers, the way a cocky guy might flash a twenty-dollar bill at the valet stand in a restaurant.

"Thanks," Hildy said. "You just saved my favorite pair of pants."

The door next to hers opened. Hildy finished her business quickly so she could thank her savior face-to-face. She was standing at the sinks, so Hildy saw the back of her head first: stick-straight blond hair in one of those cool ultrashort bobs that would have looked ridiculous on someone with curls.

When Hildy got closer, their eyes met in the mirror. *I know you*, Hildy thought, even though the face wasn't quite right. Maybe Hildy had met this girl's sister, or she looked a little like someone on TV, or . . . they'd been roommates two summers ago at a journalism program for high school students.

Only back then, this girl—Corinne—had been in her goth phase, making her hard to recognize without the black hair dye and intense eye makeup. High school Corinne's most notable personality trait was meanness, so Hildy wouldn't have known her by the heroic restroom assist either.

So much for the day taking an upswing. This had to be a cosmic joke.

"Wow," Hildy said, skipping past the *do I know you?* song and dance. There were only so many people she could pretend not to recognize in one morning. Besides, it was evident from Corinne's expression that the jig was up.

It would have been weird if she didn't remember Hildy, considering they'd slept a few feet apart for a week. Not to mention the bit where Corinne stabbed Hildy through the heart. That had certainly left an impression on Hildy—and judging by the tension around Corinne's eyes and mouth, her memories of that time weren't terribly cheerful either. Maybe her conscience was bothering her, assuming she had one.

"You're still in journalism?" Corinne flinched. "That was a stupid question. Obviously, you are."

"*There are no stupid questions*." Hildy did a credible impression of one of their teachers from that summer, who had labored under the mistaken belief that he was deep.

Surprise flickered across Corinne's face. Had she assumed Hildy was humor-impaired, or was she expecting pistols at dawn?

"You thought I would have given up by now?" Hildy guessed, claiming the next sink over.

Corinne reached for a paper towel, averting her gaze. "I owe you an apology."

That was unexpected enough to make Hildy overlook the nonanswer to her question. Her attempt to act casual by washing her own hands was foiled when it took four tries to get the motion-activated faucet to work.

Corinne took a deep breath. "I—was not at my best that summer."

"Join the club." The irony was that before it all fell apart, Hildy had convinced herself the summer before her senior year would be the high point of her existence. She was growing up! Doing great work! Meeting interesting people! One of whom she connected with so deeply, she foolishly assumed he'd be in her life forever!

He'd never apologized, even though that betrayal was a lot worse. Corinne had been her randomly assigned roommate. Whereas Walter was (briefly) Hildy's favorite person on the planet. A rejection hits differently when it falls on you from that height.

"Do you want to get a coffee?" Hildy was almost as surprised as Corinne to hear those words come out of her mouth.

"Do you?" Corinne replied, skepticism etched in the line of her brows.

Hildy shrugged; stranger things had happened. Maybe this one small piece of her past could still be salvaged.

* * *

Plot twist: Corinne was fun to talk to. Not in the bright, affirming style of Hildy's sorority sisters, but with an understated wit that made you look forward to the next time she opened her mouth. Presumably, she'd always been the kind of person who made clever observations about the world, but that side of her personality had been hidden behind the barbed wire of her bad attitude.

Or the brambles of Hildy's insecurity.

"Are you and Walter still in touch?" Corinne asked.

Hildy tried to scoff, but it came out as more of a choke. If only she had something other than a scalding cappuccino to clear her throat. At her suggestion, they'd left the convention center in search of a real coffee shop. For the fresh air, she'd told Corinne, though her main motivation was avoiding another run-in with Walter.

"In a word, no," she finally managed to say. It was possibly the least smooth moment of her life.

"Strange," Corinne said, without any particular inflection. "I figured you would have found your way back to each other by now."

Hildy shook her head, since vocalizing wasn't her friend.

"You were so into each other." Corinne sounded like a doctor pronouncing a diagnosis. "Not quite *Wuthering Heights*–level, but borderline. It was like you were the only people in the room."

"We weren't *that* weird."

"Hence the 'not quite.'" Corinne sipped her matcha latte. (Hildy would have pegged her as more of a triple espresso type, but she was turning out to be full of surprises.) "Maybe I was jealous."

Hildy felt a stab of something unpleasant. Retroactive possessiveness, maybe. "You were into Walter?"

"Nah, I'm fully gay."

"You were into *me*?" Had Hildy misread the situation that badly?

"Don't flatter yourself." The next words emerged with visible reluctance. "It would have been nice to have a friend like that." She paused, mouth pruning. "Could also have been super annoying."

"Trust me, you don't want a quote-unquote *friend* like Walter Burns."

Corinne studied her in silence. "What about you?"

Hildy shook her head, not caring if it messed up her curls. "I don't want a friend like that either." Not anymore.

"I mean, what kind of friend were you to him?"

"Better than he deserved." Maybe not perfect, and yes, she could have been more open, but Hildy's strategic and necessary silence on certain points paled in comparison to Walter's crimes.

"Okay." Corinne didn't sound fully convinced.

"Let's make a rule. The past is the past." Hildy didn't pause long enough for her to disagree. "It's not worth dredging up and making a big thing out of it. We were naïve teenagers, shit happened, moving on. Here's to making new and different mistakes!"

"Fine by me. I already have one set of divorced parents, so it's not like I'm out here looking for more drama."

Hildy raised her mug in a toast, receiving a grudging clink from Corinne. Despite doing her best to shut down that line of inquiry, part of Hildy wanted to beg for a few more scraps before the window of opportunity closed. Who else could she ask about that time except Walter, who was obviously not to be trusted? But she also wanted Corinne to think she was tough, so she changed the subject.

"What track are you on? Career-wise."

It was Corinne's turn to look skittish. "Don't laugh."

Hildy tried to think of the most unlikely journalistic path for Corinne's personality. "You want to be an advice columnist?"

"Please. The world isn't ready. Data visualization. That's what I'm into these days."

"Infographics?"

"To use the layperson's term."

Hildy rubbed her nose to hide a smile. "That may be the most pretentious thing you've ever said to me. And you brought up Nietzsche five minutes after we met." She was unreasonably pleased when that sparked a laugh from Corinne.

"So what's your deal? Doesn't seem like you're coasting on the nepo-baby train."

Hildy shrugged, because she wasn't entirely sure that was true, or how she felt about it. She'd thought a lot more about family and money and privilege since that summer, but her views still felt wobbly and half formed. It was hard to know what you really believed until you had to test those convictions in the real world. Until then, it was just posturing.

"I don't know if I see myself at a newspaper," she admitted, shaving off a piece of the truth.

"TV?" Corinne asked.

"Definitely not. I don't want to be in charge of that many moving parts. I just want to worry about the things that interest me." She made accordion folds in an empty packet of raw sugar. "I know what I like, but I'm not sure how to put it all together yet—or if that's even possible."

"Okay," Corinne said slowly. "You realize that's vague as hell?"

On impulse, Hildy decided to test the waters. If anyone was going to drop a truth bomb, it would be Corinne. "I've been thinking about magazines."

"What, like *Vanity Fair*?"

"Not glitz and conspicuous consumption." Hildy tried not to be offended that this was Corinne's first guess. It wasn't like she really knew her—not yet anyway. "More approachable than that. Like a smart friend . . . or a really cool older female relative you go to for advice. But still a little bit glam," she added, to cover the echoing void where the word "mom" might have appeared.

"Huh." Corinne sounded more intrigued than skeptical.

Encouraged, Hildy sketched a marquee with both hands. "Watch this space." She left it at that, because it seemed wisest to quit while she was ahead. The danger of exposing a tender young dream to ridicule was that it could so easily get stomped out before it had a chance to take root.

"Do you think we would have been friends back then?" Hildy asked, both as a subject change and because she genuinely wanted to know. "If I hadn't been so hung up on Walter."

"I doubt it," Corinne said without missing a beat.

"Wow. Don't feel like you have to spare my feelings."

"You annoyed me. I annoyed me. The world annoyed me." She shrugged, the movement tight and jerky. "I've mellowed a lot since then."

Hildy let her brows creep upward.

Corinne sighed. "I liked that story you did."

"Really?" She would have been less surprised if Corinne suggested they get matching BFF necklaces.

"It sounded stupid as shit, but you pulled it off."

Hildy put a hand to her heart to show how moved she was by this tribute. *We*, she thought. *Walter and me*. That's who pulled it off. Not that he cared about the result.

"Maybe we'll work at the same place someday." She glanced at Corinne, afraid she might catch her in an eye roll of deep scorn, but her expression was pleased—in a cautious and extremely jaded way.

"Sure. You can hire me at your magazine."

It almost sounded like she was imagining it too.

NOW

26

Hildy

TWO DAYS BEFORE THE PRESCOTT-SCHAFER WEDDING

TAMNIÈS, France—When the knock sounded at Hildy's door that evening, her first reaction was *hallelujah, a break from talking about numbers with Corinne!*

Until she found herself face-to-face with a despondent Robbie, at which point the spreadsheets didn't seem so bad. She steeled herself. Time to pay the piper.

"Do you want to come in?" Hildy gestured behind her. "Corinne and I were just having a quick business chat." That was a euphemism for *making emergency plans in the likely event that our current business model goes up in flames.*

"Actually, I was hoping you could come outside. To talk to Fiona." He stuck his hands in his pockets. "It's about the wedding," Robbie finally admitted, surprising exactly no one. He glanced past Hildy at the papers spread on her coffee table, overseen by a grim-faced Corinne. "But I don't want to interrupt your meeting."

"Don't worry about it," Hildy said. "I've been waiting for a chance to apologize. Give me five minutes and I'll be right there."

Robbie nodded, still looking weighed down by his cares. "She's at the pool."

"Got it." Hildy sent him off with an encouraging smile, closing the door before turning slowly back to Corinne.

"You're coming, right?" Hildy asked, ducking into the bathroom.

Corinne set down her wineglass. "Talking people around is your area. Half the time they don't even realize it's happening."

"I mean, they sort of know," Hildy said, keeping it humble. "They just choose to go along with it because they realize it's in their best interests."

"Either that or you wear them down until they don't have any strength left to resist."

"Potato, potahto." Hildy hesitated, afraid to give voice to her fears in case it made them manifest. "What if I fuck it up?"

"You won't."

"How do you know?"

"Because that would be very bad. For our bottom line."

"And sad," Hildy reminded her. "For Fiona and Robbie."

"Yes, Dr. Seuss. And don't forget how *mad* you'll be if we get kicked off the story and Walter has it all to himself."

"Right." She shook out her arms. "Okay, I'm getting fired up."

Corinne stood to gather her papers. "Go get 'em, tiger."

* * *

Fiona was sitting on the edge of the pool with her feet in the deep end.

"Mind if I join you?" Hildy asked, kicking off her sandals.

Fiona glanced at her. "Did Robbie find you?"

"Was he not supposed to?"

Fiona swished her feet, not quite making a splash. "You probably think he's super mellow, but he has a hard time when I get upset. You know how some people can't see someone puke without throwing up?"

"Are you feeling sick?" A rocket went off in Hildy's brain, blazing a trail of hypotheticals. Is Fiona pregnant? Does she *know* she's pregnant? Was Hildy going to have to be the one to get Fiona

Prescott to pee on a stick? She tried to remember if she'd seen Fiona partaking in the wine tasting, but as usual Hildy had been too occupied with Walter to pay more than passing attention to the rest of the world.

"This is like emotional distress." Fiona touched her chest. "If I cry, Robbie starts crying. It's super intense. And then his eyes will be all puffy and bloodshot, and people will assume we don't love each other, when it has nothing to do with that. I wish we could be alone, just the two of us, instead of having all this"—she gestured at the hotel, or possibly the entire countryside—"breathing down our necks."

"Do you want to talk about it? Or I could get your sister?" Hildy wondered why Robbie hadn't sought out Maude in the first place.

"Good luck with that."

"What do you mean?"

"She's with Loïc." Fiona slid her a knowing glance. "I should have known that whole thing with your guy was a smoke screen."

"Walter isn't *my* guy."

"Sorry, I didn't mean to put a label on it if you're not there yet."

"Yeah, no, that's not—we're not together."

Fiona frowned like Hildy might be holding out on her. "Are you sure?"

"Pretty sure."

"But he's totally into you?"

Hildy's heart chose that moment to take up ski jumping. "I wouldn't say that."

"You're into him, though." Fiona didn't even have the decency to make it sound like a question.

"You know what? Let's talk about you. And Robbie! Who is such a great guy." Hildy infused her voice with maximum cheer, like a human air freshener pumping out clouds of cinnamon-scented bliss. "Which is why all that stuff I said in the cave has nothing to do with the two of you."

Fiona looked down at her feet, swishing up and down without breaking the surface of the water. "You're worried I'm going to call off the wedding."

"No! It's not that." Hildy paused to check in with her conscience, verifying that what she'd just said was true. Or if not the whole truth, at least in the ballpark. "As you may have noticed, Walter and I have . . . a history. If he says the sky is blue, I say it's purple."

"It could be," Fiona pointed out. "At sunset."

"See? You're an optimist. Usually I am too. All that dark stuff was coming from a place of panic and bitterness. Walter and I don't bring out the best in each other. Not like you and Robbie."

Fiona twisted the fringed hem of her cover-up. "So you don't really believe all those things you said?"

Hildy wondered if she was crossing a line by getting this involved, but she was a person first and a journalist second. Having a heart-to-heart with the bride wasn't that different from hand stitching seed pearls to someone's bodice fifteen minutes before she was due to walk down the aisle, which Hildy had also done. Not to mention the part where the current crisis might be a teensy bit her fault.

"All that matters is what *you* think. You have a lot more experience with love than I do."

"Actually," Fiona countered, "Robbie said we could learn from you two."

"Oh? Learn what, exactly?"

"Don't hold on to anger for so long that your love gets lost and buried and you fight all the time."

"Right." Before Hildy could point out that "love" wasn't really the right word, Fiona went on.

"I never fight with Robbie. The closest we got was when we took Viennese waltz lessons for the wedding and Robbie wanted to add a breakdancing circle in the middle. Is that weird?"

The breakdancing? Hildy almost asked, but Fiona wasn't finished.

"Does it mean we're not passionate enough?"

"Not at all! Fighting isn't fun." Sometimes it was a little bit fun, but Fiona didn't need to know that.

"Uh-oh." Fiona tilted her head at the other side of the pool, where a dark-haired mistake from Hildy's past was standing in the shadows. "Looks like he found you."

"He was probably looking for you."

"Mm, no. I could be a stack of towels right now. That's how much he noticed me." Fiona shifted her weight, leaning back on her hands. "It's nice to be ignored for a change."

That was an unexpected angle for a bride. "Is it?"

"Yeah," Fiona admitted. "This whole week, I feel like every conversation is the dentist's office."

"Painful?"

"All up in my face. Open wide, Fiona! We want to poke around your private business with stabby metal things. Keep smiling! A little bigger! Are you happy? How happy? Show us!"

Hildy let the dust of Fiona's speech settle before replying. Big emotions deserved their own space. "It does suck, to feel like you're a blood bag and everyone is a mosquito. The love of the masses doesn't keep you warm at night." She'd never been a bride, but Hildy's time as a so-called celebutante had taught her more than enough about the sensation of having your life on display.

"Especially when the one person you want to be watching you isn't." Fiona's voice trembled.

Oh shit. Was she pining for someone else? Hildy could deal with logistical snafus and mood swings all day, but the human heart was trickier to wrangle.

"You mean—?" Hildy made it sound like she was confirming something she already knew, praying Fiona would fill in the blank.

"My mom." Fiona's eyes were damp. "*You* know what I'm talking about."

Hildy nodded, even though her answer was closer to *sort of*.

Walter chose that moment to stroll over. "Am I interrupting?"

"Walter has a mom," Hildy heard herself say.

"I—yes?"

"Lucky," Fiona sighed.

"Yeah, but look at him." Hildy nudged Fiona with her elbow. "Is *he* getting married?"

Fiona's teary gaze ping-ponged from Hildy to Walter. "Not that I know of?"

"He's not." The false alarm with Maude was already fading from Hildy's memory like a bad dream.

"I'm not," Walter agreed, waiting until Fiona looked away to shoot Hildy a *where are you going with this?* brow lift.

"See? No one has everything. He still has his mom, but he probably lives alone in a sad bachelor pad."

"So sad," Walter murmured. "Stacks of pizza boxes, and cheap posters Blu Tacked to the wall."

The desire to see for herself burst like a firework at the back of Hildy's brain, but she refused to be distracted.

"*He* isn't coming home to someone like Robbie every night." She jerked a thumb at Walter.

"True," he agreed. "He's never there."

Hildy locked eyes with Fiona. "You have so much love in your life. Think about that, instead of what you might or might not be missing."

"You're right." Fiona tipped her head back to stare at the night sky. "I am very lucky. And I hope you have someone who loves you too."

"Me?" Hildy was excruciatingly conscious of Walter listening to every word. "Um, yes. My uncle and my cousins. Several of my step-aunts." She forced herself not to glance in Walter's direction, even though her family was far from a neutral topic for the two of them. "They don't understand me, but they do love me."

And maybe that was as good as it got for most people. The idea of finding someone you could talk to about anything, who connected with you on the deepest level and adored you anyway, was a dangerous illusion. Hildy had learned that at a young age and lowered her expectations accordingly.

"I know there are people who have much less than I do. Not just in money or houses," Fiona clarified, lest they think she was out of touch. "Ugh, that's enough about me. Let's talk more about you two." She waved at Walter to sit.

He settled down a little closer to Hildy than seemed warranted. Fiona took this in with avid interest. She probably also noticed Hildy staring at Walter's calves as he rolled up his pants. Was he a runner now, or was he getting that cut from CrossFit? If only this were an interview and she had an excuse to barrage him with questions.

"So how did you meet?" Fiona asked. "Was it at a wedding?"

"Sort of," Walter began.

"It's a boring story," Hildy cut in. "Not worth repeating."

Walter leaned forward. "She's being modest."

"No, I'm being *honest*. There's a difference."

"Really? I'd love to hear you explain it."

"Good thing you're used to disappointment." Hildy forced herself to leave it at that when she realized Fiona was watching this exchange like it was the hot new drama on HBO. At least she looked entertained rather than mopey, almost as if . . . the Walter situation wasn't a liability after all. Or not at the moment anyway, when Fiona was desperate for a distraction. And what was more diverting than knowing other people's lives were more fucked up than yours?

Hildy felt the tug of an idea trying to take shape from the swirling cauldron of her thoughts. Fiona was tired of being stared at.

She wanted more time with Robbie. A distraction lightened her mood. She had doubts about her wedding plan . . .

"She's plotting something," Walter whispered to Fiona.

"You don't know that." It was a reflexive denial. Hildy's brain was running full scheme ahead.

He made a low grinding noise. "I can hear the wheels turning."

"That is not how my brain sounds." She jabbed a finger at the side of her head. "My mind is an electric vehicle."

"Scooter?" he guessed.

"Porsche." Hildy locked eyes with Walter, daring him to challenge her metaphor with gratuitous mansplaining.

Fiona pressed her lips together, stifling a giggle.

Right. The plan. That was the primary objective.

"So what is it?" Walter asked.

She turned to Fiona. "I think you need a minute to reconnect with the heart of what's happening here. We can't let all the noise and confusion obscure what matters most. Which is why I think we should go see your castle."

"Now?" Fiona's eyes were huge. "In the dark? Us three?"

"You and Robbie," Hildy corrected. "And me."

"And also me," Walter interjected.

"Plus Corinne," Hildy said, since apparently they were making it a group outing.

"We'll have to ask Maude. And she'll probably want to bring her secret boyfriend." Fiona glanced at Walter, who nodded to confirm he was cool with Loïc's presence.

"Meet by the van in fifteen minutes?" Hildy phrased it as a question, trusting everyone to understand it was really an order.

"This is so spontaneous." Fiona pressed a hand to her mouth, like she couldn't believe their audacity. "It's not even on the itinerary!"

NOW

27

Walter

TWO DAYS BEFORE THE PRESCOTT-SCHAFER WEDDING

MARQUAY, France—Hildy was onto something with this under-cover-of-darkness trip to the wedding venue. It felt romantic and cinematic, with a hint of mischief: whispering and cramming into the van as they snuck away from the hotel; headlights picking out flashes of lonely road ahead; the faint hum of the radio, playing something French. An almost tangible sense of relief and excitement emanated from the bride and groom. If the point was to soothe and reassure Fiona Prescott, the mission was half accomplished by the time they reached the bottom of the hill.

Other cultures were better at coddling brides-to-be, but Walter supposed it was the American way to make prewedding rituals an endurance test instead. If you didn't optimize every last detail, were you even trying?

Granted, there were worse fates than being fêted at an extravagant destination wedding, but Walter was getting better at seeing the real people behind the trappings of an upper-class lifestyle. He liked Fiona and Robbie, both as a couple and as unexpectedly quirky individuals. Plus, as Hildy had pointed out, there were some things all the money in the world couldn't buy.

The space between his shoulder blades burned with the urge

to turn and look at Hildy. It didn't take an ace reporter to figure out she was avoiding him, to the extent it was possible to ignore someone enclosed in the same van. Halfway across the parking lot Hildy had called dibs on the back row and announced that Corinne would be sitting next to her.

While Walter's gut had been telling him for days that the only path forward with Hildy was to sort through their past, she was clearly not on the same page. He'd have to find a different approach that wouldn't send her into a defensive spiral before they had a chance to really talk to each other. If she still wanted nothing to do with him after that, at least he'd know he tried.

The van parked in an unremarkable gravel lot between the road and the forest. You couldn't see the castle from here, though Walter supposed the towers might be visible above the tree line when it wasn't dark.

"Picture really handsome attendants at the valet stand," Fiona narrated, leaning forward to point past the windshield. "Dressed like medieval pages."

"Too bad I didn't pack my tights," Robbie said as he helped her out of the van.

Loïc and Maude were waiting for them on the grass.

"This is where the carriage will pick you up," Maude told her sister. "Can you imagine?"

"I wish we could ride in a carriage now," Fiona sighed.

Robbie stomped the ground with one foot, snorting and tossing his head. "My lady?" he said, crouching in front of his bride-to-be. He grunted as Fiona climbed onto his back, hoisting her higher as he straightened.

"Good horsie!" she chirped as he trotted away.

"I should let her borrow my riding crop," Corinne mused as the rest of the group followed the bridal couple along the trail leading to the edge of the forest.

"We'll string lights all through here." Maude gestured at the path through the trees, which was the approximate width of a car (or horse-drawn carriage).

In the absence of hanging lanterns, flashlights flickered like fireflies from the cell phones in every other hand. A hushed quiet fell once they set off through the trees. Walter wondered if Hildy was spooked by the darkness or the rustling branches, but didn't want to embarrass her by asking.

"There used to be wild boars in these woods," Maude informed them.

"Oh goodie," Hildy muttered.

"It makes a delicious sausage," Loïc added, like that would offer some consolation. Yes, you got gored, but on the upside: charcuterie!

The forest felt like something out of a fairy tale. Walter had been to plenty of outdoor weddings, but the backdrop of "nature" was always groomed within an inch of its life. This was an actual wilderness, as if the forest might decide at any moment to retake the narrow strip of land.

A prickle of awareness alerted him that Hildy was staring.

"Why are you looking at me like that?"

"I'm trying to imagine you with horns."

"Like . . . a devil?"

Her curls swished as she shook her head. "Like one of those dark fae lords who lures you into the woods and you don't find out until book five that he's actually trying to kill you."

Walter had questions, but one rose to the top. "And? How do I look?"

She shrugged. "I think you could pull it off. You have the hair for it."

He had no idea if that was an insult or a compliment, but the fact that Hildy was talking to him felt like progress. As if sensing his eagerness to prolong the conversation, she sped up, not slowing until Maude and her archaeologist were between them.

"At least she likes your hair," Corinne whispered, hurrying past him to catch up with Hildy.

When they emerged from the forest, the castle was a shadowy mass in the distance, rising out of the rock. Between the edge of the trees and the base of the cliffs, Maude had created an enchanted garden. Walter angled the light from his phone at hedges that had been clipped into cloud-like puffs and sloping curves.

"There's a labyrinth over there." Maude indicated a series of concentric gravel paths that petered out into a grassy verge.

"This is incredible," Hildy said. Walter wondered if she was also drafting descriptions in her head.

"I had to work with what was already here," Maude explained, toeing the line between modesty and pride. "Like those urns, and some of the shrubs. It was an interesting challenge, to shape the plants and give them room to breathe, instead of ripping everything out."

"It is magnificent." Loïc's tone dared anyone to argue.

Maybe if Walter had an accent Hildy would let him talk.

Fiona patted her fiancé on the shoulder, and he lowered her to the ground. "What do you think?" she asked Hildy.

"It's fairycore Versailles meets *Where the Wild Things Are*," Hildy pronounced, answering Walter's question about whether she had her journalist's hat on tonight. "You could say your vows right there, at the center of the circle." She pointed at the half-finished labyrinth.

"I love the symbolism," Walter chimed in. "You found your way to each other, on a winding path full of twists and turns."

Hildy cleared her throat, silently warning him to cool it with the double meanings.

"That would be cool." Fiona sounded wistful. "Except Daddy wants us to get married in the Great Hall, so we're just having the pre-reception out here."

"At least you don't have to worry about rain. And we can come back outside after." Maude pointed at the sky overhead, where an almost perfect moon had risen above the trees. "It's going to be completely full the night of your wedding. Can you imagine? The trees bathed in silver—like the moon came to watch you get married."

Fiona bit her lip. "Doesn't crazy stuff happen during the full moon?"

"If you're a werewolf," Corinne muttered, grunting when Hildy elbowed her in the side.

"I googled the top ten things that can go wrong at a wedding," Fiona continued.

"Fee, you didn't!" Maude looked horrified. "That's like diagnosing yourself on WebMD."

"I know you want to protect me, but I need to face reality. If there's a norovirus outbreak, or a bat infestation and then we all need rabies shots, or my whole face is a giant cold sore, I'm going to have to deal."

"Every wedding is perfect in its own imperfect way. You wouldn't believe some of the things we've seen." Walter glanced at Hildy, who gave a shrug of affirmation.

"Like what?" Fiona asked.

"Well," he stalled, thinking he'd have to dig for an example. But it slid to the front of his mind as if it had happened yesterday. "There was a couple who had a big plan for a theme park wedding." From the corner of his eye, he saw Hildy tense. "Only the groom got sick—"

"What kind of sick?" Fiona interrupted.

"Cancer," Walter replied. "That was actually how they met."

"They both had cancer? Do they die at the end?" Fiona fanned a hand in front of her eyes. "Because I don't think I can handle that right now."

"She was his doctor."

"He's burying the lede," Hildy said before he could go on.

"They went to the same high school. They were even in a musical together—"

"Now who's burying the lede?" Walter interrupted.

"They *re-met* at the hospital," Hildy continued, raising her voice. "And then they had the wedding there."

"In the hospital? Like, at his bedside? I think that happened on *Grey's Anatomy*."

Robbie nodded, like he vaguely remembered the episode.

"It was actually in the cafeteria," Hildy informed them.

Walter held up one finger. "I think they called it a canteen."

"Thank you for that vitally important distinction." Hildy didn't roll her eyes, but the sentiment was there.

Fiona's gaze swung between them. "You both wrote about this wedding?"

"Yes," Hildy answered, giving Walter a look when he would have said more. "And it was one of the most memorable weddings I've ever seen. They didn't let anything get in the way of having the ceremony they wanted. The challenges made it more meaningful."

"You think we don't have enough challenges?" Fiona asked.

"Not at all," Walter assured her. "But I also don't think you have too many challenges. You have just the right amount."

"I know a guy who got married in an old train yard," Robbie said.

"Was it like that warehouse party we went to in New Haven?" Fiona grabbed his arm. "Remember that weekend?"

"Yeah! Parts of it. And the wedding was supercool." Robbie frowned briefly. "A couple people had to get tetanus shots after, but it was totally worth it!"

Fiona shook herself. "I'm sorry I got all up in my head about this. At least we have our health, right?"

"Such a good point, babe."

"Do you want to frolic?"

"Always!"

They took off across the grass, leaping and laughing.

"Those crazy kids." Corinne sighed, watching them gallop toward the trees.

Hildy mimed drawing a curtain. "Let's give them their privacy." She turned her back on the young lovers, considering the looming shape of the castle instead.

Walter took a casual step in Hildy's direction, and then a few more. "About earlier—"

"I'm working," she said.

"Right now?"

"Yes, Walter."

She said it with such conviction, he had no choice but to back away. Maude and Loïc were whispering to each other in French, so he approached Corinne.

"What's your strategy here, Romeo?" She indicated Hildy with her chin.

"Keep blundering along and hope something miraculously changes?"

Corinne slow-blinked at him.

"I didn't say it was a good plan." He hesitated. "Do you have a better idea?"

"Depends what you're trying to achieve."

Walter had to laugh at that. As if he knew! He wanted to uncover . . . *something*. A truth or a secret or a solution, even though a parting salvo seemed more likely, given their history. Maybe it would come as a relief, to put an end to his fascination with Hildy after all these years. His heart didn't exactly soar at the thought, but then a lot of things that turned out to be good for you sounded awful at the outset. Fish oil, for example.

Actually, that stayed awful. He wanted more than that. "You think I should walk away and let her have the story?"

"Would you do that?"

"I don't know." He wasn't even sure where the idea had come from. "Would she do that for me?"

"One, you're asking the wrong person. Two, Lord knows you maniacs would manage to get your wires crossed, and I am not here for some 'Gift of the Magi' clusterfuck."

Before Walter could mount a defense, Fiona and Robbie came trotting back, breathless and sweaty.

"I love it here," Fiona announced, spinning around. "I love the moon, and the grass, and the trees, and the castle up there, and the smell of the flowers. You did such a good job, Maude!"

Raising her arms over her head, she turned a cartwheel. It felt like the exclamation point at the end of a sentence.

"Can't do that in a corset. Or with a twenty-foot train!" She gave a sudden bark of laughter. "My headdress would be so jacked up right now."

Robbie attempted a cartwheel of his own, though his knees never straightened past ninety degrees. "I could probably do that in a tux, but I might split my pants."

"And that would be fine," Fiona told him, "because weddings aren't supposed to be perfect." She turned to Walter and Hildy with an expectant look. "Right?"

"Right." Walter suppressed a faint premonition of doom. He had an inkling those two might have taken the wrong lesson from this evening's outing. There was a difference between rolling with the punches and flashing your wedding guests.

"I wish we could get married right now." Fiona threw her arms around Robbie's neck. "I feel so light and free!"

"Just—hold that truth in your heart," Hildy suggested. "Ignore the noise and remember what matters. Before you know it, you'll be on your honeymoon, looking through pictures and reminiscing about how great your wedding was. And it will be totally amazing, because it's *yours*. Not to mention, look at this place. I've seen a lot of wedding venues, but this one takes the cake." She stole a glance at Fiona. "Do you want to head back to the hotel now, get some rest?"

Robbie rubbed Fiona's back with one hand. "What do you say, babe?"

"Can we stay out here a little longer?"

He fished the keys to the van out of his pocket and tossed them to Corinne. "Fee and I will get a ride with Maude."

"Shotgun," Hildy called, hurrying past Walter.

The drive to the hotel was mostly silent. When they arrived, Corinne put the van in park and turned off the ignition before resting her forehead against the steering wheel.

"We survived," she said, sitting upright again. "That was a good night's work. Strange, but effective."

"I hope so," Hildy mused. "For their sake. I like Fiona—and Robbie. He seems like a good guy."

"Pretty solid," Corinne agreed. "If you're into that kind of thing."

"The goofy golden retriever type?"

"Men."

Hildy made a noise of agreement. "At least with Robbie, what you see is what you get. How many other guys can you say that about?"

Walter wondered if they had forgotten he was there, or didn't care. When Hildy started to climb out of the van without so much as glancing his way, he unbuckled his seat belt and hurried after her.

"Can I talk to you?" he asked before she could escape.

She stood perfectly still, keeping her back to him. "I'm tired. Can it wait?"

"Whatever you're going to do, take it inside." Corinne gave Hildy a little shove in the direction of her room.

"Fine," Hildy sighed. She trudged down the paved path, unlocking her door and going inside without looking back.

When he stepped tentatively into her room, she was sitting on the bed with her arms crossed. "So?" she prompted. "I'm listening."

"I think we should finally talk about it. It's time." Past time, more like, but he didn't want to open on a sour note.

"Talk about what?"

"That summer."

She looked away. "Why?"

"I think we need to."

"What do you want from me, Walter? Is this a step on your healing journey? I'm sure you can evolve without me."

"I want us to be honest with each other." He kept his voice calm, even though he knew she was trying to push his buttons. "About what happened."

"Bad shit. Period, end of story."

"It wasn't all terrible, Hildy."

"Really? I don't remember."

If it wasn't for the trembling of her chin, Walter would almost have believed she was telling the truth.

THEN

28

Hildy

TEN YEARS AGO

TAMPA, Fla.—Sweet freedom. She'd made it here at last.

Hildy's first dramatic inhale filled her lungs with a smell best described as future sinus infection, but that was a minor detail, like the dingy walls and ancient twin beds. The squalor was a means to an end: independence, knowledge, control of her own life. She would sacrifice a lot more than comfort to get where she wanted to go.

Comfort *and* privacy, assuming the black garbage bag on the other bed contained her absent roommate's belongings—as opposed to actual trash.

Maybe she was sharing these narrow walls with someone who objected to luggage for political reasons. There were probably a lot of crusading-activist types here for the fellowship. You had to be interested in the world to want to report on it. Even though reporters were supposed to be neutral bystanders, most of them secretly believed their work had the potential to change lives.

Doubt flittered like moth wings at the back of her mind. Was Hildy really one of the twenty best high school journalists in the entire country? Could she hold her own with the nineteen other "rising stars" for a highly competitive weeklong summer intensive that would make or break her college applications, and by extension her entire career?

Her family certainly didn't think so. They'd tried to talk her out of going, right up to the moment she left them behind at airport security.

Okay, that stiffened her resolve. This was her opportunity to prove them wrong. Maybe the last chance, before they shoved her onto the conveyor belt leading to a future more in line with their expectations.

"I can do this," she announced to the empty room. "I will do this."

A sarcastic huff from the doorway was Hildy's first indication she wasn't alone.

"Great," said a girl whose obviously dyed black hair showed several inches of blond at the roots. Hildy couldn't tell if the look was intentional, or she was overdue for a trip to the salon. "I got the one who talks to herself."

The garbage bag made more sense in the context of its owner. The other girl's look was designed to be in-your-face edgy, in that classic "don't you dare look at me" style: black nails, tattered denim shorts, T-shirt cut to fall off the shoulder, barely tied combat boots, a necklace made of . . . paper clips? Maybe she'd stolen them from an office supply store, in the true spirit of anarchy.

On the other hand, she'd obviously put a lot of time and effort into crafting this punk rock girl persona, which was the teensiest bit contradictory. Notice me! Stay away! There was some aesthetic whiplash happening—not that Hildy planned to kick off their week of cohabitation by mentioning that fact.

"I'm Hildy." She held out her hand, then worried a handshake reeked of capitalism and the patriarchy.

"Hildy Who Hears Voices." The other girl left her hanging while she studied Hildy's clothes. *Sue me for wearing a sundress in freaking Florida in July*, Hildy thought. As if that revealed something about her character. This would be so much easier if they could sniff each other like two dogs squaring off at the park. Get the dominance thing settled and move on.

"Corinne." Her roommate sighed like she begrudged the necessity of even that much politeness. But she did pump Hildy's hand once before letting go. That seemed like a victory, however small. Maybe they wouldn't spend the next six days giving each other the silent treatment.

"Where are you from?" Hildy asked.

Corinne flopped onto her bare mattress, tugging her garbage bag closer so she could root around inside. "Can we save the icebreakers for tomorrow? I'm meeting some friends like five minutes ago."

Hildy waited for an invitation to tag along, smiling in case Corinne glanced over, but her roommate was busy throwing clothes onto her bed. And the floor. Since her body language did not say "ask me about my social life," Hildy was left to guess how Corinne already had friends when the program hadn't even officially started.

"I'm going to unpack," she informed Corinne, who spared her a *did-I-ask?* glance.

Whatever. The point of this week was to work. And net*work*, but surely there would be easier targets than Corinne, who tapped the doorjamb with her knuckles as she sped off to do her thing. Why knock on the way in when you could be different and make it a goodbye instead?

Maybe Hildy needed a signature gesture to set herself apart. She pictured herself winking uncontrollably. That would for sure win friends and influence people.

But hey, that was a tomorrow problem, and she still needed to tackle today. The itinerary made it sound like most people would be eating with their families tonight. Which wasn't an option for Hildy, since she was flying solo. By design rather than abandonment, since she couldn't risk letting her relatives loose anywhere near here, but it still promised to be a lonely evening.

Not a big deal! There must be at least one or two pizza places that delivered to the college dorm where all the fellowship kids were staying. Her uncle had offered to put her up in a hotel instead, but Hildy wanted the full experience. By this time tomorrow, she'd have a whole day of workshops behind her, and plenty of people to hang out with. Maybe she and Corinne would bond over breakfast, if her roommate consumed anything more substantial than black coffee and snark.

Hildy frowned at the bed not covered in Corinne's clothes. When female business leaders talked about claiming your space, they probably didn't mean a plastic-covered brick of a twin mattress in a rundown dorm, but everyone had to start somewhere. She pulled out her phone, murmuring as she typed: "How to make a bed."

* * *

Who knew you were supposed to wash brand-new sheets before sleeping on them? On the off chance it wasn't a scam concocted by Big Detergent, Hildy felt compelled to follow the multistep instructions she'd found online. The only problem was that laundry was not among the skills she'd planned to acquire this week, reasoning that it would be easier to pack extra underwear than waste crucial reporting time washing her own clothes.

That was fine! She could roll with a change in plans, because she was a mature and resourceful person who conveniently had nothing else going on this evening. How hard could it be? Put the clothes in the big hole and add detergent . . . once she acquired said detergent. After that she'd worry about the array of dials and buttons. (Although seriously, why were there so many? You'd think it was a small aircraft.)

You found the laundry room, Hildy reminded herself. Step one, in the bag—no thanks to the RA who was supposed to be on duty at the deserted front desk. It would have been nice to think someone knew where she was in case this basement lived up to its potential as a crime scene, but oh well!

The imaginary trailer for a *Who Killed Hildy?* podcast had barely started playing in her head when the lights switched off, plunging the laundry room into darkness. The package of sheets made a slapping sound as it hit the ground, but it wasn't loud enough to drown out her whimper of alarm.

"Shit," said a voice from the other end of the room.

The lights flickered back on, and Hildy forced her lungs to expand. She had the strap of her purse stretched between her hands like she was about to strangle someone. Good to know her crisis response was fight rather than flight.

"I'm really sorry," the guy hovering at the base of the stairs called out. "I didn't realize there was anyone down here."

"That's okay. I have a strong heart."

"I'm Walter." It sounded like another apology. His shoulders hunched like he felt bad for taking up so much vertical space, which reduced the creepy factor of him being male and blocking the exit. It also helped that he was wearing cargo shorts and a ratty T-shirt, as opposed to a long black robe with a scythe in one hand.

"Hildy," she yelled back. "Are you by any chance here for the Pachner Fellowship?" Because he did not seem laid-back enough for college.

"Yeah. You?"

She nodded before bending to retrieve the sheets. "I don't suppose you know how to work these things?"

"The washer?"

"I'm not familiar with this model." Or any others, but he didn't need to know that.

As Walter slouched across the laundry room, Hildy took a closer look. He was not what most people would call hot, but the potential was there, once his weight caught up with his height. His hair had the opposite problem—too much volume, in the wrong places—a relatable issue in this humidity. (Hildy suspected she looked like she'd been struck by lightning.) Was his skin perfect? No. But if you looked past the scattering of pimples, the long straight nose and dimpled chin would likely be handsome on his grown-up self.

When he smiled, Hildy got a sneak peek at future Walter's charm. Her fingertips tingled—though that was mostly relief at the thought of having a friendly face to look for tomorrow morning.

"Do you have quarters?"

"What?" Hildy struggled to jump from her current train of thought (*isn't it strange how you can tell just from looking into someone's eyes that he's smart*) to unzipping her purse.

Walter frowned at the handful of coins she dropped in his hands. "For the washer," he said gently.

It was the mildest possible correction, but Hildy felt her face heat anyway. Of course he wasn't asking her to pay him. She scooped the quarters out of his hand, blush intensifying at the slightly sweaty skin-to-skin contact. To her relief, the coin slot was easy to find, now that she knew to look for one.

"I feel like I should get a gumball out of this," she said, dropping in a quarter.

He put a hand on her arm when she started to shove the coin slot into the machine. "Better put your clothes in first." Walter averted his gaze like she might be holding a pile of G-strings and push-up bras.

"It's just sheets," she reassured him. "I haven't even slept on them yet."

"You're washing clean sheets?"

"Thank you! It's bizarre, right? Is this why adults are so stressed? Their lives are filled with made-up chores."

He nodded slowly, like he was giving her theory serious thought. It was a nice change from home, where everyone smiled vaguely when she talked, as if they were indulging her childish babble while counting down the seconds until they could bail.

"Does your mom still do your laundry?" Walter asked.

Although she didn't detect any judgment in his tone, Hildy felt the need to set him straight. "She's not in the picture."

"I'm sorry."

"It happened a long time ago. Not exactly breaking news."

"Still."

"I never really knew her." Hildy was going for *it's all good! I'm not a human tragedy!* Judging by Walter's expression, the attempt had backfired. She balled up the sheets and dumped them into the washing machine. "What's next?"

He hesitated only briefly before accepting the subject change. "Detergent."

Walter looked Hildy up and down, from the bare floor next to her feet to her empty hands and slim purse. It felt like a practical inspection rather than a pervy one, but she would have gladly given him one of her remaining quarters for his thoughts.

"They have some down here." He led her to a banged-up metal cabinet. To Hildy's surprise, Walter pulled a set of keys from his pocket and unlocked the doors. There were shelves full of cleaning supplies inside, including industrial-sized boxes of laundry detergent.

"You're like the James Bond of laundry," Hildy observed as he scooped some bluish-white powder into a plastic measuring cup.

He snorted at that. "Not exactly."

"Then why do you have keys to the secret supply cabinet?"

"I'm helping out at the dorms when we're not in class. My scholarship is actually a work-study deal. To cover the room and board."

She was relieved he didn't ask about her family's ability to pay out of pocket for this program, since Hildy had no desire to go there.

"So you know the lay of the land."

"I guess?" Walter shrugged before heading back to the washer. "It's not like they gave me the nuclear codes."

Modesty was a rare quality in Hildy's world. She found his lack of hype refreshing. It made him seem trustworthy, on top of being handy to have around.

"Walter."

"Hmm?"

"Do you know anyone else in the program?"

"No."

She smoothed her hair. "Do you want to do it with me?"

His hand jerked, shooting granules of laundry soap onto the floor. "What?"

"There's going to be a group project." This was the one useful piece of advice she'd gotten from her cousins. "We could be partners."

Walter closed the lid of the washer and turned a dial. "You want to work with me?" he asked over the sound of water filling the machine.

"That's the general idea."

When he didn't respond right away, Hildy braced for rejection. Maybe she'd come on too strong, when she should have played it cool.

"You don't even know who else is going to be there," he said at last, sliding her a look she couldn't read.

"I have excellent instincts." Or at least she hoped that was the case. Will to power and all that. "But if you don't want to—"

"I do."

"Good." She gave him her full-wattage smile. "I think this is the beginning of a beautiful friendship."

His mouth opened and then closed again without making a sound.

"That's a line from an old movie." As opposed to someone trying way too hard to turn this into a cheesy moment.

Walter smiled, a little shy, and Hildy's embarrassment faded. Clean sheets *and* someone to sit with tomorrow? Things were looking up.

* * *

"Hi," Hildy said, a little out of breath, as she sank into the empty chair on Walter's right the next morning. A toothpaste misfortune had forced her to change her entire outfit, hence the later-than-planned arrival.

Corinne leaned past him to give Hildy a sardonic look. "Nice of you to join us."

Oh, goodie. Her mysterious and hostile roommate was sitting with Hildy's only friend. "You two know each other?" She crossed her fingers the answer was no.

"Me and Wally go way back," Corinne replied, before Walter could get a word in. "Scholarship kids stick together." She raised her eyebrows, daring Hildy to pretend to be one of them.

"We met yesterday," Walter said. "Corinne was locked out."

Hildy wondered if he would say something similar about her. *We met yesterday. She didn't know how to use a washing machine.* That was okay, because he was about to see her in her element.

She surveyed the rest of the room, sizing up the competition. One or two other loose clusters had formed, including a band of private school types who had clearly been acquainted for longer than a day. They reminded Hildy of her cousins, from the tips of their gelled hair to the leather laces on their boat shoes. No doubt they assumed the prize was theirs for the taking and had already written off the rest of the group for not looking like they'd traveled here by yacht. It was going to be a pleasure to wipe the floor with them.

A newspaper landed on the table in front of her. Hildy snapped to attention, making quick eye contact with the woman who was passing them out. She was old enough to have silver threaded through her shoulder-length dark hair, and her expression, while stern, lacked the tightly wound quality of a copyeditor. Probably a department head, judging by her age and air of command. Too intense for features, and not outdoorsy enough for photography or sports, so Hildy's money was on the metro desk.

Her fingers tapped, nervous energy spilling over. *Let's go, let's go, let's go.*

"You okay?" Walter asked.

"I'm excited," she whispered back, not softly enough to keep Corinne from rolling her eyes.

Hildy tuned her out. Why should she be ashamed? This was about to be adrenaline central. The program was always structured as a competition, and Hildy knew they worked in teams, but beyond that the curriculum varied every year. They could be asked to produce cutting-edge digital media or dig through old records on a cold case. Whatever it turned out to be, she was ready.

She hoped.

The woman who'd dropped off the papers joined a shorter man in a wrinkled button-down at the front of the room, crossing her arms as he gave the welcome speech. When he stepped aside, she took his place at the podium.

"Each of you has a copy of today's morning paper," she said. "Your assignment is to choose one item from any page and write a long-form follow-up. We're looking for insight, originality, and depth. Do not regurgitate what's already there." Lowering her reading glasses, she speared them with a warning look before continuing.

"You'll be working in groups of at least two, because this is a collaborative business. Your deadline is five PM Thursday, but I suggest you meet with the copydesk and design department well before that. Faculty will be available for consultation." She glanced at her watch. "Your time starts now."

The rustle of newsprint filled the room. It sounded like a wind machine had been switched on. Hildy understood why people were flicking through the pages like their lives depended on it. They wanted to find the juiciest material and claim it first.

But this wasn't a speed-reading contest, and Hildy didn't intend to go the obvious route by choosing a crime or a scandal. The smarter play would be finding a nugget of gold in an unexpected place—something everyone else had overlooked. She took a deep breath before diving in.

The first group was out the door by the time she got past the A section.

"Hildy?" Walter's voice wobbled a little, like he was trying not to sound nervous.

"Don't worry," she told him, without looking up.

"Did you see the piece about someone illegally dumping cooking oil in the retention pond?"

She hmmed an affirmative.

"We could try to track down the fast-food bandit?"

"I like that," Corinne said. "Who is the Fry Guy? Or girl. We could make it pulpy. Put people at the scene. *Midnight. The Arby's parking lot. Rusty water drips onto the stained pavement.* You know?"

"Give me a minute." Hildy turned to Sports. Not her first choice, but you had to keep an open mind.

Another group left, chattering about finding someone with a boat. Corinne made an exasperated noise.

"Dude, everybody is going." It was clear she was talking to Walter, and Walter only. "We should see if we can join those guys. Drugs! Smuggling! Gators! That's real news."

Hildy was on the last section of the paper, a few thin pages away from the classifieds. She split her focus between Community News and the conversation unfolding between Walter and Corinne. If he ditched Hildy now, she'd have no choice but to fall in with another group, where she'd be at the bottom of the pecking order. They'd probably have her ordering lunch and checking facts.

Her finger stilled near the bottom of the page while she waited for Walter's response.

"I'm sticking with Hildy," he said.

"Good luck with that. Wait up," Corinne called after a departing group, not wasting another second on either of them.

"Thank you," Hildy said. They were the last two left. "You won't regret it."

She slid the newspaper over to him, tapping the relevant text.

"It's a wedding announcement." The frown was audible in his voice. Was Walter being a snob because a wedding was too frou-frou and feminine to be worth reporting on? If he turned out to be a closet misogynist, this partnership was going to be over before it started.

"And?" Hildy prompted. "Did you read it?"

"'So-and-so and so-and-so, together with their families, are delighted to announce their wedding, which will take place at Disnée World'—" He looked up from his read-aloud. "D-I-S-N-É-E? With an accent? Is that a typo?"

"Keep going," Hildy urged.

"'Disnée World,'" he repeated, "'located in the fifth-floor cafeteria at First Presbyterian Hospital.' Huh." His frown was different now, more intrigued than worried. "'After the ceremony, Carlee will complete her residency in oncology and Carlton' . . . Is it not weird that their names are Carlton and Carlee?"

"You're burying the lede." She flicked her fingers at him to go on.

"'And Carlton will continue treatment for kidney cancer.'" His eyes met Hildy's. "Shit. Do you think that's how they met?"

"That's what we're going to find out."

Walter glanced at the story again. "It's happening this afternoon."

"Yep. Let's get cracking." Hildy tucked the folded newspaper under her arm before grabbing her bag and starting for the door. Walter hurried to catch up.

"We're crashing a wedding?" he asked, pitching his voice low.

"No, we're going to *insinuate* ourselves into a wedding reception," she corrected. "With our charisma and charm."

"Speak for yourself."

Hildy's mouth froze in an *O* of surprise, which she tried to play off with a hair toss. "Why, thank you."

NOW

29

Walter

TWO DAYS BEFORE THE PRESCOTT-SCHAFER WEDDING

TAMNIÈS, France—"So we worked on a story together. A thing that happens every day, in newsrooms all over the world. Whoop-de-do." Hildy twirled a finger in the air. "It was a long time ago."

"It was more than that."

She leaned back on her elbows, legs crossed. "Do tell."

It felt like a dare, as if Hildy was waiting for him to say the wrong thing so she could kick him out. Walter edged the narrative forward, a man walking on an icy sidewalk.

"We went to a wedding together. And it was uplifting and beautiful and meaningful." He could see Hildy getting ready to call him out for being a sap, so he added a pinch of salt. "Also, a bit strange."

"Yeah. Weddings are like that."

"All weddings have lab techs in dwarf hats doing a group dance number?"

She lifted a shoulder, totally blasé. "Maybe they should. Why don't you suggest that to Fiona and Robbie?"

Walter was aware she was trying to provoke him into veering off course. He also knew Hildy liked to protect herself by hiding behind a show of attitude, because she didn't like to feel vulnerable—which meant he had to go there first.

"Happiness. That's what we found in that cafeteria." He paused before going on, letting her wonder whose happiness he was talking about. "Honestly? I thought it might be sad. Here were these two people who didn't get their dream wedding, and now they had to party in a cafeteria, and their whole future was uncertain—but it wasn't like that at all. They were *incandescent*."

"Or you were blinded by all the sparkly fabric."

Walter ignored her grumbling. He knew Hildy didn't believe that. "They were overjoyed they'd found each other. They had the most important thing, and nothing else mattered."

"Found each other twice," she corrected, "which made it even more . . ." Hildy broke off, realizing she was arguing the wrong side.

"Magical." He held eye contact until she looked away. "It was a total rush, covering that wedding."

"You did hit the soda fountain pretty hard."

"It wasn't the Mountain Dew, Hildy. It was *you*." He thought of what he'd told his mother on the phone that night: *I don't know how to describe her, because I've never met anyone like Hildy before.* Ten years on, he had yet to encounter another person who went straight to his bloodstream like a double whiskey and Coke.

She was silent long enough that he thought maybe he was getting through to her, until she spoke again. "And what happened after that, Walter?"

"You had a craving for pie."

THEN

30

Walter

TEN YEARS AGO

TAMPA, Fla.—"Turns out you're kind of wild," Walter said as they walked back to the dorm after the wedding.

She wrapped a curl around her finger. "What was your first clue?"

"Maybe when you had the gift shop wrap that box of candy to make it look like a wedding present."

"It got us in the door, didn't it?"

"I'm sure you would have talked your way in without the props. Like when that old lady asked who you were and you said, 'Do you know Cousin Jimmy?' Just like that." He snapped his fingers, still in awe of her nerve.

Hildy shrugged like it was no big deal. "That was slick, wasn't it?"

"Maybe you should join the CIA."

"Nope. It's the news biz or nothing for me."

"You're pretty awesome at it."

"No regrets about your choice of partner, partner?"

"Definitely not."

She bit her lip, and Walter remembered he was alone with a cute girl. He'd done his best to keep that awareness tucked away at the back of his mind while they were working, but it was harder to ignore now that it was just the two of them, without the background noise of a packed cafeteria.

"That was a fun wedding." Hildy bumped him with her elbow, and Walter was almost sure she'd done it on purpose, though it could have been because the sidewalk narrowed around a garbage can.

"I wouldn't know."

She stopped walking to stare at him. "That was your first?"

"Yeah." He hoped she wouldn't ask what other major life experiences he was lacking, because the list would get embarrassing very quickly.

"Weddings are like the Fourth of July in my family. You don't even want to know how many step-aunts I've had."

He wasn't sure whether she expected him to be impressed or scandalized, so Walter waited in silence for his next cue.

"It's funny they met when they were our age," Hildy mused.

When the bride and groom found out Walter and Hildy were high school students working on a project together, there was a lot of oohing and awwing, hands to mouths and hearts in their eyes. It turned out Carlee had played Cinderella in their school's production of *Into the Woods* while Carlton understudied the role of her prince. They'd lost touch after graduation, until Carlee started a rotation on the oncology ward where Carlton was undergoing cancer treatments. And now they were married—though obviously Walter and Hildy would add more detail to the finished story.

"Can we go in there?" Hildy was pointing across the street at an old-fashioned diner. "And have coffee and pie like gritty old newshounds?"

"It's kind of late—"

"You can have decaf, grandma." She grabbed him by the hand, not letting go until they were inside. The contact was so distracting, Walter forgot to worry about his bank balance, though he wasn't in a position to casually eat out, unless the restaurant featured a drive-thru and a dollar menu.

"Look, they have Dutch apple!" Hildy bounced with excitement. "We're definitely getting that."

He tried to surreptitiously check the price, but there wasn't a sign.

"My treat," she announced. Walter wondered if he'd given himself away, but Hildy was studying the laminated menu she'd plucked from the abandoned hostess stand.

"You don't have to—"

"I'm not," she interrupted. "My uncle gave me an emergency twenty for the trip, but I didn't need it because you showed me the secret laundry detergent stash. So basically we're even." Hildy closed her menu. "You're giving me the look."

"What look?"

"Like my head is a fortune cookie and you're trying to read what's written inside." She tapped her temple. "It's your interview face. You're going to be really good at this, you know. I can tell."

"Yeah?" His smile was at least half relief that she hadn't called him out for staring at her. It would be easier for both of them if he kept his crush under wraps.

The waitress led them to a booth with squeaky vinyl seats, dropping silverware and two menus on the table.

"Real food or straight to dessert?" Hildy's lips pursed as she studied him. "If you can't decide, go with the grilled cheese. Not too little, but not too much. He'll have a grilled cheese," she informed their waitress, after a split-second glance at Walter. "And fries. Coffee for me, and a slice of that pie. With two forks. Please," Hildy added, flashing her dimples.

Their server seemed to appreciate the decisiveness, collecting their menus with a nod of respect.

"I'll eat it if you don't want it," Hildy assured Walter when they were alone.

"Grilled cheese sounds good."

"I know. It's a classic for a reason."

As with most things about Hildy, he found her bossiness charming. It reminded him of his mother's cat, poking you with a velvet paw until you remembered you were wasting valuable time that could be spent scratching under his chin.

"To us," Hildy said, raising her glass of ice water in a toast. "We make a good team, don't you think?"

He inclined his head in agreement, and also to hide his blush. "We still might not win. The judges are probably looking for coverage of serious issues. Future Pulitzer stuff. As opposed to a feel-good story."

"Then we'll just have to change their minds." She unrolled her silverware, arranging it next to her plate. "So no one will be able to underestimate us ever again."

"Plus we'd have twenty-five thousand dollars for college," Walter reminded her. "And priority admission to J-school."

"That too." She folded her hands on the table. "So what are you thinking?"

"For college?"

"Our story."

Right. They were here to work. Walter thought fast. "We could be inside Carlton's body, like we're describing what's happening in his cells, and then it cuts to stark statistics about how many people get sick every year, the likelihood of recovery—all that."

"Whoa." Hildy blinked at him. "That's kind of dark for an article about a wedding."

"Okay, what about starting right before they get the diagnosis? Maybe he's even waiting for the doctor to arrive."

"But then it's a disease story." Hildy sat back as the waitress deposited their plates.

"What were you thinking?" Walter asked, reaching for the ketchup.

Hildy waited until he'd blobbed some onto the plate to steal one of his fries, dipping it before taking a bite. "We don't want it to be all sunshine and rainbows. That's a fair point." She angled the remains of the french fry at him. "But we also want to capture how it actually felt to be there, really bring it to life on the page. And I was not getting bummer vibes."

"Me neither," Walter admitted, though he wasn't sure how much of that had to do with Hildy's presence.

"I think a story can be uplifting *and* truthful."

"You're an optimist."

"I don't know about *that*. I'm not out here with bluebirds circling my head."

"That would be awkward."

"Right?" She grinned at him, and Walter felt like he'd landed on Park Place. "I'm just saying there's more to life than misery."

Sitting across from Hildy, he was inclined to agree. Regular life could be magical, under the right circumstances.

"I wonder if we could find their high school drama teacher. Or the guy Carlton understudied." Her nose wrinkled as she grabbed another fry. "That's getting off track, isn't it? This isn't a showbiz memoir."

"I thought it was a good idea." Walter dabbed at his mouth with the paper napkin, worried he was sporting a chin full of grease from the sandwich. "Although other people might be less interested in the high school element than we are."

"That's the fairy tale of it." She nudged her pie plate to the middle of the table, turning one of the forks so the handle faced him. "Destiny and second chances and 'oh, our paths kept crossing for a reason. We were meant to be!' People love that stuff."

"Even though it's not very realistic?"

"Um, they just got married?"

"Yeah, but you don't usually stay with a person you meet in high school."

"I'm sensing baggage. Do you have a tortured relationship history we need to talk about? Because I'm all ears."

"Uh, no." He huffed a laugh. "Not a lot going on in that department. I wasn't talking about myself."

She held up a finger. "Before you start spilling, if you're a stress eater we're going to need another piece of pie."

Walter fiddled with the strap of his watch. He could dodge the question. They'd just met and might never see each other again after this week. Somehow, that made it easier to tell her the truth. "My mom got pregnant with me her senior year."

Her expression didn't change. "And your father?"

"Who?"

"Right." She hesitated like she had something to say but wasn't sure how it would be received. "You know what? We'll talk about my stuff later. My family stuff, not my love stuff." She broke off a piece of pie crust with her fingers, keeping her eyes on the plate. "I don't have a boyfriend. In case you were wondering."

The fact that she was not only single but had chosen to volunteer that information was the best news Walter had heard all day. He felt floaty with hope, like a bobbing helium balloon. "Do you think it's possible to meet the person you're meant to be with when you're our age?"

"Are you asking if I think Carlton and Carlee are going to make it?" Hildy frowned. "You want to put some foreshadowing in the story? Like 'they seem so happy now, but the future remains uncertain,'" she intoned in a dramatic voice.

He shook his head. "It was more of a philosophical question."

"Wow, okay. Going deep." She took a careful sip of water, like she was stalling for time. "In theory, I guess. I feel like I know myself. I could conceivably turn into someone completely different when I'm thirty-five or forty but hopefully not? I think I'd miss me."

Walter nodded. It was a more thoughtful response than his ridiculous question deserved.

"We could start with today," Hildy offered. "See where it leads us."

It took him several tries to find his voice. "We—what?"

"Open at the wedding, go big on the descriptions, and then flash back to high school. But we don't gloss over all the hard parts, because we want it to have a little gravity, like you said. Our story," she added, waving at him. "Earth to Walter."

"The wedding. Got it." He picked up his ballpoint, trying to look like he was focused on the task at hand. When he flipped back through the last few pages of his notes, a line jumped out at him. "I jotted something down. While we were there."

"Let's see." She tried to drag the notebook to her side of the table, but he held on.

"It's probably too cheesy."

"How will I know if you don't let me see it?"

Reluctantly, he lifted his hand. Hildy grabbed the notebook and flipped it around. "Is this shorthand?"

"My handwriting sucks."

"Read it to me." She shoved it back at him.

"Once upon a time, a kingdom traded science for magic and a white coat for a wedding gown fit for a queen." He forced himself to look up. "Too much alliteration?"

She leaned across the table, tapping the back of his hand with her index finger. "That could be our first line." Her smile was as slow and warm as syrup over a fresh stack of pancakes. "I'm going to start calling you Walt as in Disney."

"Why?"

"Because he made the magic happen. That's all I know about him, so hopefully he wasn't a total deviant." She shrugged an apology, just in case. "Might leave the metaphors to you."

"I was actually named after Walter Cronkite. The news anchor."

"I'm going to pretend you didn't just mansplain media history 101 to me."

"Sorry. I'm not used to being around people who care about

this stuff." Nor had he realized how cool it would be to share your weird obsessions with someone.

"For your punishment, you can sit there and watch me eat another piece of pie."

"Agony," he agreed, quoting Carlton and Carlee's favorite song from *Into the Woods*.

NOW

31

Hildy

TWO DAYS BEFORE THE PRESCOTT-SCHAFER WEDDING

TAMNIÈS, France—"That was our first inside joke." Walter's eyes were wide and hopeful, like the babe in the woods she'd mistaken him for back then. This time, Hildy wasn't fooled.

"Talk about selective amnesia."

"I remember everything," he insisted. "Every hour of every day we spent together."

They'd been more or less inseparable. The excuse was that they were working on their project, but there had been long stretches where journalism was the furthest thing from her mind.

"The classes," Walter continued, like he was working down a list, "the cocktail party full of boring old people that was somehow fun. The makeover."

"I helped you pick an outfit. It wasn't a *makeover*." Not like the glow-up he'd had since then.

"I remember walking home with you one night and wanting to hold your hand, but I didn't know if it would be okay. And then we got to your room, and I was desperate to kiss you."

"But *you* were the one who worried it would get messy if we broke up before we finished our project. Like I was some kind of drama queen."

"That wasn't what I was thinking at all."

She waved at him to go on.

"I was afraid if we crossed that line, I wouldn't be able to think about anything else. Forget the story, forget everything."

"As if I would ever let a personal relationship get in the way of my work," Hildy scoffed, before recalling certain incidents of the last few days. "Shut up," she said, though Walter hadn't spoken beyond an eloquent lift of the brows.

"You agreed with me," he reminded her. "Because you didn't want anyone to make assumptions about you, since people are dicks about women in business. We *mutually* decided to wait . . . but it wasn't easy. At least not for me. I couldn't get enough of you."

She tried to keep her face hard and unyielding, but the memories were like pollen, irritating her eyes and making the back of her throat itch. For that one shining week, working with him had been as easy as breathing. Some people fought you at every step: You say up, I say down. Being with Walter was more like the improv game she'd played in family therapy. Instead of a world of "no," everything was "yes, and!"

Do you like this headline? Yes, and we can use this photo!

Does that metaphor work? Yes, and it ties back to the Cinderella theme!

No one had ever "gotten" her as quickly as Walter. She didn't have to explain things twice or fill in the gaps between one idea and the next leap of logic to bring him up to speed. They pushed each other, and the story kept getting better.

And it wasn't just the work. She'd liked Walter, period. His quickness, the subtle sense of humor, the way he looked at Hildy like she was already the type of bold and brilliant person she'd always dreamed of becoming. In her mind, reporters as a type were more in-your-face go-getters, yelling out questions and speaking truth to power, but Walter didn't seek the spotlight. If anything, he seemed more comfortable letting her take the lead.

Or so he'd let her believe. She swallowed, but the bitterness didn't fade. "Too bad we didn't keep it professional."

He stared at her in disbelief. "That's your takeaway?"

"Well, that is when it all went to shit." Leaving Hildy feeling like the world's biggest idiot.

"Maybe it was worth it."

"Which part?" She held up a hand when he started to answer. "Let's just say mistakes were made and leave it at that."

"I don't want to leave it."

"You could have fooled me."

THEN

32

Hildy

TEN YEARS AGO

TAMPA, Fla.—One of Hildy's special gifts was taking something that was already pretty great—hanging out with Walter, his hair, their story—and raising it to the next level. It was instinctive, the way tennis must be for someone sporty. Ideas popped into her brain without conscious effort: a tweak here, more emphasis there. Sometimes her head felt like a crystal ball. *Ping!* Another gem of inspiration shimmering into place.

Her latest brainwave was perhaps her most daring idea yet.

Sex. With Walter.

As a concept, it was both obvious and brilliant. Trust, attraction, limited supervision—the conditions were ideal for her first time. Clearly the universe wanted them to do this. Especially since it would also be Walter's first time (she was pretty sure), so Hildy wouldn't feel self-conscious about her lack of experience. Or worry that he might forget her after this week, when they went back to their separate lives. You never forgot your first.

Hildy didn't have anyone she could ask for tips on staging a seduction, so she was winging it. She wanted tonight to feel classy and sophisticated to show Walter he was important to her—that she cared enough to pay attention to the details. Hence the trip to

Victoria's Secret, and the cans of cranberry juice cocktail (Walter's favorite) chilling in the mini fridge.

This was definitely not what her uncle had in mind when he booked a hotel room in case Hildy couldn't handle the dorms, but she was all about making the most of the resources at hand. She'd proven she could rough it, and now she needed privacy, because if she asked her charming roommate to make herself scarce, Corinne would come back after five minutes, just to be a contrarian. And from everything Hildy had read, this would take longer than that.

He knocked on the door promptly at eight.

"Hi," she said, hoping the breathlessness sounded sultry rather than nervous.

"I got your note." Walter held up the folded square of paper, sending a wave of fragrance in Hildy's direction. It was possible she'd gone overboard with the perfume. "Is everything . . ."

He trailed off, and she watched his gaze flit around the room, taking in the low lighting and soft thump of music in the background. Hildy stepped out from behind the door, giving him a glimpse of her lacy purple nightie. Walter's eyes went wide.

"Am I interrupting?" he asked, hovering on the threshold.

She frowned, wondering how the scenario could have been any more obvious. Maybe she should have gotten a piece of posterboard and written LET'S GET IT ON in bubble letters. Grabbing him by the wrist, Hildy tugged Walter into her hotel room, slamming the door behind him.

He glanced over her shoulder, and Hildy saw him take in the full picture: the sheets neatly folded back, a trail of rose petals leading to the bed, the plastic hotel ice bucket on the desk with two cans of Ocean Spray.

"You. Uh." He paused to take a breath. "You were waiting for me?"

"Yes, Walter." In more ways than one, but she wanted this moment to be sexy, not sappy. "Is this okay?"

He nodded, still blinking more than normal, like she'd just set off a strobe light in his face. Hildy edged closer, placing her hands on his shoulders. That triggered a response, his arms coming around her waist. She felt the warmth of Walter's palms through the satin at her hips.

"We finished the story." She wasn't whispering on purpose, but they were standing so close a normal voice would have felt like shouting.

Walter made a low murmur of agreement.

"You know what that means?"

His gaze strayed to the bed. "Possibly?"

Hildy tried to think of something saucy to say to erase any lingering doubts, but a smile broke free instead. When he smiled back, she forgot about planning her next move and stretched up to kiss him.

Walter's mouth was warm and soft, with a hint of sweetness from the peanut butter and banana sandwiches he made himself for dinner every night. She was ready for it to be awkward, since they'd never done this before, but kissing Walter was as easy as having a conversation with him. Except their lips were less far apart—and all the parts of them below the chin were touching too.

The press of Walter's body against hers felt so good, Hildy couldn't stop straining to get even closer. She needed an assist from gravity, and a lot less clothing. When she reached behind her to untie the halter neckline of her nightgown, Walter put a hand on her arm.

"Let me do that."

She shivered as his fingers skimmed up her back, slowing when they reached the midpoint. A crease formed between his brows as he moved his hand from side to side.

"Something wrong?" Maybe she had a previously undiagnosed spinal condition.

"I can't find your bra."

"I already took it off. You don't wear them under pajamas."

His blush intensified. "Sorry. If you'd given me more notice, I would have done research."

She was focused on walking backward without letting go of him, so it took a second to catch on. "Like porn?"

"No!"

The light went on. "You were going to interview people. About sex. A little fact-finding mission. Maybe loop in a librarian."

"Forget I said anything."

"Not likely." She kissed him again, because he was so earnest, and she could.

"Speaking of preparations," he said, when they were standing next to the bed. "I don't have any, um—"

"I have some. From the dorm."

"Okay. Wow. I should have known you'd be on top of things."

"And you're cool with this?"

He laughed, just a little, so she could tell it wasn't aimed at her. "I keep waiting to wake up."

Hildy reached around him to pinch his butt. "Still with me?"

Walter nodded.

"Then I guess it's not a dream."

She kissed him again, keeping her hand low and tight on his behind. Now that she'd blazed that trail, it was fair game—and Walter's ass felt like a safe place to start before things really escalated. There had to be a graceful way to ease onto the bed without either of them chipping a tooth. Hildy was attempting a slow sag when her phone buzzed.

"Ignore that," she told Walter, breaking away long enough to drop onto the edge of the mattress. She patted the space next to her thigh.

He sank down beside her, and Hildy managed to get them horizontal without too much struggle. They stayed like that for a while, lying on their sides, facing each other, lips and tongues together while their hands wandered. She wanted to close her eyes and savor the feeling of Walter touching her, but couldn't seem to stop her own restless exploration, from his ears to his shoulders and chest. When her fingers brushed against the button at the waistband of his shorts, Hildy pulled away just far enough to look him in the eye.

"It's actually a snap," he whispered. "Not a button. Just FYI."

"Thanks for the heads-up."

"Any time."

Her fingers had just started tugging on the pull of his zipper when the hotel phone on the bedside table rang, the sudden burst of shrillness startling them both. Her hand jerked, bringing her knuckles into contact with a sensitive part of Walter's anatomy. She wasn't experienced enough to know whether his yelp meant she'd hurt him, or the opposite.

"Should you get that?" His voice was slightly strangled.

As much as she wanted to ignore the call, Hildy was afraid whoever it was might come knocking if she didn't answer. Sighing, she rolled over and grabbed the receiver.

"Hello?"

Ten seconds later, Hildy's insides had turned to ice. The freezing sensation spread from her stomach to her heart and then to her face. She was dimly aware that Walter was watching her with concern.

The person at the front desk was waiting for a response. Hildy needed a defibrillator for her brain.

"Tell him . . . I just got out of the shower," she stammered, with none of her usual flair for ad-libbing. "I'll be down in ten—fifteen minutes. Tell him not to come up," she added, with a sudden stab of panic.

Hildy let go of the phone. She had considered beating herself to death with it, but she didn't have the strength—or the time.

"Hildy?" Walter asked, placing a tentative hand on her arm. It was a sympathetic gesture, as if she needed another sign that the romantic portion of the evening was over. "Is everything okay?"

"My uncle's here."

He scrambled to his feet. "Here—at the hotel?"

"I told him not to come. It's so typical of him to show up anyway."

"He wanted to be here for the awards?"

Hildy shrugged. Uncle Richard would claim he was there to support her, but he undoubtedly had other reasons for making an appearance. Throwing his weight around, glad-handing a few cronies, being fawned over—the usual.

"That's kind of nice," Walter pushed back, ever so gently.

"Is it, Walter?" She cast a significant glance at the front of his shorts, still gaping open. He adjusted himself before zipping up his fly. Now all he needed was a duffel bag to hide the evidence of what they'd been doing.

"What's the plan?" He looked around the room, from the tangled sheets to the trail of rose petals. "Do you want me to help clean up?"

She shook her head. "I need to get dressed and get down to the lobby before he decides to come up here."

"Do you want me to leave?"

Hildy could tell he wanted her to say no, but she wasn't ready to introduce him to her family. That would require more preparation—on both sides. She'd been a little too focused on getting Walter naked to worry about explaining her life story.

"Sorry," she said, as if that would soften the blow of kicking him out.

"That's okay." He leaned in, pressing a quick kiss to her lips. "I'll see you later?"

It was a classic Walter response: hopeful but trying not to push. Hildy's heart squeezed with affection. "I'll call you."

She wanted it to be tonight, but there was no telling how long it would take to manage her uncle, and Hildy was tense enough without worrying about Walter waiting for her.

He hesitated in the doorway, sending her a last fleeting smile. "Good luck."

The second she was alone, Hildy had the strangest urge to throw herself on the bed and cry. But that was silly. She would handle the situation like a mature and competent adult, and then she and Walter could finish what they'd started.

There was no reason to feel like she'd just lost something precious.

NOW

33

Walter

TWO DAYS BEFORE THE PRESCOTT-SCHAFER WEDDING

TAMNIÈS, France—"You never did call." It might be a small thing in the grand scheme of their past, but Walter still wanted to know why she'd ghosted him.

Hildy shook her head, like she couldn't believe he'd had the audacity to go there. "I wonder why?"

"So do I," he said slowly.

She smoothed her skirt over her knees, avoiding his gaze. "Does it matter?"

"I'm just trying to understand your side of the story."

That got her attention.

"*My* side?" Hildy's eyes flashed. "I thought we were on the same side, Walter. That's the problem."

"Then why did you leave?"

"How could I stay after—"

"After what?" he prompted, when she broke off.

She leaned forward. The tension in her posture suggested she'd come to a decision, and Walter had better get ready. "I came to the dorm to find you."

"When?" Had he somehow missed her? And by how much? How fucked up to think a few minutes had changed the course of his life.

"Later that night."

"I didn't see you."

"No." Hildy let the silence grow heavy. "But I heard *you*."

THEN

34

Hildy

TEN YEARS AGO

TAMPA, Fla.—As soon as she ditched Uncle Richard, who was more than happy to watch golf tournament reruns in his room once she showed him how to work the TV, Hildy headed straight for the dorm. The RA on duty told her Walter was on the patio, a fancy name for the slab of concrete behind the building where a pair of decrepit wooden picnic tables awaited those willing to risk a backside full of splinters.

She decided to surprise him. That would get things back to fun and flirty mode, as if the interruption had never happened. After creeping out the door, Hildy ducked behind the low cement-block wall that separated the building's mechanical systems from the rest of the courtyard.

The "boo!" was already forming in her throat when she realized Walter wasn't alone. The smell of cigarettes should have been her first clue. It might as well have been a cloud of brimstone.

"Where's your girlfriend?" Corinne taunted, with the slight sneer that was her conversational baseline.

Hildy risked a quick glance through one of the square gaps in the wall. Their faces were angled away from her, making it unlikely one of them would look this way.

"She had some family stuff." Walter didn't seem bothered by

the "girlfriend" part, even though Hildy was pretty sure it had been meant as a dig.

Suck it, Corinne! I am *his girlfriend!*

It was a funny way to find out, but Hildy wasn't complaining. Her mind was zooming into the future, thinking about long-distance relationships and the logistics of making it work beyond this summer. A daunting prospect, but college was only a year off and she knew how she felt about Walter. Besides, when had Hildy ever backed away from a challenge?

"I guess there are a lot of VIPs in town for the awards banquet," Walter was saying when she tuned back in.

Corinne grunted, like she was too cool to care about that kind of thing, even though Hildy knew her roommate was as ambitious as anyone in the program. She'd probably have copies of her résumé safety-pinned to her shirt.

"You know who I saw tonight?"

Don't say it, Hildy silently urged him. She couldn't be that unlucky. The whole point of hustling Walter out of the hotel had been to avoid this very situation.

Her roommate exhaled a plume of smoke. "Who?"

"Richard Johnson. Of Johnson Media." Walter shook his head, like he was trying to make the information fit. "I would have assumed they'd send an HR person or maybe a junior editor, not the head of the whole company. Do you think he might actually consider hiring people from this? *If* they win."

Even over the chorus of *oh shit* ringing in her head, Hildy could hear the vulnerability in Walter's voice, hope barely masked by his attempt to sound chill.

Corinne snorted. "I wouldn't think you had to worry about that."

"Thank you?" There was a question mark at the end, because it didn't exactly sound like a compliment.

"Come on. There's no way you aren't going to win. Johnson

Media probably bankrolled the program. Of course they're going to give Hildy Johnson the prize. That's how the world works. It's all about who you know."

No! Hildy wanted to howl into the echoing silence. The whole reason she'd been so careful to scrub any mention of her family from the application was that she wanted to earn this on her own merits. She hadn't even told her uncle about it until she'd been accepted, so he couldn't "accidentally" influence the selection committee.

"I assumed that was your angle, cozying up to her from the jump." Corinne stubbed out her cigarette on the table. "I'm curious, did she come right out and say, 'my uncle is a media tycoon, you should work with me' or did you figure it out and approach her first?"

It was like watching a stack of plates slip out of someone's hands in slow motion. Hildy couldn't do anything but wait for the whole thing to come crashing down, shattering into shards.

"Good for you or whatever." There was a hint of respect behind her roommate's cynicism. "I should have clocked it sooner, just from how she acts."

How the fuck did Hildy act?

"All queenly and shit," Corinne continued, as if she'd heard the silent question.

Since when did using actual luggage qualify as uppity? It wasn't as if Corinne knew about Hildy's allowance . . . or her hotel room.

Unlike Walter. Why hadn't he asked any questions about how she'd pulled that off?

She thought about standing up and confronting him, but wasn't sure her knees could support her weight. Besides, if she stood up now it would only make her look shadier for sneaking around and spying on them—even though she hadn't intended any of this.

When Walter finally spoke, his voice was as flattened and dry as a callus. Hildy barely recognized it.

"I'm a reporter. It would have been pretty stupid of me to overlook something like that."

He knew? All this time? Only the fear of giving herself away kept Hildy from toppling to the ground.

"Too bad I missed my chance to get on the gravy train with you," Corinne said, with what almost sounded like admiration. "That was a smart play."

Walter shrugged, like he was too modest to toot his own horn.

"I thought maybe it was a sex thing."

"No," he said, after a slight hesitation.

But they'd come *really* close. Hildy closed her eyes, imagining how she'd feel right now if they'd gone all the way. Except this moment wouldn't be happening if they were still in her hotel room, so Hildy would still be in the dark about Walter's true motives.

"I can't believe you had to do a wedding story, though." Corinne made a gagging sound. "Rich people, man. What's next, a society ladies' tea party?"

Walter made a noise that was somewhere between a *ha* and *ugh*. All the effort they'd put into their project, Hildy's pride in their work, dismissed like it was nothing—a sham on his part, bringing himself down to her level.

So sorry you had to go slumming with a human-interest feature, she thought bitterly.

"Did she introduce you yet?" Corinne asked. "To her uncle."

"No."

"Huh."

It was a loaded *huh*. Walter swallowed the bait. "What?"

"People like that see someone like you or me as a pawn. We're useful until we're not. I'm going to go out on a limb and guess she had you doing the heavy lifting on your quote-unquote group project. Who actually wrote the story?"

"I did most of the writing," Walter admitted.

Which was true, but not the whole picture! Hildy had been an equal partner, planning and researching, editing every line, not to mention taking point on the art and design. It was her freaking idea in the first place, though apparently that was nothing to brag about.

"And who gets the credit?" Corinne pressed.

"It was going to be a joint byline."

"Damn." Her roommate tutted as if Walter had revealed something scandalous. "She really made you her bitch. I guess that's one way to launch a career you're going to spend taking credit for other people's work."

Hildy waited for Walter to defend her. He *knew* she wasn't a slacker. Making fun of her taste, and her talent, was bad enough. Talking shit about her work ethic was an outrage.

"She didn't even need this program. Much less the fellowship." It sounded like Walter was talking to himself, adding another black mark to the list of Hildy's crimes.

Corinne huffed as if she felt his pain. "I'm sure you know what you're doing, and maybe she promised you some super sweet deal for being her ghostwriter, but I'd watch my back if I were you."

"Why?"

"Better make sure she doesn't cut you out. I don't know about you, but I'm not here to let some trust funder use me. We may not have money, but we have brains and talent. And integrity."

Hildy didn't miss the unspoken implication: unlike *Hildy*.

What had Walter said earlier, about waiting to wake up from a dream? Somehow everything had turned upside down, and now Hildy was living a nightmare. When your favorite person gave voice to your worst fear, it was like having a full orchestra echo your inner soundtrack of self-doubt.

You don't have what it takes. No one will ever like you for yourself. Everything about you is mediocre and forgettable.

"I won't let that happen," Walter said.

"You're tougher than I thought."

"You have to be, in this business."

"Unless you have everything handed to you. Cigarette?" Corinne asked, like the two of them were best buds now.

Walter shook his head, already standing. "I need to take care of something."

"Her stuff isn't in our room. I wouldn't be surprised if she already bailed. Probably had a cotillion to get to."

"I don't care where she is . . . or what she's doing." Walter's voice was hard. "I'm going to make sure she can't do any more damage."

For the rest of her life, Hildy would associate the feeling of having her heart carved out with this exact moment: the roughness of brick under her hands, muggy air, aching quads from crouching for so long, cigarette stink—and the sound of being betrayed by someone she considered her friend, her colleague, her creative partner . . . and maybe more. Hildy had been brushed aside and underestimated before, but this was her first taste of scorn.

If she hadn't heard it with her own ears, Hildy wouldn't have believed Walter was capable of speaking with that kind of contempt—least of all about *her*.

She waited until the door closed behind them to pick herself up off the ground. So much for her fairy tale.

The only Cinderella moment Hildy was going to get was running the hell away.

NOW

35

Hildy

TWO DAYS BEFORE THE PRESCOTT-SCHAFER WEDDING

TAMNIÈS, France—“I lied,” Walter said as soon as Hildy finished.

It wasn’t a denial, much less an apology—or writhing on the floor, tortured by regret.

“I know.” She kept her chin up, willing her voice not to waver. “You were using me the whole time. Another person who only cared about my last name, or who I could introduce them to.”

“No!” He was agitated now, suave adult Walter replaced by the splotchy red face and shaky voice she remembered from his insecure teen self. “I was lying to *Corinne*. You had to know that. I’m no good at pretending.”

“Unlike me, you mean?”

“Hildy.” His voice broke on her name. “I was hurt and humiliated. To find out you were playing me and I was too infatuated to notice? I couldn’t admit to that.”

“How could you think for a second that I wasn’t serious about the work? Or that I just wanted to coast on my name? That’s bullshit, Walter. You *knew* me. And that’s who you rejected. *Me*. Not my uncle or his company or a pile of money.”

“I didn’t say it made sense.” Walter stood to pace, hands clasped at the back of his neck. “Even before that, I wasn’t in my right mind. Being around you was like being high. I couldn’t trust my own perceptions. It was so much easier to think it wasn't real than to believe that . . . it was. But it was, wasn't it?" His voice dropped to a whisper at the end.

Hildy could feel the heat of his gaze, a thousand times more potent than his interview face. But she wasn't one of his subjects, and she didn't have to answer his questions. This was her story too, and she was fully capable of telling it like it was.

"It doesn't change the fact that I showed myself to you, and you said, 'no thank you.' To everything about me."

Walter shook his head. "That's not what happened."

"Then explain to me why you withdrew from the competition." She still remembered the shock of learning he'd dropped out. That had been the final blow, when Hildy would have sworn it couldn't get any worse.

"Because you took your name off our story," he said, as if it should have been obvious.

"What choice did I have? You accused me of being a freeloader who was taking credit for other people's work. I had to show you how wrong you were by doing the opposite!"

"I thought you didn't care about me, Hildy. That was the killer." He pressed a hand to his chest, like he could still feel the ache.

"And I thought you didn't want to be associated with our shitty story, and you were humoring me because of who I was." She hesitated before admitting the rest. "You probably didn't even want to do . . . the other part."

"I would have crawled over broken glass to be with you." He waited until she looked at him, as if eye contact would make it harder for him to lie. Did he think she'd forgotten how easily he fooled her before?

"Try to spin it," she dared him.

"I wasn't going to win by myself for a story we wrote *together*. It was your idea!"

"That's so stupid! You could have had a full ride to journalism school. What the fuck!" Unable to contain the urge any longer, Hildy crossed the room to shove him in the shoulder.

Walter grabbed her hand when she tried to pull away. "That's not the only thing I lost."

This time, he let her go when she tugged her hand free of his grasp. Hildy took a step back. It would be easier to keep her thoughts in line if he wasn't touching her.

"And then out of the blue you start covering weddings, like suddenly human-interest stories aren't beneath you after all. 'Let me show you how it's done, silly socialite.' Though I guess that was an improvement over you writing about *me*. What was that about, Walter? You had to make sure to put me in my place, over and over again?"

He rubbed a hand over his jaw. "I don't even know where to start."

"Then let's not. We're not going to get anywhere by reliving some really shitty memories. As if once wasn't enough. Why don't we move on to the next super fun item on your agenda, like stabbing ourselves under the fingernail with rusty tweezers? Maybe some light dental work? At least that would be productive."

After another heavy exhale, something resembling a laugh punched out of his chest.

"Are you mocking me?" Hildy felt like a cat, ready to hiss and unleash her claws—or hide under the furniture until her dignity recovered.

"No." Walter spread his hands, a gesture of what looked like helplessness. "I can't believe we both walked away. I'm not sure if that counts as doing the right thing for the wrong reasons or vice versa."

It was a valid question, though Hildy had no intention of admitting that to him. "I just had a terrible thought."

"About then? Or now?"

"Both," she decided, after a moment's reflection. "What if we suck at this?"

"Talking to each other?"

"Figuring out the truth—which is pretty much the main job of journalists." Hildy shuddered at the prospect of her entire career being rooted in delusion. "No, I'm not going to neg myself. I know I'm awesome. And you're . . . not bad. At your job."

He sketched a mocking half bow. "So where does that leave us?"

Hildy felt like they'd just stepped out of a darkened movie theater and were standing on the sidewalk adjusting to daylight. "Right now?"

"Tonight, yes. And tomorrow. And after."

The words were neutral enough on the surface. And yet Hildy felt the temperature in the room tick up a few degrees, a slow simmer of possibility in the air.

"As in, are we still dagger-to-the-throat, or will we magically get over it like we've been lobotomized?"

Because it wasn't as if he'd prefaced all of this with an impassioned speech. *Oh, Hildy! How I yearn for you! The reason I'm dredging up this unpleasantness is that I've carried a torch all these years! Let's kiss and make up!*

He was probably doing some kind of therapeutic exercise where he had to make peace with his past so he could move forward to a normal relationship untainted by a tragic legacy of mistakes and misunderstandings. And who could blame him?

"The thing is, Walter, we tried to clear the air—"

"A little," he countered.

She let that slide for now. "I can't flip a switch and *abracadabra* forget all the things we said and did to each other."

It was as if her emotions had been taken out of their boxes and thrown around, making it impossible to tell which feeling went where. They were still there, vast and oceanic, but all Hildy could do was let them surge around her and hope she didn't drown.

No one had ever made her *feel* the way Walter did.

"There must be part of you that's still angry," she insisted. Hildy saw the instinctive denial form on his lips before he caught himself.

"I don't know. Honestly? I think all these years I've been trying to get your attention. Making my big stand, writing about you, competing with you—there's a pretty clear through line. *Notice me, Hildy. I'm right here.*"

"Like Ben Seward."

Walter shook his head. "Is he a tabloid guy?"

"No, he was a kid who used to chase me around the playground in second grade and pull my curls. 'Hildy, what's wrong with your hair?' *Yank*! All the adults were like, 'Isn't that cute? He has a crush on you! Be nice to him.' Which is what every little girl longs to hear: Better start placating the incels early!"

"And I remind you of him?"

"No. I never liked Ben Seward. He ate his boogers."

"A low bar, but I like to think I clear it."

Hildy refused to puff up his ego by agreeing. Besides, they were losing the plot. Again.

"I don't think it matters *why* we acted the way we did. It doesn't change the fact that we did real damage to each other. Compared to what, a *week* that was . . ."

"Perfect," he supplied, when she faltered. The look in his eyes dared her to deny it. Rather than perjure herself, she stayed stubbornly silent—which had the unfortunate effect of allowing Walter to go on.

"My whole life I had this constant list in my head. If only I was taller, or smarter, or faster, or my hair didn't stick up, or my knees weren't bony . . . but all that went quiet when I was with you. For the first time, I was glad to be exactly who and where I was." Walter paused, and Hildy knew he was waiting for her to say something: *yes, I understand*, or *it was the same for me*. But she couldn't, because she suspected it wasn't quite true. Walter hadn't made her feel *good enough*. She'd been unstoppable. Superpowered. It was as if he saw the person she'd planned to become once she got her shit together and stopped breaking out.

"That must mean something," he prodded when she didn't respond. He tried to hold eye contact, but Hildy looked away after a few scorching seconds. "Being with you was so easy, Hildy."

"Until it wasn't," she reminded him, ignoring the traitorous thump of her heart. "And it stayed that way for a long, long time. So who's to say which one was real?"

Walter hesitated. "What are the options?"

"The hating or the . . . not hating."

"I never hated you, Hildy."

"You could have fooled me."

"Come on. You know that's not what we do. Our fights are—"

Electric. Invigorating. Almost as big a rush as holding a finished copy of my magazine. "Childish," she said.

"Thrilling," he countered.

"See? We can't even agree about this. Not to mention the part where we're still competing for this story. You think that's going to be smooth sailing?"

"I think people can change. If they want to. And aren't stubbornly determined to assume the worst. There could be more to the story. A second act."

Also known as taking the risk of running her heart through the garbage disposal all over again. Because even if they hadn't really hated each other all these years, they'd both been deeply wounded. She was saved from having to admit she was afraid by a knock on the door.

"Oh good, you're both here!" Fiona said when Hildy answered. "See, Robbie? I told you they were hooking up."

"And I said there was too much tension for you to already be sleeping together," her fiancé filled in. "But I should have known Fee was right."

"What can I do for you?" Hildy asked, ignoring Walter's presence at her back. He couldn't just stand beside her like a normal person or hover at a respectful distance. She was pretty sure she could feel his breath tickling the nape of her neck. When she slid a foot back, intending to step on his toes, he grabbed her waist as if she'd slipped.

"Careful," he murmured, right into her ear. Because of course he was practically glued to her back now. Walter must be trying to make an argument with his body that he hadn't been able to sell with his mouth: *There's still something between us—and it's not animosity.*

As if being attracted to him had ever been the problem!

Fiona and Robbie exchanged a significant look.

"We wanted you to be the first to know. Since it was your idea." Fiona took Robbie's hand, arm swinging as if she could barely hold in her excitement.

"Which idea would that be?" Hildy asked, feigning calm.

"Getting married on our own terms." Fiona spoke with unmistakable pride. "We don't need the live peacocks, and a light show, and an orchestra, and a twenty-course tasting menu as long as we have each other."

Robbie nodded his support. "I want to marry Fiona the way she wants to get married."

"Wild and free! No shoes! No cameras! No passive-aggressive great-uncles!" Fiona sounded like she was warming up for a poetry slam.

When Walter's hand tightened at Hildy's waist, she couldn't tell if he was having a nervous spasm, or she'd swayed from the sensation of a trapdoor opening under her feet.

"Tell me more," Hildy said, as if they were discussing what Fiona had ordered for dinner. "What exactly are you envisioning?"

"Just like tonight." Fiona let go of Robbie to squeeze Hildy's shoulders. "Thank you so much for suggesting we go out there. It made everything so clear!"

Robbie gave an emphatic nod. "What she said."

"I love you so much!" Fiona threw herself at her fiancé, kissing him with an enthusiasm that made Hildy instinctively back away to give them privacy—sending her right into Walter's arms.

It felt a little like support, his warmth and strength there to prop her up. That was comforting but also confusing, because it was Walter.

"So you still want to get married at the castle?" Hildy asked when Fiona and Robbie were finished tonguing each other.

"Oh, for sure!" Fiona confirmed. "That part is perfect. We could go back right now!"

Robbie pointed at her, as if he'd never heard a better idea. "I'll grab the rings!"

"Hold that thought," Hildy said before Robbie could take off. "Could you give us one second?"

She bumped Walter backward so she could close the door, then sagged against it.

"What are we going to do?" he whispered.

"Why are you asking me?"

"Because you always have a plan."

"For ruining the wedding of the century and making an enemy of the man who could tank both our jobs? Not so much," she hissed. Though of course she did have the beginnings of an idea; Hildy was shocked, not dead. "We need to stall. Buy ourselves a few more hours."

She yanked the door open, relieved Fiona and Robbie were still there. "Hey, guys! Super exciting concept, but you know what would be even better?"

They shook their heads.

"Picture this: sunrise, birds singing, a new dawn. The sky turns pink and yellow behind the castle, slowly lighting up the trees. New life, rebirth, a brand-new day. Champagne and warm croissants.

It's pure, it's fresh, the symbolism is—" Hildy kissed her fingertips. "Chef's kiss. What do you think?"

Fiona turned to Robbie. The two of them had a telepathic conversation for a few seconds before Fiona screeched, "Yes! I love it! Plus we'll be able to see each other!" She turned to Hildy with an expectant air. "So like in a few hours? I don't actually know what time the sun comes up."

"Love the energy," Hildy said. "But I was thinking the sunrise after that—your actual wedding day. So you can be well rested."

"Excellent point." Walter grabbed Hildy by the shoulders, like a coach getting ready to send her back into the game. "Let's all get some sleep before the big day!"

"Okay. We're definitely going to 'rest.' Just like you!" Fiona winked at them before taking Robbie by the hand and dragging him away.

"We are so fucked," Hildy said when they were out of earshot. "We should never have told them about Carlee and Carlton."

Despite the gravity of the moment, Walter smiled. "I guess we're both still hung up on the past."

"Such as it was."

"You can admit it. We were good together, Hildy. I bet we still could be."

Maybe he was talking about journalism, but Hildy couldn't help glancing in the direction of the bed.

His brows shot up.

"We don't have time for that," she reminded him.

"So if time wasn't an issue—"

Hildy pressed a finger to his lips. "Hush. All this talk about second chances is giving me an idea."

NOW

36

Walter

TWO DAYS BEFORE THE PRESCOTT-SCHAFER WEDDING

TAMNIÈS, France—"I'm all ears," Walter said. Few things were more stimulating than having a front-row seat to one of Hildy's brain waves. Since he also happened to be cooking up a separate plan that depended on the success of hers, he was doubly intrigued.

"I've been talking to Fiona about this wedding for months, right? And yes, she's freaking out now—which I totally get—but a lot of this stuff was her idea. That girl was *pumped* about the bagpiper and her crystal shoes and the guys in lace-up shirts serving hors d'oeuvres."

"And the carriage," Walter reminded her.

"Exactly. The list goes on. These are things she's going to be sad to miss—*if* she misses them." She arched her brows, inviting him to guess.

"You're going to talk her out of the secret sunrise wedding?"

Hildy shook her head. "I'm going to gently encourage her to do both."

"Two weddings?"

"The little one and the big one. Private and public. The first will be for them, and the second will be for the world."

"Including us?"

"Yes. Assuming we manage to coax the runaway bride and groom back into the fold. Then we can worry about how all of this is going to play out in print."

"I have faith in you."

Her eyes narrowed.

"What? It was a compliment."

"You're being very chill about this."

"The weddings, plural?"

"That and how I tabled our other conversation." She was watching him closely, so Walter lifted a shoulder, affecting unconcern.

"I understand. Work comes first."

"Really? You're cool with pushing all that aside, no more fruitless trawling through our past?"

Walter could have pointed out that working together was how everything had started, so if anything was going to help them rediscover the harmony of the early days, it would be a joint project. But that would have been counterproductive. Hildy didn't want to hear it right now, so he wasn't going to rush her. If the long game was what it took, that's what Walter would play. What was another few days compared to a decade?

"You've given me a lot to think about," he said mildly. "Plenty of new information that I should probably let simmer."

"Like how I'm not actually the worst?"

He shook his head, not willing to cop to something he'd never really believed. "More like how you were feeling. And why. But we both have a lot riding on this, so I'm ready to lock in. What can I do?"

"You're going to take orders from me?"

"It wouldn't be the first time."

"You're not worried I'm going to screw you over?"

"I thought you said we don't have time for that."

"We don't," she said.

"Speaking of collaborations—"

"Here it comes," she muttered.

"What if we did the story together?"

She looked at him like he'd lost his mind. "Exclusivity is the whole point."

"Is it?"

"How would that work with your job?" she pressed. "Your editor is never going to let you moonlight for another publication."

He picked up one of the random decorative objects in the hammered copper bowl on the coffee table, pretending to inspect the surface of what appeared to be a wooden egg. "Then maybe I'd quit."

"Oh no you don't," Hildy said at once. "I'm not messing up your life again. I don't want to be your personal wrecking ball. Not that we're talking about that!" She glared at him as if he'd tried to trick her into revisiting the subject of their past. "We can help each other by making sure the wedding happens. After that it's every journalist for herself."

"If that's what you want."

"Seriously, Walter! What is this?"

"I thought we were making plans?"

She huffed in frustration. "Why are you being so agreeable?"

"I'm showing you we don't always have to fight."

"Yeah, except I'm starting to get twitchy, so the clock is ticking. Also, your case is flimsy as hell. Need I remind you that you can't write a trend piece based on one example?"

"I can think of other times we weren't mean to each other." He waited until she glanced at him, not quite able to hide her interest. "Those minutes behind the coatrack come to mind."

She turned away, but the side view only made the pink of her cheeks more apparent.

"I better go." He stood, taking a few slow steps across the plush rug until he was standing in front of her. "I don't want to make you uncomfortable."

Her chin lifted in defiance. "I'm totally relaxed."

"Glad to hear it." Walter extended an arm, knowing she'd take it as a dare.

Hildy reluctantly placed her smooth, slender hand in his. He wrapped his fingers around hers, enjoying the sensation of skin against skin for several stuttering heartbeats before shaking her hand.

"Go, team," he said quietly.

"Yes." She yanked her hand free, hiding it behind her back as if she feared he might lunge for it. "I'll talk to Fiona," she said briskly. "I already have a bunch more arguments lined up."

"That's what you've been thinking about this whole time?"

"Maybe." It would have been more convincing if she'd managed to meet his eyes.

"Top secret intel?" he guessed.

Her mouth worked like she was trying to force out the words. "I'm going to remind her about her sister's business. This would be a huge boost for Maude's retreat center. Whereas if the wedding doesn't happen, it'll have the taint of failure." She hesitated. "Does that sound like emotional blackmail?"

Walter pondered for a moment, so Hildy wouldn't think he was being glib. "Only if you're getting Fiona to act against her own interests."

"No, I honestly believe she'll be much happier in the long run if she goes through with the extra wedding."

"Then I guess I'll talk to Robbie."

"What's your angle?"

"I was going to mention the fire-eaters and the roasted pig."

"Everything flame-related," Hildy translated.

Walter gave a solemn nod. "That and the horses, obviously. Man stuff."

She'd find out about the rest soon enough.

* * *

Walter finally caught up with Robbie at the hotel restaurant midmorning. Fiona's fiancé was wearing a baseball cap and sunglasses like he was trying to go incognito, but the effort was undermined by the faded letters on the back of his old jersey spelling out his last name.

"Hey, Robbie."

He jumped, spilling coffee on his plate of melon slices and smoked duck. "Scared me," Robbie said. "I thought you were Fiona's dad. Or my dad. Or one of my uncles. Or the pastor."

Walter was beginning to wonder how long this list would go on when Robbie shook himself, mustering a pale shadow of his usual grin.

"That's just how it is, right? Everybody means well."

"Yes," Walter agreed, though he wasn't entirely sure what they were talking about. "Do you have a minute? I was hoping we could chat."

"You too?" Robbie sighed. "I mean, yeah. No problem." He gestured at the empty place setting across the table. Most of the other guests had been whisked away on a boat cruise, or kayaking if they wanted something more athletic, so they had the place to themselves.

"How are you holding up?" Walter asked, watching Robbie reach for the dish of sugar cubes before changing his mind.

"Good." Robbie sipped his black coffee, wincing a little. "You can just dive right in, you know. I don't need the whole warm-up."

"I'm sorry?" Walter's best guess was that Hildy must have already spoken to Fiona.

"You want to give me some man-to-man advice, right?" Robbie

calmly sliced his melon into bite-size pieces. "Before I get married. And become a man."

The "disguise" suddenly made sense. "I take it you've been getting a lot of that?"

Robbie nodded. "Mostly about investment strategies."

"I wouldn't be the one to speak on that."

"Sometimes it's about other things." Robbie speared a piece of melon with his fork. "Holidays. In-laws. Gift-giving. Communication styles. Sex."

"That's . . . very personal."

"Yeah. I didn't know Pastor Chris had it in him. But I guess he hears a lot of stuff, from counseling married couples."

On balance, Walter thought he'd prefer advice about the stock market.

"And then I feel bad," Robbie continued, dabbing his mouth with a napkin, "because they don't know about the—" He glanced behind him before mouthing the words "secret wedding." "It's like I'm being dishonest even though I'm not saying anything."

"A lie of omission."

Robbie looked impressed. "I guess that's part of your job, knowing the words for everything."

"That's actually what I wanted to talk to you about."

"Improving my vocabulary?" Robbie grimaced at the prospect of adding yet another item to his Becoming a Man checklist.

"Keeping secrets," Walter corrected. "Maybe there's a way you don't have to feel bad."

"That sounds nice. Between you and me"—he pointed his fork at Walter—"I've been a little worried we got caught up in a moment and it snowballed. Me and Fee tend to get excited about stuff and go all in, like 'yes, let's do this!' And then later we look at each other like, 'wait, why did we think we wanted a hydroponic garden?' It's a lot of work. And you have to keep doing it, over and over."

Walter nodded. That tracked with what he knew about gardening—and Robbie and Fiona.

"And that's fine if it's something we do with our balcony," Robbie continued. "We can change our minds. There will still be tomatoes in the world. But with the wedding, people came all this way. They're going to be disappointed." He looked to Walter for confirmation.

"There could still be tomatoes. Figuratively speaking." It seemed best not to linger on that moment of brilliance, so Walter hurried on. "Let's look at the big picture. As someone who's been to a lot of these things the last few years, I've had some realizations about weddings, and relationships, and priorities. There are parts that seem important in the moment that don't matter in the long run." He broke off when Robbie raised his hand. "Yes?"

"So you *are* giving me life lessons?"

"I'm building to something concrete."

"Oh, good!" Robbie sent a longing look at the breadbasket.

"Why don't you have a piece, with some of this fresh butter?"

"Is that the advice?"

"It's not *the* advice. That was more of a general suggestion. Don't deny yourself things you really, really want."

"As in this actual bread or is that another metaphor?"

"Both." How many motivational speeches had the poor guy listened to this week? Walter needed to keep it simple if he didn't want to lose Robbie. "Weddings can be chaotic. You're caught up in something that takes on its own momentum. Like a cyclone. It's totally natural to think, 'Wait, whose wedding is this? Why does it matter if we have this color napkin or that one? I'm marrying a person, not a three-ring circus.'" Walter pretended to juggle invisible balls. "That's how it is for *any* wedding, so multiply by a thousand for you and Fiona."

Robbie paused in the act of buttering a slice of bread, brow furrowing. "So sneaking away *is* a good idea?"

"Maybe. Partly. But there's more to it. There's the choice you made—this person, more than anyone else, forever. That's between the two of you. This is the moment where you acknowledge that you found someone you're crazy about. Partly because they make you that way, but it's also that when you met her you realized, 'that's it for me. I'm done. She is better than the best I could ever have imagined. I'm going to hold on as long as I can.' Because it's impossible to imagine feeling that way about anyone else."

Walter's thoughts tilted, tumbling from this table to wherever Hildy was right now. How long had it taken him to understand that no matter what he told himself was going on between them, part of him had never let go?

"Totally," Robbie said, forcing Walter's attention back to the present. "That's Fee for me."

"The thing about the wedding is that it's a chance to build this whole support system around you. This is your inner circle, of family and friends and people who are invested in your happiness, coming together in this kind of ring of strength. Like at a castle."

Robbie set down his bread, brushing the crumbs off his hands. "And the moat is like the outer circle. Business associates and our parents' friends?"

Walter nodded as if he'd been about to say that very thing. "You're giving all of them a gift, by letting them share your joy and excitement."

"And a really good dinner."

"That too. But you're getting something in return. It's not just symbolic, the power of a community that's rooting for you and witnessing your commitment to each other. All those people are there to lift you up and strengthen this bond between the two of you, by seeing it and believing in it."

"Like little kids believing in fairies." Robbie popped the rest of the bread into his mouth before taking a sip of coffee. "So what I'm hearing is that you *don't* think we should do the secret wedding?"

"What I'm proposing is . . . actually, it's Hildy's idea."

"She's smart."

"Very," Walter agreed.

"And pretty." He gave Walter a sly look.

"That's not really relevant to the matter at hand, but yes."

"Okay." Robbie shook his head, laughing under his breath. "*Relevant*. I like that."

"Hildy thinks you should have the secret wedding *and* the other one," Walter said, all business. "As planned."

"Get married *twice*?" Robbie made an effort to lower his voice. "Is that even legal?"

"Think of it as a vow renewal. You say 'I do' quietly, for the two of you, all woodsy and natural, and then you say it again, in front of your community. And they're like a chorus that amplifies your voices, you know?"

Robbie grabbed another piece of bread. "And nobody would be sad."

"It flows both ways," Walter agreed. "The giving and the getting."

"Like the QR code we have on the place cards for people to donate to the World Wildlife Fund. I guess we'd miss out on that too, if we don't have a wedding."

"You'd also be doing me a solid." Walter swallowed the strangeness of confiding in Robbie Schafer, of all people.

"Because of your story?" The heartbreaking part was that Robbie didn't even sound disillusioned, as if being a pawn in other people's moneymaking schemes was part of life.

"This is more of a personal situation."

"It's about Hildy," Robbie guessed, lighting up with interest.

Walter nodded. "I'm kind of hoping seeing your wedding will soften her heart—toward me. Make her feel optimistic about love."

"That would be so cool!" Robbie shoved him in the shoulder. "If my love for Fiona was so powerful, it was *contagious*."

Walter didn't see any need to clarify that it wasn't the falling he and Hildy had trouble with; that had been accomplished ages ago. The issue for them was being brave enough to admit how they felt—and do something about it.

"That's the magic of weddings. Two people who love each other, standing up and telling the whole world. What's more powerful than that?"

Robbie blinked at him, a slight furrow between his brows. "That's beautiful, man."

"I learned it from Hildy. She once told me that you can see everything good about people at a wedding." And some of the bad, but he didn't need to remind Robbie of that. "Before that I didn't really get it, you know? I thought it was just a party with funny clothes."

Robbie leaned back in his chair. "You really like her, don't you?"

"Yeah, I do."

"But does *she* know that?"

"I don't know," Walter admitted.

"Then you gotta fix that, stat. You don't want to waste any more time." Robbie stood, gathering his dishes. "Damn, that felt good."

"The carbs?"

He shook his head. "Giving somebody else advice for a change."

NOW

37

Walter

THE DAY OF THE PRESCOTT-SCHAFER WEDDING

MARQUAY, France—The rising sun painted the ancient stone of the castle walls in soft pastels as Fiona Prescott married Robin Schafer in an enchanted French garden.

That was how Walter might start the story—if he were writing it. Set the scene, transition into a few tantalizing details about the clothes ("the bride was resplendent in her favorite nightgown") and styling ("a crown of wildflowers, still wet with dew, picked by Ms. Prescott and her sister"). In the next paragraph, he'd jump back in time to Robbie and Fiona's first meeting, followed by the obligatory mention of her famous father, so-and-so of Prescott Industries, and their upper-crust zip codes and educational achievements.

But Walter wasn't reporting on this wedding, and neither was Hildy. They had both agreed to cover the other "wedding" instead, keeping this one hidden from the world.

He looked to his right, where Hildy was standing with a bottle of champagne dangling from one hand, lit from behind by the warm light of dawn.

"What do you think?" he asked.

She brought the bottle to her lips before offering it to him. "About the bubbles? Breakfast of champions."

"About the Prescott-Schafer wedding." He took a judicious sip.

It wasn't the time to overindulge. Walter needed his mind and his body to be fully alert if the rest of the morning was going to play out the way he hoped.

"Magnificent," Hildy said without hesitation. "Wedding of the year."

"Is it everything you imagined?"

She smiled, and his heart lurched in his chest. "It's more."

"Is this the kind of wedding you'd want?" In all their previous run-ins, Walter had never dared to ask. Now it seemed vitally important for him to know.

"Oh no, I'd need a much bigger castle than this. With a helipad." Hildy pressed her lips together in a vain attempt not to laugh.

"You never thought about it?" He kept his tone light, even though he was burning with curiosity. "As many weddings as we've been to, you must have opinions."

"I always have *opinions*, Walter. It doesn't mean I keep a scrapbook under my bed with 'My Dream Wedding, by Hildy' spelled out in fuzzy stickers on the cover."

"That just tells me you're too embarrassed to share. Is it a theme wedding? Are there costumes?"

"If I ever get married—and that's a big *if*—the wedding will depend on the person. It's not like I'm plunking some rando into my puppet theater. Insert Spouse Here."

"That sounds reasonable."

She paused with the neck of the bottle halfway to her mouth. "Are you doing that agreeable thing again?"

"No, Hildy. I'm just plain agreeing with you."

"Oh."

"I know. Someone should alert the media."

She fished her phone out of her pocket. "Note to self: On this date at way-too-early o'clock, Walter Burns finally acknowledged my superior reasoning skills."

He was tempted to give her more reasons to gloat, just so she'd keep looking at him like that, but he needed to build his case in a semiorganized fashion. Hildy liked a plan. Or at least, she liked *her* plans. Walter would have to hope she could appreciate one that happened to be about and for her, even if she wasn't doing the scheming. Maybe it would be a nice change of pace, like when someone made a humble home-cooked meal for a professional chef.

Fiona and Robbie came scampering over from their labyrinth walk, hand in hand and glowing with happiness. Their bare feet were speckled with grass.

"I love my secret wedding," Fiona informed them, not for the first time.

"Secret time, secret place." Robbie shook his hips to a beat only he could hear.

"Secret vows." His bride touched her lips before pressing her hand to her heart, as though tucking away the words only she and Robbie had heard before Maude used her hastily obtained online credentials to pronounce them husband and wife. "And I don't even have to be sad it's over, because I'm having a whole other wedding."

"Bonus wedding!" Hildy held up her free hand for a high five.

"With all the pretty horses," Robbie chimed in, spinning his bride.

"I'm going to be sitting there getting my hair done, and while everyone messes with me, I'll be hiding the best, biggest secret." Fiona turned to Robbie, taking his other hand like they were about to play ring-around-the-rosy.

"We got mar-ried," she chanted.

Robbie quickly joined in, breaking off only to throw a hopeful look at Walter. "Do you have any maracas?"

He shook his head. Procuring predawn croissants and champagne and transportation and sneaking the bride and groom out of the hotel—especially on top of Walter's other preparations—had exhausted his resourcefulness.

They watched Fiona and Robbie waltz across the grass. Maude and her Frenchman had already wandered off, ostensibly to look at an interesting shrub, but they weren't fooling anyone. Walter wondered if Hildy had noticed they were the last two people who hadn't paired off. When he snuck a glance, she was raising the champagne bottle to her lips.

"Oops," she said. "Last sip."

"That's okay. I was done."

"I wasn't worried about that. You don't know the French rule about finishing a bottle?"

"I must have missed that day at finishing school."

"I'll give you a hint, Man of the People. It's like catching the bouquet." She raised the bottle, squinting at the green glass. "Might be a couple of drops left. I should give this to Maude, so she can be the next one headed down the aisle."

Walter plucked the bottle from her hands, upending it into his mouth. The barest hint of sweetness hit his tongue.

"Problem solved," he announced, setting the bottle on the grass.

She blinked at him. "Okay, then. Let me know where to send your gift."

"I will." He offered her his hand. "Can I have this dance?"

"There's no music."

"I'll hum." He kicked off his shoes. "I hear dancing barefoot in the grass is something everyone should experience at least once."

"Maybe I do it all the time. I could be the scourge of golf courses everywhere."

"But you've never danced with me." He let a hint of challenge creep into the words.

"Fine." She tossed her hair, a gesture he recognized as Hildy's version of cracking her knuckles. "If you insist."

When she stepped into his space, he was tempted to forget

about dancing and pull her closer, but he suspected this conversation would go better if they were in motion. The physical side of their relationship had always been less thorny than the talking part, which was borderline ironic for two people who made their living from words.

Walter spun her in the direction of the forest, humming under his breath. It took Hildy a few bars to recognize the tune.

"I guess it is a Whole New World for those two." She looked over her shoulder at the distant forms of Fiona and Robbie, waltzing toward the castle. "I didn't realize you were such a sap."

"I'm feeling optimistic."

Hildy squinted up at him, as if she sensed a hidden meaning. "About marriage? Or your career?"

"I've been thinking," he said, dodging the question.

"Don't hurt yourself." She winked at him, and Walter sent up a silent wish that Hildy would hold on to that playful energy a little longer.

"It's about what you said—that we've done too much damage to each other. I disagree."

"Of course you do," she huffed, as if that proved her point.

"You didn't make my life worse, Hildy."

"That's empirically incorrect."

His hand flexed against her lower back, drawing her closer. "What do you think my life would have looked like if I hadn't met you?"

"You would have won the fellowship! Just for starters."

Walter shook his head. "How? If you weren't my partner, I would never have done a wedding story. And I definitely wouldn't have had the confidence to start my own group. Without you, I would have been the fourth name on a mediocre article about a traffic stop or a zoning violation. Maybe I would have come away thinking I wasn't cut out for journalism. I could be an accountant right now."

She frowned like he'd been holding out on her. "Are you good at math?"

"It's a hypothetical, Hildy. I'm trying to say that I wouldn't be who I am or have a job that lets me travel the world and eat cake for a living if I'd never met you. So you can tell yourself it was all a mistake, but the way I see it is that you made me feel like I could do anything. When I thought you didn't give a shit, it hurt, yes. It also fired me up. Competing with you, trying to get your attention? That pushed me more than anything. And every time our paths crossed, that was a day I felt fully alive. Everything else was filler."

He watched expressions play over her face like clouds racing across the sky on a windy day: surprise chased by doubt, a flicker of fear, and what might have been a trace of hope.

"I don't think anger is the real reason we've been circling each other all these years," he said, pressing his advantage. "Do you want to know my theory?"

"You may as well tell me." She tried to sound pouty, but Walter wasn't fooled. He could feel the tension in her body.

"Because we both know we haven't gotten the full story." They had reached the edge of the woods, the trees offering the illusion of privacy. Walter stopped moving but didn't let go.

"All this time, we've been chasing the truth," he said.

"Which is what?"

"I don't know exactly. I need your help to figure that out. But I can tell you right now that you didn't ruin my life. And I definitely wouldn't have been better off without you." Just the thought of a life without Hildy made him shudder.

"What are you saying?" she asked in a small voice.

"I want to try something different—if you're game."

"Like what?"

"Can I kiss you?"

"Right now?"

"It's a wedding. People always kiss at weddings."

"If you're the bride and groom."

"That seems so limiting." He let go of her hand to gently draw his thumb along her cheekbone. "You need a reason? Kiss me because you want to. And it's been too long. And I've probably been in love with you for ten years."

She rose onto her tiptoes, holding on to his shoulders. "Probably?"

"I'm trying not to scare—"

She cut off the rest of his sentence with her lips.

The next time his conscious brain surfaced, Hildy's dress was pushed up around her hips and he had backed her against a tree. It took Walter several breaths to remind himself that ravishing Hildy in the woods was not the plan. The first time they slept together was not going to involve bark burn.

He eased back a step, gesturing between them. "You can't tell me there's nothing there." Walter reached into his pocket and pulled out a note. He'd spritzed it with his cologne for the full effect.

"What is this?" she asked warily.

"An invitation." Walter felt as if he'd handed her his heart instead of a folded square of paper. "The ball is in your court."

NOW

38

Hildy

THE DAY OF THE PRESCOTT-SCHAFER WEDDING

TAMNIÈS, France—*I'll be waiting for you in Room 9.*

That was it: the full contents of Walter's supersecret message. Except not really, because there were a lot of invisible layers at play. This was clearly a callback to the note she'd left him all those summers ago. Apart from the room number, obviously—and the fact that it smelled like grown-up Walter instead of seventeen-year-old Hildy's excessively sweet perfume.

She also doubted he'd answer the door in a lacy purple nightie. *If* she knocked.

Assuming he was really committed to the reenactment bit, Walter was basically asking her to have sex with him. Except they weren't clueless teenagers anymore, which honestly sounded like a bonus. Hildy had no desire to relive the nerves and fumbling of her actual first time, much less their thwarted hotel hookup.

Back then, her motive for taking that step with Walter had been a muddle of affection and attraction alongside a healthy dose of wanting to get it done, so she could be an official member of the Sexually Experienced Club. The idea of sleeping with Walter affected her in a very different way now. It was grounded in her body, an immediate rush of heat at the thought of his naked weight on top of her. Or underneath; the image varied. While that mental movie played out, it was easy to ignore the faint alarm bells ringing in the background.

Until she remembered that this was *Walter* she was fantasizing about, sweating and moving and breathing. If she did this with him, Hildy would be letting her guard all the way down. Which was a lot scarier than dropping her panties.

She slid that trepidation to one side of the scale. On the other, there was the fact that she wanted this—wanted *him*—a lot.

Hildy was still contemplating during her long, scented bath, and the meticulous moisturizing that followed. (Things she would have done anyway, due to the thigh-high slit on the dress she planned to wear later, at the "real" wedding that was actually a dupe.)

Could it be that Walter was right about their past not being a toxic dumpster fire? He was good at getting to the heart of a story—at least as a reporter—which made it hard to dismiss his argument out of hand. Plus, it was appealing to think she hadn't been the bane of his existence.

As for Walter's role in *her* life . . . if she looked past the hurt, Hildy could admit that some of the hard parts had been good for her. Without Walter's judgment in the back of her mind, she wouldn't have worked so hard to become independent. It would have been too easy to rely on her family's money, even at the cost of compromising her vision. Hildy might not have started *Life, Styled* if she wasn't so determined to prove she could do it. And she was *fiercely* proud of that magazine—the way she imagined a mother who actually wanted to raise her child would feel about a beloved daughter.

There was a staircase in her brain, one step leading to another and then another. If she hadn't been a blight on Walter's prospects, and vice versa, it opened a window onto a different view of her past. Maybe waking up every day bouncing out of her skin at the thought of seeing him again wasn't the worst mistake of her life.

Did that mean she could have it back? All the spark and delight and wonder? When she tried to remember how it felt to be that young and innocent, Hildy pictured Fiona and Robbie frolicking through the meadow, all soft and fresh and full of hope.

Except turning back the clock to their teenage dream wasn't an option for Hildy and Walter. She'd been partly right too, about the lingering marks of experience, but being older and wiser wasn't all bad. Hildy liked this version of herself, a little sharper and more sophisticated. And she was not indifferent to the adult edition of Walter, with his confidence and a strength that went beyond the physical.

At the same time, Hildy had a hunch that underneath the good hair and tailored clothing, traces remained of their younger selves. She wasn't sure if it was a remnant of her adolescent brain that kept drawing her back to Walter or something less immature. Either way, part of her could not stop wondering: *Maybe this time?*

* * *

"Hildy," Walter said when he opened the door. It sounded more like a sigh of relief than a greeting.

He moved to the side, and she stepped past him. Eight AM was a funny time for an assignation, but since when had they done things in the normal order? There was enough light filtering through the drawn curtains for her to see the trail of rose petals leading to the bed. Music played faintly in the background.

Her throat tightened. Walter remembered. More than that, he'd made an actual effort to recreate the scene.

"When did you do all this?" Hildy tried to sound unaffected even though she was melting on the inside.

"Before the wedding."

"So, in the middle of the night?" She had a vision of him creeping through the hotel garden plucking rose petals under cover of darkness.

Walter glanced around the room as if seeing it through her eyes. "Is it too cheesy?"

"It's the perfect amount of cheese."

He rocked back on his heels, looking everywhere but at her. "Well, thanks for coming."

It felt like they were communicating via translator, with a slightly artificial lag between sentences. Having made up her mind to be here, Hildy didn't want to waste time dancing around the issue. "It's weird, right?"

"What is?" he asked.

"Us. Like this."

"Standing ten feet apart?"

"That's part of it."

Walter took several steps in her direction. "Better?"

"I don't know." Somehow Hildy had envisioned them tumbling into bed without needing to discuss it. Right now that seemed as probable as bungee jumping without a harness. They were too busy choking on this strange new *politeness*. "Do we just hit the reset button? Different era, commencing now."

"We can ease into it. There's no hurry."

"It's been ten years, Walter. We're not exactly rushing things. I just . . ."

"You just what?" he prompted, when she didn't finish the thought.

"I'm not sure how to act. Are we supposed to be serious now? What are the rules?"

He nodded slowly, brow creased in thought. "You want something more formal to mark the occasion. Like a treaty?"

"Or a parade. And speeches. For Armistice Day." It was a funny mental image, even though the last thing they needed was more pressure. She smoothed her hands over her hips, watching him track the motion with his eyes. At least she had his full attention.

"It wasn't like this in the woods."

"Yeah, well." Enchanted forests didn't come with a bunch of

expectations. There were no beds daring you to find out whether the reality of sleeping with Walter Burns could possibly compare to ten years of sexual tension. They needed a way to get past this last barrier between them.

Hildy crooked a finger at him. "Come here."

Walter pointed at himself.

"Yes, you." She indicated the spot directly in front of her. When they were standing toe-to-toe, Hildy placed her hands on his shoulders. Walter ducked his head to kiss her, but she leaned away. "Wait."

"You want to talk more?" To his credit, it sounded like a sincere offer, despite the pinch of resignation around his eyes.

"Wouldn't that be a role reversal?" She was tempted to torture him by pretending, but that wasn't the game she wanted to play right now. "Are you sure you've let go of all our troubles? No lingering resentments or festering grievances?"

He looked down at her hands, which had moved to his top button. "I—no? Nothing festering on my end."

Hildy nodded as she undid the first button. "Then you won't mind if I double-check."

His throat moved as he swallowed. "Be my guest."

"I'll need to be thorough," she warned, undoing another button.

"Touch me anywhere you have to." He lifted his chin. "I can handle it."

"You're very brave," she murmured, running a finger down the center of his chest. Walter shivered. "You okay?"

He opened his mouth to speak before opting for a nod instead.

When she had slipped the last button free of the fabric, Hildy spread her palms over his stomach, sliding them up and over his rib cage, past the wild beating of his heart to the smooth muscle of his shoulders. The shirt slipped down, and he eased his arms free of the sleeves.

Hildy took a moment to appreciate Walter's upper body with

her eyes before running her hands back down to his stomach. She pressed one thumb into the hollow of his belly button.

"Find anything?" he asked, choking back a laugh.

"All clear so far." Her hands settled at his waist. "Looks like the only thing you've been hiding are these muscles."

"You've seen me without a shirt before."

"I know. But that was incidental nudity. Now it's *for* me." She slid a finger across his nipple, just because she could.

"I was always for you."

Walter was deliberate with language, so she knew his use of *I* instead of *it* wasn't an accident.

"Hildy."

She wet her lips. Was he waiting for her to make a declaration in return?

"I should do you now," he said, eyeing her dress. "To keep things equal."

It was a fair point. She held her arms out to the side, silently offering permission. *Have at it.*

Walter reached for the bow at her neck. "It's like a present I get to unwrap."

"I thought you were going to say it's like checking each other for ticks."

"Am I that much of a downer?"

"I wish," she sighed. "It would have been easier to resist you."

"Is that so?" The pads of his fingers skimmed her bare shoulder. "You have the softest skin I have ever touched."

Hildy suppressed the urge to tell him about her new body oil. He probably wasn't looking for product recommendations right now. Turning her back, she shimmied the dress down to her waist, glancing at him over her shoulder before cutting her eyes in the direction of her bra strap. "A little help?"

There was a faint pressure, followed an instant later by the relief of the band loosening.

"Smooth."

"I've been practicing."

"Department store mannequin?"

"My apartment is full of them. I hope you don't mind a little competition." His arms came around her from behind so she could feel his laughter against her back.

Being wrapped up in Walter made her whole body feel like softened wax. She'd been right to think they needed to shed those last scraps of restraint, so they could finally come together like this, skin to skin, slow and careful so they both knew it was a deliberate choice, not a momentary madness.

Or maybe her libido talked a good game when all it really wanted was to get him naked. Sometimes Hildy was a mystery even to herself.

Whatever. It was working out well. "The end justifies the means."

He kissed the back of her neck, a slow press of breath and lips. "I'm glad you think so."

When the rest of Hildy's clothes had joined Walter's in a pile on the floor, she turned in his arms, watching him lose the battle not to stare at her breasts. She hadn't really expected him not to enjoy her body, but Walter's transparent admiration felt like bathing in milk and honey.

"Hildy." He pressed his face against the curve of her neck, inhaling deeply. "I'm afraid you're going to wreck me. In a whole new way."

She knew exactly what he meant. Because it wasn't just today they were looking at. Once they broke through the dam of old wounds, the only thing stopping them was . . . them.

"I don't want to screw this up," she whispered, as if that would keep him from hearing the vulnerability in her voice.

"Sex?"

"All of it."

Walter shook his head. "It's you and me, Hildy."

"What does that mean?" If he was referring to their track record, it wasn't exactly an auspicious sign.

"Have you ever felt this way about anyone else?" He looked right into her eyes.

"No." There wasn't even a close second.

"Me neither." Walter slid his hands down to grasp her hips. When he pulled her closer, a familiar heat flared, her body craving more of his touch. "Don't think of it as a shocking twist. Maybe we were always headed for this moment."

"It took us long enough." Hildy shook her head at the thought of their mutual bumbling. "What were we thinking?"

"Maybe the problem is that we weren't thinking."

"Or thinking too much." The back-and-forth felt like slipping on a favorite sweater.

Walter took her hand, turning it over to press a kiss to her palm. "Hildy."

"Walter." She tried to copy his inflection but wasn't sure it had the same panty-melting effect.

He brushed his lips over the pulse point in her wrist. Was he planning to dismantle her inch by inch?

"Are you teasing me?" she demanded. "I thought we put that behind us."

"This is the fun kind of teasing. Not that it wasn't fun before," he added, when she started to protest.

Hildy summoned her sternest expression. "Okay, but we don't have all day."

"I've been waiting half my life for this. I was planning to take my time." As if to illustrate, he gently bit her earlobe.

"What if we get interrupted? *Again*." It felt weirdly freeing to mention the past so casually after all these years pretending their history was dead and buried.

He wrapped his arms around her, lips finding hers in an

open-mouthed kiss. "We should have a few hours at least. It's still early."

"How about this?" Hildy countered, holding his chin in place with her thumb and forefinger. "One time fast so I don't lose my mind, and then you can go slow."

"If that's what you want."

She should have known he was capitulating too easily. It turned out Walter was humoring her when he promised not to make her wait. Then again, it was hard to complain while reclining on a bed of rose petals as he kissed his way down her body.

Hildy felt like a goddess. Except this goddess was very much on the physical plane as opposed to floating in some distant Olympus. A goddess on vacation! She thought of a line from the old-fashioned wedding vows that had always struck her as surprisingly racy for a church: *with my body, I thee worship*.

As his mouth ventured to ever more sensitive places, she felt cherished—and insanely turned on. "Walter."

"Hmm?"

"What are you doing?"

"Living out my teenage dreams."

That distracted her. "Is it— I mean, am I like you imagined?"

He lifted his head. "How could the real you ever be less than the fantasy?"

"I don't know. But I'm kind of a competitive person."

Walter grinned. "You don't say."

"Just trying to be honest."

His palm traced the curve of her waist. "Nothing compares to the Hildy I can touch. The Hildy whose heart I can hear beating." He brought his cheek to rest against her chest. It probably sounded like she had a hummingbird trapped inside her rib cage.

"What if you let me be in charge?" Walter lifted his head to kiss her collarbone. "Just for a few minutes? Then you can go back to ruling the world."

It was an intriguing proposition, especially when his tongue flicked the hollow at the base of her throat. Walter hadn't told her to *calm down* or *loosen up*. He was offering to take care of her, because he understood how she was wired. When was the last time Hildy had yielded control to someone else?

Somehow she knew this wasn't a power play. Walter wasn't trying to score a point or assert his dominance. He was asking her for permission. Could she rely on him to take over for a little bit, so she could concentrate on the feeling of his mouth traveling inch by torturous inch from her hip to the delicate bones of her ankle?

What would it feel like to let go?

Walter sat back at the end of the bed, settling her leg on his lap. His thumbs massaged the ball of her foot as if he knew she was still holding on to a last thread of tension and was determined to work out every scrap of resistance. "What do you say, Hildy?"

It took a few seconds for her to access her verbal abilities. "About what?"

He kissed her instep. "Do you trust me?"

That was the question, wasn't it? The big one, lurking behind everything else two people might ask each other. She felt a fleeting impulse to close her eyes or turn her head, going inward to avoid his searching gaze, but it wasn't time to hide. There was no more winning or losing side, no advantage to claim. They were in this together.

After all these years, the answer turned out to be simple.

She smiled at him. "I do."

They both knew how powerful those two little words could be.

NOW

39

Hildy

THE DAY OF THE PRESCOTT-SCHAFER WEDDING

TAMNIÈS, France—"Walter, are you awake?"

"I am now."

They'd fallen asleep eventually, despite the daylight seeping into the room. He stretched his arms over his head before lowering one over Hildy's side to pull her closer. "I'm not a teenager anymore, Hildy. I need some recovery time."

"This is about work. I have an idea." She felt his energy shift, less sleepy now and more alert. But he didn't let go of her.

"I'm listening."

"I figured out a way we can both do our stories. You can do the newsy version—who what where, and how it went down. Here it is, on the record. Boom."

"What does that leave for you?"

"*Life, Styled* is going to do a deep dive on the backstory. The Prescott sisters, their relationship, two paths diverging—marriage versus starting your own business, the eternal struggle—and it all culminates in the wedding, complete with exclusive full-page color photos. Or does it?"

"I'm guessing no."

"Exactly." She threaded her fingers through his, holding their linked hands over her heart. "You think the story's over, but then you turn the page and it's about what comes after. Maude starting her business. Maybe finding love of her own. We'll go big on the castle. I'm thinking a sweepstakes, a lucky reader and her best girls winning a deluxe trip to France. Fully sponsored, obviously. Airlines, restaurants, shopping spree."

"Wow."

"I know. And Mr. Prescott can't bitch because both of his daughters get the spotlight."

"When did you come up with all this?"

"You mean, was I planning the next issue of my magazine while we were having sex?"

His shoulders moved in a shrug she felt against her back. "Not to be insecure, but I thought I had your full attention."

"You did." She kissed his hand. "This came to me while I was falling asleep."

"It sounds amazing, Hildy."

"I know. And much more our brand—exploring different facets of a woman's life, centering relationships that go beyond the romantic. Etcetera." Even though she couldn't see his face, Hildy sensed the worry wafting off Walter. "What is it?"

"I just want to make sure it's not because of . . . this. You didn't change all your plans because we slept together?"

She pushed away just far enough to roll onto her back. "Yes, you ensorcelled me with your magic wand. I am no longer capable of independent thought." Reaching up, she pressed a finger to the crease between his brows. "Give me a break. I'm still the boss of me, Walter. You are lucky enough to be witnessing me at the peak of my powers."

"Very lucky," he agreed, slipping a finger into her hair and wrapping it in one of her curls.

"I'll grant you that it's possible the sex enhanced my creativity. It felt like I reached a higher state of being a couple of times there."

"Does that make me your muse?"

"Let's not get ahead of ourselves."

"But it is something you should do regularly," he said, as if he were a doctor dispensing medical advice. "To keep yourself in top form."

"Like flossing my teeth?"

"Exactly." He lowered his head to kiss her shoulder. "I'm glad you told me."

"It's nice not being rivals, isn't it?"

"Very. Also, I was going to text my editor in a few hours to tell him I'd lost the story."

"Ha!" She poked him in the chest. "Too late, loser. Somebody beat you to the punch. How does it feel to come in second *again*?"

"Honestly? Pretty great." He gave an exaggerated shiver. "Except my lower back is a little cold. I don't usually sleep naked."

"Poor baby." Hildy reached over him to grab the edge of the sheet, tucking it up under his chin. "All these things I still need to learn about you. Are you a one leg in and one leg out person? Full burrow?"

"Depends on the season. You'll have to stick around to find out."

She wormed her way under the sheet, pressing herself against him. "You know what always makes me think of you?"

"Sunsets?" he guessed. "Wild horses? Piano ballads?"

Hildy shook her head. "Washing my sheets."

"Seriously? I'm going to have to up my game."

"You know exactly what I'm talking about." She tickled her way up his rib cage. "Don't pretend you forgot our meet-cute."

Walter grabbed her hand and brought it to his lips. "It rings a bell."

Some Enchanted Evening

By Walter Burns

MARQUAY, France—Even the peacocks were on their best behavior when Fiona Prescott and Robin Schafer exchanged vows in a remote pocket of the French countryside, watched over by the approximately three hundred guests fortunate enough to receive an invitation to a social event billed by many as "the wedding of the century." The bride and groom appeared remarkably carefree during a ceremony their wedding designer described as a "blend of medieval pomp and enchanted-forest whimsy."

The medieval part came courtesy of the real-life castle painstakingly restored for the occasion by the bride's family, under the watchful eye of local historic preservation experts. As for the whimsy, credit the opulent setting, the perfect summer evening, and the effervescent bride and groom, who had to pause several times during their first dance to allow for laughter. Who needs champagne when you have that much joie de vivre?

"Mom always said this was the most romantic place in the world," the bride said. "And she was so right. Being here was a magical experience, and not just for me and Robbie."

"Love was definitely in the air," the groom agreed, presumably in reference to other romances rumored to have sparked—or rekindled—during the lead-up to the main event, a weeklong foray into luxury travel with a side of personal enrichment.

When not dining on local delicacies, guests were ferried among cultural attractions including prehistoric caves and ornamental gardens, culminating in the reveal of the top secret wedding venue: a castle fit for a fairy tale.

Even the most guarded observer would have been hard-pressed to describe the Prescott-Schafer wedding as anything but a happy ending for a love story that first began years ago.

See ENCHANTED, page A7

INTO THE WOODS: THE OTHER PATH

By the staff of *Life, Styled*

In fairy tales, a handsome prince rides to the rescue, with an occasional assist from a wand-wielding godmother.

This isn't that story. It's not about the princess, or her prince, though you will get to see a castle. Imagine this: Your sister is starring in the wedding of the century. Where does that leave you, the hardworking—and relentlessly single—older daughter?

For Maude Prescott, the answer was complicated. Was she happy for her sister? Yes. But you don't have to be living the jealous-sibling archetype to feel the sting of comparison.

"I'd do anything for Fiona. Claw through the proverbial wall of thorns if she needed help. But I did feel like people were looking at me in this pitying way. Poor Maude, the lonely old crone!"

A sibling's choices may not be a referendum on where we stand in our own lives, but when it comes to major milestones, it's hard not to assess our own progress against someone else's yardstick, especially once extended family weighs in with unsolicited commentary.

So how do you make peace with being on a different path? For Maude, it started with a mindset that will be familiar to many of us: *I may not have the perfect romance, but I'm killing it at my job*. As the savvy readers of this magazine are well aware, "having it all" is a dangerous myth that exists to make women feel perpetually inadequate.

And then her story took a twist, as often happens when a determined woman ventures into the woods—in this case, a literal forest. Maybe we don't all meet and marry the water-polo-playing scion of a shipping dynasty. That doesn't mean a dark and brooding love interest isn't waiting in the wings. Even a plant witch with plenty of her own magic is allowed to want love.

But we're getting ahead of ourselves. Once upon a time, there was a different story. Not the one you're thinking of. It starts at Kew Gardens, the summer Maude Prescott turned seven. Her mother took her on a trip to England, while toddler Fiona stayed home with their father. That was the moment Maude discovered that plants spoke to her.

We don't always recognize these forks in the road when we first happen upon them. Years may pass before the pattern of our lives reveals how "then" shaped "now," especially if we have our eyes fixed on the horizon. Often it's not until experience forces us to take stock of the past that we observe the seeds of destiny taking root.

A whim, an instinct, a chance encounter . . . a plant bending toward the sun: Whether you believe in fate or making your own fortune, there will be signs of what's to come, no matter how many detours obscure your progress. Sometimes the longest journey is finding your way back to where it all began.

(CONTINUED on page 73)

Turnabout Is Foreplay: A Wedding Reporter Ties the Knot

By Corinne Vega

When my colleagues Hildy Johnson and Walter Burns asked me to write their wedding story,* did I say, "Moi? Impossible! I am but a supporting player in the epic saga of your love!"

No. My first thought was this: Finally, a chance to share my truth.

Do you ever think about how the other people in *Romeo and Juliet* felt, watching those two fools screw up their lives? Let me tell you: It's exhausting.

But they got there in the end. Roll credits.

Kidding!

I first met Walter and Hildy at a summer journalism fellowship for ambitious and high-strung rising high school seniors. They were awkward; we all were. But beyond the questionable personal styling, one thing stood out about those two: They were super into each other from the jump. We're talking cartoon heart eyes, slo-mo saxophone solo, the works. It was obvious to everyone. Some might say sickeningly so.

In hindsight, it was cute. At the time, it felt like watching a movie where you know the ending, but the characters have no clue, so every day they wake up and do the teen romance equivalent of checking out the weird noise coming from the basement in the middle of the night.

Speaking of basements, I can exclusively report to the readers of *Life, Styled* that the proposal took place at the scene of

* Just kidding, I totally volunteered. You're welcome.

their very first meeting. What a lovely sentimental gesture . . . it would have been, if they hadn't met in the creepy subterranean laundry room of a rundown college dorm. I'm sure the dust bunnies were impressed.

Oh, the ring? Burns proposed with a custom piece made from a vintage typewriter key (the question mark, of course) which is just on the right side of twee, in your correspondent's humble opinion.*

But let's slow it down for a second, because there are miles of hard road between the innocence of youth and putting a ring on it, and I wouldn't want you to think they didn't work for their HEA. I have my personal theories about the psychological factors that kept them apart for so long, but "couples therapy" isn't part of my job description, so let's just say they both had some growing up and getting over themselves to do. You can't trust someone else until you learn to trust yourself, etcetera and so on; somewhere there's a Hallmark card with their names on it.

After years of heated professional rivalry, punctuated by occasional episodes of public indecency, it shouldn't have surprised anyone that the turning point in the Johnson-Burns relationship came while they were both on assignment. And not just any assignment, but the biggest story of their careers: the Prescott-Schafer wedding in the south of France. (Can confirm both were 100 percent focused on the work, as opposed to their personal drama.†)

Something shifted on that trip, and it wasn't just a mattress. Was it the wine? The scenery? The romantic ambience? Or did they finally figure out how to have an adult conversation?

* I would personally prefer my engagement ring to be delivered in a glass of Domaine Gabby blanc de blanc. I'm not picky about the stone.

† Is the irony coming through? I sincerely hope so.

Who can say! All we know for certain is that by the time they returned to the States, Johnson and Burns were a done deal. He quit his job to become both a reporter-at-large and member of the editorial board for *Life, Styled*, while maintaining an active freelance career that gives them enough alone time to "miss each other," according to Burns.

How do two people who made their names covering the ultraluxe wedding scene get married? At the local courthouse on a Tuesday afternoon, accompanied by a half dozen of their nearest and dearest, including yours truly. The photographer was a friend of the bride's named Jefferson Jones, accompanied by award-winning *Life, Styled* columnist Libby Lane. Visual artist Jean Harrington, best known for her album cover designs, presented the couple with a custom caricature of the two of them on the cover of this very magazine, alongside their rescue cat, Rosalind. The champagne was ample and of extremely high quality, courtesy of the charming and talented proprietress of Domaine Gabby (visit her website for all your sparkling wine needs).

Word on the street is that the (revoltingly) happy couple plans to honeymoon at an undisclosed location in the Dordogne region of France, aka the place they finally got their shit together, once they put the next issue of *Life, Styled* to bed.

Probably literally, in their case.

Acknowledgments

One of my favorite things about travel is how quickly the golden haze of nostalgia falls like a curtain over the actual indignities of hauling your mortal body through time and space. As far as I'm concerned, our family vacation in France three summers ago was an unbroken string of magical moments, during which no one was ever jet-lagged or lost or ill. So thank you to Fred and Gilly for making the trip with me, and to Ahmed, Claire, Amaël, and Elias Diallo for joining us on your Tonton's dream archaeology/gastronomy holiday!

Thanks also to: The pastries! The castles! The painted caves! The crêpes! The charming villages! The fabulous Airbnb that was also a producer of artisanal duck delicacies! I hope this book captures at least a soupçon of the beauty and delight of southwestern France.

This also seems like an opportune moment for a merci to the French side of my family, who welcomed me as a belle-fille twenty-five years ago this summer. My belle-mère, Yvette, is especially missed, though her sweetness and artistic spirit live on in Marie and Lucile and Pablo and Gilly.

On the publishing side, I am grateful to Alyssa Maltese and the rest of the Root Literary team for welcoming me into the fold. I'm extra delighted to be agency siblings with my friend who is basically family, Megan Bannen. There is no way I could have survived the last three years of deadlines without your support as a

CP, cheerleader, and Midwestern Cher, gently reminding me to *snap out of it* when the occasion demands.

My gratitude to everyone at St. Martin's Press for their invaluable assistance on this book (and the two preceding titles that featured a younger Hildy waiting for her turn in the spotlight): Anne Marie Tallberg, Jen Enderlin, Meryl Levavi, Chrisinda Lynch, Kejana Ayala, Brant Janeway, Zoë Miller, Lesley Allen, Soleil Paz, Ginny Perrin, and Joy Gannon. A special shout-out to Olga Grlic for the summer dream of a cover.

Kelly Stone deserves gift baskets, spa days, and monuments for her editorial work on this book, but I'll start the tributes with this paragraph. Thank you for not panicking when I sent you the first draft of this book—a shadow of its future self. Somehow in the midst of juggling two separate projects (cf. *Flirting with Murder*, out now!), you managed to give me the space and the support to try something new with this story, and to keep working at it until we got it right. I am so grateful for your smarts and your enthusiasm, as well as your faith in me. You'll be relieved to hear that I'm done experimenting with multiple timelines . . . for now!

To my writing community in Lawrence and beyond, and to my beloved and unwaveringly supportive family: thank you!

And finally, happy anniversary to my tour guide, language coach, personal DJ, and resident expert on prehistory. Merci mille fois for going on this adventure with me, Freddy Bear! Can you believe it's been twenty-five years?

Maybe one of us will remember the date this time!

ABOUT THE AUTHOR

Frédéric Sellet

Amanda Sellet is a former journalist and the author of rom-coms for teens and adults, including *By the Book,* which *Booklist* described in a starred review as "impossible to read without laughing out loud." She loves old movies, baked goods, and embarrassing her teenage daughter.